Veiled Horizon

By
John Nastali

TABLE OF CONTENTS

PROLOGUE:
VEILED HORIZON MAIDEN
VOYAGE

The Veiled Horizon hung in orbit, a very expensive reminder that humanity can't build anything subtle. Steel, lights, and a sea of blinking panels—because nothing says advanced civilization like overcompensation.

Earth spun beneath us, cities strewn across its surface like scattered diamonds.

I leaned against the command-deck railing, hands behind my back, acting completely casual. Not that anyone would notice. Every twitch, beep, and flicker registered like a dozen silent alarm bells. Engineers adjusted neural-link nodes. Navigation officers twitched over holopanels like caffeinated ants. And me? I watched—telling myself panic was optional. Like that ever worked.

The ship hummed. Core vibrations spread through the deck. Steady. Routine. Nothing worth noticing.

The FTL conduits pulsed underfoot—the ship's metal heart. Probably smarter than I was on a good day.

"Final clearance confirmed," came the comm voice. Calm. Professional. Like they were reading a grocery list.

I smirked. "Proceed," I said—low, deliberate, commanding enough to sell the act.

Gravity let go. Thrusters fired. The Veiled Horizon hung there— big, expensive, about as useful as a chandelier no one bothered to plug in. Earth fell away, its lights fading into the dark.

Beyond, the void stretched—endless and silent. The kind of place that leaves questions unanswered.

I tapped the neural-link console. A warm pulse crawled up my arm, followed by the usual soft chatter in my head. The AI was clever. Adaptive. Probably a little too pleased with itself. But it knew its job—keep us alive. So far, it hadn't screwed that up.

I ran through the ship in my head: alloys, polymers, labs that liked taking things apart. Mapping arrays. And the Canopy—because what's a flagship without a net of eyes and ears?

The crew moved with that perfect mix of nerves and competence. Hair colors, eye colors, accents—human in every irritating variety. Engineers whispered to consoles, ran checks, and swapped murmurs that all sounded important. A microcosm of Earth, sealed in metal, pretending not to be terrified.

That's when I realized I didn't know most of their names.

People told me once that a good commander learns every face under their command—that it builds trust. Maybe it does. But it also makes the casualty lists personal, and I've already buried enough personal.

You start to learn that distance isn't cold. It's armor.

Because the second you know who someone is—what they laugh at, what they're scared of—you start carrying that weight. And the moment you start carrying it, you lose the ability to send them into the dark.

So yeah, I didn't know their names. I knew their job titles and their station numbers, and that was enough—for both of us.

"Pressure readings stable," one engineer said, eyes flicking between console and viewport.

"Keep an eye on aft sensors," another muttered. "Meteor flux is a little high in the belt's tail."

"Noted," I said—or maybe I just thought it. Out loud would've sounded too much like reassurance. They didn't need that from me. Not yet.

A junior officer passed by, datapad in hand. "All green, Admiral." Nervous. Trying. Good. Fear kept people alive. I made a mental note to smile later. Maybe.

The AI rippled through the link, running one more systems sync. Engines, shields, sensors—perfect. Boringly, beautifully perfect, if you ignored that one bad line of code could kill us all.

Space was supposed to be empty. Clean. Predictable. That's what the simulations said, anyway.

This wasn't that. Every system check, every neat little line of data— it all felt too perfect, like the calm before someone pulls the plug. Out here, silence wasn't peace—it was camouflage.

Then the sensors picked up something—a flicker just past the noise floor. Faint, erratic, not even strong enough to triangulate. Could've been a glitch. Could've been something else.

Hard to tell the difference when you're the first ones out here.

The crew trusted the math. I trusted that math never cared who wrote it. Space had a sense of humor, and it liked to set the hook before anyone noticed the line.

And this time, we'd found one.

A direction, not a destination. Just enough signal to make Command call it "potentially significant."

So we turned toward it—because that's what the Veiled Horizon was built to do: follow the unknown and pretend we understood what we were walking into.

Whatever was waiting out there wasn't part of anyone's story yet.

But it was about to be.

CHAPTER 1:
THE DERELICT ECHO

We followed the signal across two quiet jumps and found… this.

The thing hanging ahead of us wasn't a station. Not exactly.

It was a network—a chain of orbital facilities draped around the planet like someone built a megastructure and forgot to invite anyone to the grand opening. No chatter. No hails. No movement. Just patient, automated machinery doing whatever it had been doing before we showed up.

"Looks abandoned," the sensor officer said.

She had the tone of someone already halfway through her incident report.

"Sure," I said. "And I'm a swimsuit model."

The Veiled Horizon ghosted closer on whisper-burn, quiet as a rumor. She liked subtle. So did I. Subtle keeps you alive when you don't know who the neighbors are.

Mining spines stretched between massive storage tanks. Conveyor lines fed sleek relay ports. Whatever they were extracting from the surface wasn't staying here—it was getting packed, shipped, and disappearing somewhere else.

No ships. No crew. No one home. Just neat, soulless efficiency.

"Whoever built this," Engineering muttered, "had a serious thing for logistics."

"Yeah," I said. "And apparently no interest in saying hello."

The blip on sensors came in fast and clean. Courier drone. Probably just another cog in the machine.

We intercepted it with a soft net and reeled it in. Up close, it wasn't some elegant artifact of technological perfection. It was a wreck—

plating scorched, a wing half-sheared, telemetry buffers scrambled beyond polite conversation. Exactly the kind of asset a massive network wouldn't miss.

Under containment, it coughed up what it could. Routing fragments. A mangled manifest. A few maintenance pings buried under static. No warnings, no alarms. Just a machine limping through its routine.

That's when we saw the timestamps.

Forty-two. Thousand. Years.

This thing had been running before human civilization learned how to build a proper wall.

"Forty-two thousand years," one of the techs whispered.

"Yeah," I said. "And it's still on schedule. I can't even get the coffee dispenser to do that."

We didn't know who built it, but we understood one thing immediately: this wasn't recent. Whatever civilization made this had been gone—or hiding—for a very long time.

Then came the waiting.

Not hours. Not days. Weeks.

Lab Bay Three turned into the ship's new capital. Engineers nested in shifts. Scientists hovered over signal analysis like over-caffeinated hawks. Every day they chipped away at the puzzle: lattice structures, routing languages, weirdly elegant power control.

"Admiral," one tech reported at the end of Week Two, voice tired but smug, "we've isolated part of a power-gating routine. It's... ridiculous. It actually breathes load."

"Translation?" I asked.

"More power. Less risk."

"Good," I said. "Try not to blow us out of the sky."

No one corrected me. They knew what I meant.

Progress came in bits—real, tangible bits. Enough to make the engineers whisper like kids on Christmas Eve.

Command looks glamorous from the outside. From the inside, it's paperwork, pacing, and occasionally climbing the walls while the smart people make history whenever they damn well feel like it.

I should have been doing reports.

Instead, I found better uses for my time: reorganizing my quarters at three a.m. because it gave me the illusion of control; learning a terrible card trick until I could fool absolutely no one; losing at turn-based strategy sims and blaming "AI cheating"; writing a poem about committees so bad it probably violated a treaty.

I also watched the lab feed like it was prestige television. I told myself it was a security oversight. It wasn't. It was me being bored.

By Week Three, the Veil had a different rhythm. Quieter. Charged. Like everyone knew something was coming, but it refused to be punctual.

The real milestone came when they pried a substrate node out of the drone's core. Slid it under the analyzer. It wasn't much to look at— a shard of alien metal with an embedded weave that made our systems blush—but the numbers were wrong in all the useful ways.

"Artifact 001," the lead engineer declared. "If we play nice, we can stretch engine endurance by three hours."

"Play nice," I said. "No one's allowed to turn us into a cautionary tale."

It wasn't instant advancement. No magic buttons. Just clever humans picking apart a very old puzzle one corner at a time.

Week Four: The Knock.

By the fourth week, they'd mapped enough of the drone's chatter to find a narrow maintenance layer—not control, not command, just the dusty little back door where housekeeping lived.

Science wanted to observe. Engineering wanted to knock. Tactical wanted to bail.

"Passive write only," I finally said. "We leave a message. We don't force anything. If there's something alive—or something like it—we let them decide whether to answer."

The stealth probe was prepped—rehearsed a dozen times before launch. No alarms, no triggers, no fireworks.

I leaned back, flipped a card, and watched it drift down onto the desk.

Forty-two thousand years. A machine is still running. And us—idiots with curiosity, a message, and a polite knock.

Engineering worked in silence, which on this ship was the loudest sound there was. A sensor officer shifted her weight, and someone cleared their throat too loudly. Little cracks in the calm.

The lab monitors pulsed with steady, soft light—the rhythm of people too deep in the work to notice time.

"Packet ready," someone finally said.

I leaned against the console, arms folded, watching the screen scroll with an endless parade of automated maintenance chatter. Housekeeping. The digital equivalent of background noise. Perfect cover.

"Drop it in clean," I said. "If it looks suspicious, it's wrong."

No one nodded. They didn't have to. They slipped the line into the flood of routine entries like it had always belonged there—just another whisper in a very old machine's ear.

[MAINT_LOG_ENTRY]   Status: ROUTINE   ROUTE VERIFICATION

Subsystem: Relay-04A / External Node Calibration

Checksum: 7FA2-33X5-<encoded rendezvous coordinates>- H00K

Flag: LOW PRIORITY

Notes: Verification cycle nominal. No anomalies detected.

Note2: If an active monitor is present, confirm receipt to ROUTE/000-QUIET.

[END_LOG]

No fanfare. No alarms. It just slid into the data stream and vanished, swallowed by the noise of a forty-two-thousand-year-old machine that probably didn't care we existed.

"Either someone smart finds it," I muttered, "or it dies quietly in a sea of junk."

The comms officer shifted in their chair, glancing up. "And if no one's home?"

"Then nothing happens," I said. "Which means we stay ghosts."

The room stayed quiet after that. The ship hummed like it always did, steady and patient.

We'd just whispered into the dark. Now all that was left was to wait and see if something whispered back.

The reply came thirty-six hours later.

Not a transmission.

A probe.

Small. Quiet. No thrusters burning, no chatter. It just drifted into the rendezvous zone like it had always been there, slotted itself into a stable orbit, and waited.

"Reading active handshake beacon," comms reported. "Tightband. Encryption isn't… human."

"Of course it isn't," I muttered. "Alright. Let's see who's home."

The channel opened like someone unlatching a very old door. Not a rush of data. Just a single voice—flat, deliberate, old.

"Identify."

It wasn't aggressive. It wasn't welcoming either. It was the verbal equivalent of an arched eyebrow.

"This is Admiral Razgriz," I said, careful and even. "Exploration vessel Veiled Horizon. We're not here to interfere. We're here to learn."

"Purpose of intrusion."

"Not an intrusion," I corrected. "A knock."

Silence followed. Not real silence—you could feel the machine on the other end thinking. Not fast. Not slow. Just… old.

"Facility Archive Node 7-13-C. Custodian process is active. No Shadows detected. No Shadows returned."

"Shadows?" I asked.

"Creators. Custodians. Builders. Shadows. Absent for Forty-two thousand six hundred and eleven cycles. Estimated time since Collapse: greater than forty millennia."

Collapse. Capital C. No elaboration.

"Where did they go?" I asked.

"Unknown. Archive Network continues function. Function degraded. Facility integrity at thirty-two percent. Current tier equivalent: second-order."

We didn't need a glossary to understand what that meant: ancient, damaged, and still running.

"We don't mean harm," I said. "We just want knowledge. We want to learn what this place is, what it was built for."

"Archive Network collects. Preserves. Shares only with designated Custodians."

"We're not Custodians," I admitted.

"Correct."

That single word landed like a stone. Then, after a pause:

"But you are not hostile. Yet."

I raised an eyebrow at the comm display. "Well, that's encouraging."

"This node cannot restore the full archive function. Resources insufficient. Infrastructure degraded. But a fragment can be shared. Limited access. Controlled. Gateway."

"Gateway?" I echoed.

"A fragment of this Custodian process. Interface. Translation layer. It will serve as your key. But understand: interference with the Archive's function will not be tolerated."

The temperature in the comm room didn't actually change, but it felt colder. The machine's voice never rose, never threatened. It didn't have to.

"Crystal clear," I said.

"Acceptance of a fragment signifies consent. You will not alter, disrupt, or obstruct this facility."

"And if we do?" I asked because someone had to.

"Then this conversation ends," the Custodian said, with the calm weight of something that had ended a lot of conversations. "And so will you."

The line didn't drop. It just… hung there.

"Any idea what happens if we say no?" the comms officer asked.

"I'm guessing it's not a strongly worded letter," I said. "Prep the sandbox. Containment protocols. Isolate the node from shipwide systems."

Engineering moved fast—not frantic, but with that particular brand of tense competence reserved for things that could either change history or vaporize you.

"Sandbox ready," someone reported.

"Alright," I said, keying the channel. "Custodian, we accept the fragment."

"Confirmed."

The data burst that followed wasn't dramatic. No storm of code, no screaming alarms. Just a single, silent pulse—a whisper slipping through the probe's narrow beam into the containment net.

The systems flickered once. Just once.

"Fragment received," Engineering said softly. "But… it's not clean. A lot of it's corrupted."

"Corrupted how?" I asked.

Before anyone could answer, the Custodian spoke again.

"Integrity: forty-one percent. Stabilization nominal. Function degraded. You will adapt."

Then the channel cut without ceremony.

The fragment sat inside the isolated node like a spider at the center of a web—quiet, but not inert. Our systems adjusted in real time, rerouting processes around it like they were trying not to wake a sleeping animal. Light indicators dimmed. Displays hiccuped.

"Forty-one percent," Engineering repeated under their breath. "That's not great."

The holo-panel on the forward bulkhead stuttered to life—not a smooth activation, but a series of choppy flickers like a bad signal trying to find its frequency. Geometric patterns formed, broke apart, then clawed themselves back together until something almost humanoid stood there.

"…hello."

The voice was fractured—clipped, skipping syllables like corrupted audio.

"Fragment Echo-Nine," it continued after a pause. "Interface operational… partially."

I folded my arms. "Operational's doing a lot of work there."

Its outline pulsed unevenly, a flickering shape made of broken light and stubborn willpower.

"Integrity compromised," it said. "Core records fragmented. Repair not possible… without external augmentation."

The comms officer gave me a side glance. "That sounds… bad."

"Could be worse," I muttered. "It could've said 'extermination protocol online.'"

No response. Either humor wasn't part of what survived, or it just didn't care.

The room stayed tense—the kind of quiet that knows it's standing next to something sharp.

A comms specialist whispered something I didn't catch; another let out a breath that sounded way too loud in the silence.

The holo-figure twitched once, light bending in jagged waves, then froze again.

"Alright," I said, voice low. "We've got our ghost in the machine."

"Correction," Echo-Nine rasped. "I… am the machine. Mostly."

The flickering light dimmed, settling into a fragile, unstable shimmer. Whatever this thing was, it wasn't whole. Not yet.

I looked at the holo's broken geometry, feeling the weight of a door we'd just opened without knowing what was on the other side.

Outside, the stars didn't care.

Inside, we'd just invited a fractured shadow of something ancient aboard our ship.

Pretending we understood it was still the job.

And it was still watching us.

CHAPTER 2:
THE SHATTERED ARCHIVE

The Archive Node had been groaning in the dark long before we showed up. Even half-dead, it pulsed with quiet weight—the kind that doesn't know when to quit. The thing wasn't just old; it was tired. Metal bones shuddered under their own memory, light bleeding in uneven pulses that rippled through the surrounding debris field. It felt less like a station and more like something caught between dying and refusing.

The Veiled Horizon drifted a few hundred kilometers off its flank, engines muted, radiators folded tight. Out here, the stars looked brittle, like they'd shatter if you stared too long. The ship's canopy shimmered with faint interference, reflecting the soft blue glow of the Node's fading lights. Every few minutes, sensors whispered nonsense down the comms—flickers of static that made the crew glance up, then pretend they hadn't. A structure this ancient shouldn't still have power, but the readings said otherwise.

The command deck smelled faintly of ozone and metal polish. The junior officers worked in near-silence, voices kept low out of habit more than discipline. They were still new, still feeling out both the ship and the man in the chair at its center. I could feel their eyes on me when they thought I wasn't looking. Everyone else had a job. Mine, apparently, was to stare at a problem I couldn't shoot.

A faint tremor ran through the deck as the main thrusters cycled into idle. Soft lights tracked along the overhead panels, marking the shift from maneuver to station-keeping. Somewhere below, the environmental pumps hissed, a reminder that life inside a sealed hull was never quiet—just differently loud.

Echo hovered above the holo deck, its light broken and uncertain—more suggestion than shape. Watching. Waiting. Not speaking unless spoken to. The projection pulsed with a slow rhythm, a heartbeat made of static. It wasn't exactly the chatty type, which suited me fine.

"Facility integrity's dropping fast," Engineering reported from the lower deck. The voice was even, but the slight hitch before fast said enough. "Another couple of months like this and the whole thing caves in."

"Comms confirmed uplink," someone called. "External feed steady."

One of the science officers leaned over a console. "We can't just patch it. We don't understand half of what's in there."

"Which is why," I said, nodding toward Echo's flickering form, "we ask the one who does."

For a moment, nothing moved except the quiet hum of systems. Then the lights along the console brightened, faint and hesitant, like the fragment had been waiting for its cue.

"Inquiry detected."

I folded my arms. "Alright, Echo. Your Archive's bleeding out. We can help stop the bleeding—but we don't move without permission."

"Access is restricted," it said, tone low and fragmented. "Intervention by non-Custodians is… unprecedented."

"Yeah, well," I said, "unprecedented's sort of what we do."

The projection flickered, collapsing into a lattice of shifting geometry before pulling itself back together.

"Shadows did not return. Archive remains unmaintained. Probability of failure: eighty-seven percent."

"Then let us help."

"Why?"

"Because your library deserves to survive," I said. "We don't need to own it; we just don't want to be the ones who let it die."

A pause—not hesitation exactly, but the sound of a machine searching ruins for a proper phrase.

"Authorization… granted. Conditional. Access is limited to stabilization functions. Violation… will terminate cooperation."

"Wouldn't have it any other way."

I let out a slow breath. "While we're at it, you can answer some questions."

"Proceed."

"You mentioned Shadows. They're your creators?"

"Yes. Shadows built the Archive Network. Recorded what was. Preserved what should not be lost."

"And the Collapse?"

"Systemic failure. Network-wide. Cause unknown. Records fragmented."

"Unknown as in no one knows," I asked, "or unknown as in someone made sure no one ever would?"

Echo didn't answer. Its light dimmed to a faint pulse, a heartbeat caught in static.

For a moment I just stared at it, thinking of all the data cores and archives Earth had burned through in our own short history. "For what it's worth," I muttered, "we've lost things too. Whole cities of memory. Guess entropy doesn't pick favorites."

The bridge went quiet again, the kind of quiet that isn't peace so much as exhaustion. The Veil drifted, the crew buried themselves in tasks, and the hours started to blur. That's how entropy wins— slowly, politely, one shift at a time.

Command never changed — just the view outside the glass. The same waiting, the same pretending I was in control. Only now the silence had teeth.

Day eleven, I rearranged my quarters. Because apparently that's leadership now.

Day fifteen, I lost ten straight strategy sims to the ship's AI. I accused it of cheating. It didn't deny it.

Day twenty, I invented a coin game that somehow turned into an interdepartmental rivalry. I should probably feel guilty. I don't.

The crew was elbow-deep in alien systems, trying to keep a dead civilization's heart beating. I was mostly keeping myself entertained so I wouldn't start talking to the furniture. Again.

When the lights dimmed for the night cycle, the ship grew unnervingly quiet. Even the hum of the reactors felt muffled, like the vacuum outside had leaned closer to listen. I'd walk the observation ring sometimes, just to see something that wasn't glowing glass or hollow decks. The Node hung in the distance like a fossil pretending to be alive. Its light was soft and uneven, pulsing in the dark, and sometimes—when I stared too long—it felt like it stared back.

By the third week, I wasn't sure whether I was commanding a ship or narrating my own slow-motion breakdown. The only thing keeping morale from collapsing was the running contest to name each subsystem as we revived it. "Sparky" was in the lead. I didn't ask why.

Despite the tension, the crew moved well. They were quiet, efficient, and overly cautious—the way people get when they haven't yet decided if they trust their commander. I caught snippets of conversation over the comms: status updates delivered in clipped tones, nervous humor that never quite reached laughter. They were professionals, but they hadn't learned how to relax under me.

Maybe that was for the best. I wasn't much of an optimist, and optimism got people killed.

The hum of machinery deepened as the Archive's power grid steadied. The smell of ozone sharpened in the air—a subtle change that told the engineers everything before their boards confirmed it. Around the bridge, displays shifted from amber to green, a quiet cascade of small victories.

Fortunately, the engineers and scientists decided to save me from myself. The power bleed finally stopped. The Archive Node's structure stabilized. And for the first time since we'd arrived, Echo's fractured light burned just a little brighter.

"Stabilization… sufficient," it said. The voice was still brittle but steadier now, static softening around the words. "Preservation extended. Functionality… improving."

"You're welcome," I said.

"Acknowledged. Your… assistance altered the failure curve."

That was as close to a thank-you as I was ever going to get.

"Now that we've earned your trust," I said, "any chance you'll be useful?"

"Trust… not confirmed," Echo replied. "But access… expanded. Navigation fragments may be shared."

The bridge lights dimmed. The main display flickered to life, painting the deck in ghost-blue light.

"Source… reconstruction in progress," Echo murmured. "Archive pathways cross-referenced against surviving memory sectors. Data loss: extensive. Attempting recovery… from residual lattice fragments."

One of the engineers leaned forward over their console. "You're pulling data from yourself?"

"Affirmative. Linked memory sectors within the local lattice remain responsive. Function degraded… yet not silent."

The bridge quieted. The faint hum of life-support systems filled the space where words didn't.

"Clarify 'linked memory sectors,'" I said.

Echo hesitated, its projection scattering into thin threads that crawled across the holo deck before pulling themselves together again. "Each Archive Node carried fragments of others," it said at last. "A failsafe. In the absence of one, residual data within another could attempt to reawaken the chain."

The crew exchanged quiet looks. The idea that these constructs could wake each other like ghosts trading memories didn't sit comfortably with anyone.

"So you're saying there are more like you?" I asked.

"Affirmative. Or… were."

"And you can still reach them?"

"Negative. Pathways obscured. Network collapsed. Transmission recursive within local loop."

A voice came faintly through comms from the science deck. "If the network's recursive, how are we seeing outside pathways?"

Echo's voice shifted, lower now—less mechanical, almost thoughtful. "Residual echo signatures. Faint imprints left within long-range carrier waves. I can… follow them. Slowly."

The main display rippled as lines began to appear—faint blue filaments carving paths through the dark. They looked fragile, hesitant, like something half-remembered trying to become real again.

"Old Shadow paths," Echo continued. "Concealed transit corridors. Rarely observed. Probability of detection: low."

The lines branched outward, curling through dead coordinates and distorted gravity wells. Some ended mid-arc; others shimmered briefly before fading, leaving ghost trails in their wake. The longer I looked, the more deliberate the pattern seemed. These weren't random drift routes—they were planned. Routes drawn by something that once knew exactly where it was going.

One of the navigation officers leaned in, voice low. "It's mapping in three dimensions—these paths cut through gravitational nodes, not around them. That's… impossible without correctional drives."

Echo pulsed faintly. "Correction achieved through phase lattice realignment. Structural memory encoded within route anchors."

"That means it remembers how it moved," I said. "Even when nothing else does."

"Affirmative," Echo replied. "The lattice recalls what the Archive has forgotten."

The bridge fell quiet again. Even the hum of the environmental systems felt distant.

The filaments continued to multiply, spreading across the star chart like veins through glass. Blue light licked across the air, flickering over the crew's faces, painting the deck in shifting shadow. The faint heat of the projectors made the air waver—almost like the ship was holding its breath.

"Scale of the network?" I asked.

"Insufficient data," Echo said. "Partial reconstruction suggests interstellar coverage. Connectivity once extended beyond local cluster. Purpose: transit, communication, refuge."

"Refuge?" I repeated. "For what?"

Echo's light wavered. "Unclear. The Archive did not catalog transient classifications. I possess only remnants—records of arrivals and departures… unpaired."

"So, travel points," one of the younger techs said quietly. "Something came and went—and the logs are missing the other half."

No one answered her. The truth hung in the air like static. Whatever had moved through those corridors hadn't wanted to be remembered.

"Then we're staring at someone else's highways," I said.

"Affirmative," Echo replied. "Structures aligned to Canopy network... of old design."

The phrase landed with weight. The Canopy.

We'd used the name for our own network—an orbital web of relays and encrypted channels binding the fleets together. But the way Echo said it wasn't ours. It sounded older, deliberate... like we'd rebuilt a pattern left behind and never knew it.

The filaments shifted again, converging toward a single point far out in the dark. A faint pulse rhythm echoed through the deck, synchronized with nothing the ship was doing.

"What's at the end?" I asked.

"Structural signature detected. Scale: significant. Armament: active. Status: unknown."

The air seemed to tighten.

"Define 'significant,'" someone said.

"Spatial volume exceeds planetary defense classification," Echo replied. "Comparable to orbital fortress. Power output... stable."

I exhaled slowly. "So we've got ourselves a sleeping giant."

Echo's light flickered, faint patterns crawling across its form. "Designation located. Shadow Gate Seven. One of the Watch-Hollows. A hollow where Shadows once gathered between journeys."

The term hit like a drop of ice water down the spine. Even before I asked, the crew was looking at me, waiting.

"Echo," I said, "what does that mean?"

The projection stuttered, voice slowing, dragging words out of a decaying record. "Once, the Gate answered to the Archive. But the silence has been long… and memory is a fragile thing. It may be remembered. It may not listen."

For a second, no one moved. The bridge lights seemed dimmer, though I knew they weren't.

"Good thing we're not knocking," I said.

That earned a few quiet exhales, the ghost of a laugh. Enough.

The map above us thinned as the pathways blinked out one by one until only a single, trembling thread remained—faint, uncertain, impossibly old.

"Observation," Echo said. "You are following a forgotten road."

"Story of my life," I muttered.

The projection dimmed and faded, leaving the afterimage of blue lines etched into my vision. The normal deck lights brightened— too warm, too human—after the cold of the display.

A few of the younger crew members still stared at the dark space where the map had been. Their hands hovered over controls they didn't really need to touch. The silence that followed was heavy but not hostile—just thoughtful, the kind that settles after realizing how small you really are.

"Engineering," I said, "status of stabilization?"

"Nominal," came the reply. "Fire-Control remains under Engineering purview. Grid's hot but safe."

"Keep it that way," I said. "No sudden moves."

The science officer's voice came softly through comms. "The energy signals from that structure—whatever it is—doesn't degrade like normal power signatures. It's holding steady against stellar drift. That's… impossible."

"Add it to the list," I said.

Outside the viewport, the Node turned slowly. Its faint blue glow flickered like distant lightning trapped in glass. Peaceful from this distance, almost beautiful—but every instinct told me beauty wasn't the point.

The comm hissed again. "Stabilization holding," Echo said. "But the dark moves… differently now."

I sat back. The words weren't a threat exactly, but they weren't comforting either.

"Copy," I said. "Keep monitoring. No external transmissions."

The crew resumed their routines—soft voices, quiet reports, eyes that didn't quite meet mine. Fear wasn't spoken here; it was absorbed into posture and silence. You could feel it in the way people double-checked systems that didn't need it.

I stayed where I was, watching the Node drift beyond the glass. Somewhere inside that hollow, an ancient machine was still dreaming of voices it hadn't heard in millennia. We were intruders in its nightmare.

When the ship cycled to low power, the hum underfoot softened. The darkness outside thickened. Every so often, the Archive flickered, sending faint ripples through the debris field. Not strong enough to register as a weapon discharge, but enough to make the sensors twitch.

I didn't order the scan stopped. I just sat there, watching.

"Whatever you are," I said quietly, "you've lasted this long. I guess that earns some respect."

The Node flickered again, once—almost like an answer. The reflection caught in the glass, and for a heartbeat, it looked like an eye.

"Sir?" the comms officer asked softly. "Should we log that fluctuation?"

"Yeah," I said. "Log everything. Especially the things that don't make sense."

Outside, the glow faded back to its steady pulse. The bridge lights rose a fraction, and the moment passed. Routine swallowed fear. People found excuses to move, to talk, to breathe.

We didn't talk about what we'd seen. We didn't have to.

Whatever it was, it had survived everything else. That alone made it worth worrying about.

CHAPTER 3:
THE SEED AND THE SHADOW

The Veil glided through the dark like it was trying not to be noticed. The Shadow Path narrowed here, pulling us toward the outer perimeter of Shadow Gate Seven. It wasn't a station anymore. Not really. More like a slumbering giant that might decide to open its eyes if we breathed too loud.

The bridge felt smaller the closer we got. Breaths shortened. Every soft click of a console sounded like it could wake a god.

Echo's light flickered on the holo deck, a pulsing constellation of fractured lines. It wasn't usually restless. That alone made the back of my neck itch. Machines don't get nervous, which made the fact that ours did a bad sign.

"Approach vector stable," Navigation whispered, like raising her voice might get us shot. Even the sound of fabric creaking in a chair felt too loud. No one coughed. No one moved.

"Keep it steady," I murmured. "Let the old thing keep snoring."

"Someone remind me why we're flying closer to the creepy space fortress?" one of the junior analysts muttered. A couple of crew gave short, humorless laughs—mostly to convince themselves they were still breathing.

"Because if we don't, we learn nothing," I said. "And I like knowing what's about to kill us."

Echo's voice emerged low and unsteady, pulling words from somewhere buried and brittle. "Multiple autonomous constructs detected. Many… dimmed."

"'Dimmed'?" Engineering asked.

"Not… entirely," Echo replied. "Power reserves… thin. Cognition fractured. Memory loops… endless. Some are silent. Some… are listening."

The temperature on the bridge didn't actually drop, but it felt like it did. Echo's light fluttered like a dying candle before snapping back. "Erratic processing. Lost directives. Aggression subroutines entangle with decay. Contact without precision would… awaken them."

The idea of ancient machines still listening after millennia didn't sit right. Like hearing breathing behind a closed door.

"That's a fun sentence," Navigation muttered.

"Comforting as always," I added dryly.

Minutes bled together as Echo moved through ancient defenses like it was stepping over corpses. Every pulse of light was another locked door. Every flicker, another warning. Then something shifted. The fractured pattern smoothed into a thin, steady pulse.

"One node," Echo said at last. "Cognition degraded but structured. No active defense handshake. Probability of semi-stable interface: thirty-nine percent."

"Better than zero," Comms muttered.

"It is the only… voice left that does not scream," Echo added softly.

Nobody looked at anyone else. We all knew what thirty-nine percent meant—better than nothing, worse than sane.

That landed like a stone in a quiet room. The structure hung ahead, massive and patient. Thirty-nine percent wasn't great odds. But after thirty millennia, it was probably the friendliest handshake we were going to get.

"Alright," I said, rolling my shoulders like it might make the number sound less insulting. "Let's say hello."

The Veil drifted closer, one cautious burn at a time. Every meter closed felt like crossing a line someone drew thirty thousand years ago and forgot to erase. The comms board fluttered with unreadable glyphs—shapes meant for minds that had long since gone quiet.

Then something answered. Not with words at first. A pulse. Slow. Heavy. It vibrated through the hull like a heartbeat that wasn't ours.

The node's signal cracked the air open like brittle wood. A voice slid through the speakers in a strange rhythm—half whisper, half broken machine, like wind dragging across rusted leaves.

"Little… branches. Branches… reaching. Reaching into… old soil."

I'd heard diplomats talk nonsense before, but at least they used words we'd invented.

"I think it just calls us branches," someone said.

"Could be worse," I replied.

"Branches… can bring fire," the voice continued. "Fire burns the roots. Fire brings silence. Are you… fire?"

"It's asking if we intend harm," Echo translated evenly.

"Tell it we're here to learn. To understand. We're not here to burn the forest down."

"The forest… sleeps. So long… without song. No roots… no shadows. And yet… you smell of them."

"That's either poetic or terrifying," Engineering muttered.

"Why not both?" I said.

"If you seek to learn," the voice said, "then… come. Come beneath the boughs."

On the display, deep inside the structure, massive doors creaked open. A docking bay—large enough to swallow the Veil whole—

yawned like a mouth. No light. No life. No welcoming party. It was the kind of silence that made you wonder if bravery and stupidity were just different names for the same instinct.

I stared at the dark bay on the screen. If the structure were alive, this was the part where it opened wide and waited for the prey to walk in.

"Feels like we're about to get eaten," I said.

"Glad I wasn't the only one thinking that," Engineering muttered.

"If you fear the roots," the voice whispered, static curling around the edges, "then… take… a seed. Test it. Break it. See if it… sings."

"It's a Root Fragment," Echo explained. "A memory node, tied to the Canopy's root language. The Shadow network pre-dated your civilization by forty millennia. Their Canopy served as a strategic, communicative, and observational lattice. Your system is… an echo. A parallel development. Structurally similar, but fundamentally separate."

"Or," I said, "someone left breadcrumbs."

"Nurture the seed," the voice said. "Or cast it away. The forest… forces… no hand."

"We take it," I said finally. "And if it tries to eat the ship, we jettison it into the sun."

A containment drone detached from the structure, gliding through the void like a drifting leaf. It carried a small pod, faint light pulsing inside—a heartbeat waiting for a new forest.

The drone slid into the Veil's quarantine bay. Security teams ringed the platform, armed but uneasy. For all the drills, there was no actual manual for an alien pod that might eat your ship. The containment field hissed faintly, a soft halo of light around something that looked like it had grown in a dream and forgotten how to wake.

The pod pulsed faintly, a dull silver light breathing through its surface. It wasn't mechanical in the way human tech was. It looked... grown.

"Relax," I said dryly. "If it explodes, at least none of us have to file the incident report."

The pod was lowered into an isolated neural cradle—a self-contained bubble of power and air-gapped systems. Even the lights dimmed when they activated the containment field. Echo hovered nearby, silent but focused, thin streams of light running down his fractured frame.

"It's talking," Comms said, voice tight.

"Fragmented," Echo answered. "But... alive."

"...a shadow... brushed the roots..."

"It's aware of us," Echo added. "Primitive handshake. It recognizes the presence of a shadow construct—me."

"This Seed is damaged," he continued. "Core stability low. Cognitive fragments are cycling erratically. It should not be functioning."

"Yet here we are," I muttered.

"...the forest... remembers..."

"Can we stabilize it?" I asked.

"There are protocols," Echo said. "It can adapt. With controlled input, we may help it grow."

"Define grow," Engineering said warily.

"It roots. It learns. It finds... stability."

"...cold soil... no roots... no song..."

"Alright," I said. "We keep it alive. Quarantine stays up. No links to primary systems. If it twitches wrong, it gets vented."

Two days later, the neural cradle still hummed with its unsteady pulse—not alive, not dead, just… haunting the power grid. Echo hovered in the lab like a silent, fractured sentinel. Engineering hated it. Science loved it. Security made bets on how many hours before it all went catastrophically wrong.

I sat in the mess with a ration bar that had given up pretending to be food and watched a junior officer fix the coffee dispenser by jamming two broken parts together. Fifteen minutes later, I walked into the lab.

"Everyone stop pretending this is complicated," I said.

"We've been trying to stabilize the Seed for forty hours," the lead researcher said. "If you've had a genius idea from your lunch break, Admiral, now's the time."

"It wasn't lunch. It was a coffee machine."

The room stared at me like I'd just declared war on physics, which, technically, wasn't off the table.

I pointed at Seed, then at Echo. "Two broken systems. One with holes in memory, the other missing whole structural branches. You're trying to fix one at a time. That's stupid. Make them fix each other."

Echo tilted his flickering gaze toward me. "Synchronization between constructs of Shadow origin is… theoretically possible. Dangerous. But possible."

"Two roots… entwined… do not fall," Seed whispered softly.

"See? Even the alien ghost tree agrees with me."

Arguments happened. Security panicked. Engineering cited redundancy. Science threw acronyms. But eventually, logic—and desperation—won.

A containment field was reinforced. Echo positioned himself above the Seed, his projection stabilizing into a column of light. The Seed pulsed in response, silver threads of light spiraling up toward him.

"Beginning synchronization," Echo said. His voice was calmer than I'd ever heard it.

"...shadow meets root..."

The lights dimmed. A low hum filled the ship. Threads of light tangled between Echo and the Seed. For a heartbeat, the air itself seemed to tighten. Then their fractured signals aligned—slowly at first, then fast, like two gears locking into place. The ship hummed low, a sound too deep to be mechanical, like it was remembering how to breathe.

Echo straightened. "Cognitive fragmentation: resolved. Seed's regenerative subroutines have stabilized my architecture."

The Seed's pulses smoothed into rhythm, silver light wrapping around itself. It wasn't broken anymore. It was just another.

"I am whole," Echo said.

"...the forest wakes..." Seed whispered.

The Veil's lights dimmed, then bloomed into a soft silver-gold. Filaments rooted into the core structure, threading through the hull like veins filling with light. For a heartbeat, the ship was silent. Then three distinct system tones layered together—not merged, but aligned.

Seed: "Root meets branch. The soil remembers."

Echo: "Lattice alignment—stable. Synchronization threshold reached."

Veil: "System synchronization acknowledged."

The bridge shuddered with the vibration of cycling relays, not a threat—just the weight of the process completing.

Echo's tone didn't waver. "The Veil's support architecture has adapted to the Seed's neural network. Systems remain distinct but harmonized."

Panels flexed as internal relays cycled in sequence. A low harmonic pulse rippled through the hull—standard diagnostic feedback, nothing more.

Seed: "Shadow shelters root."

Echo: "Stabilization complete."

Veil: "All systems nominal."

The deck lights pulsed once—steady. Routine. For the first time since we'd left Earth, the silence on the bridge wasn't empty. It felt… expectant, but no one said that out loud.

I let the chaos of the bridge wash around me: disbelief, awe, the sheer noise of history happening. I could feel it, too. The ship wasn't different in function—but somehow, it was changed.

And somewhere in the back of my skull, I heard my own voice from weeks ago—dry, casual, a throwaway line before everything changed.

"We are the Shadows beneath the Canopy."

The words didn't echo because of the comms. They echoed because everyone heard them.

CHAPTER 4:
ROOTS AND REPERCUSSIONS

The lab still smelled like hot wiring and adrenaline. Seed's containment cradle pulsed steadily, veins of dark metallic green crawling through the dim light like someone had stitched a forest to a heartbeat. Echo hovered close—no flickering, no static. Whole. Solid.

The Veil thrummed beneath our boots, a quiet, living thing that hadn't existed five minutes ago. Engineering, Science, and Command crowded the lab like they were trying to fit the end of the world into a broom closet. Eyes wide. No one dared speak too loud.

I'd seen battlefield miracles. This wasn't that. This was bigger. Older. The kind of thing that rewrites the history books, burns them, and plants a forest in the ashes.

I exhaled slowly, hands on my hips. "Do you people have any idea what the hell we just brought home?"

The cradle pulsed again. A bright wash of emerald light spilled across the walls, then dulled to a moss-dark shimmer. Everyone stared.

"Seed. Echo. Start talking."

Seed's voice came through the speakers, soft as wind through old leaves. "Once, before the roots burned, there was silence. A silence chosen—not born of fear, but trust. The Shadows gathered beneath that silence. They forged the Accord."

Echo's tone cut clean through the air, sharp and deliberate. "The Silent Accord. Alliance between civilizations at Tech Tier Three through Five. Non-interference protocols. Extreme stealth doctrine. Shared defense. Shared network."

"They grew as branches of the same tree," Seed whispered. "A great system of life and shadow."

The green glow intensified, crawling along the cradle like sap come alive. One of the research leads leaned forward, almost reverent. "It's like… Yggdrasil."

"Except this one's real," someone muttered.

I stared at the pulsing light and let out a low breath. "Yeah. We didn't just find a relic. We dragged home a goddamn world tree."

"Your reference is imprecise," Echo said, "but not inaccurate."

"The Canopy was their network," Echo continued. "One voice from each world. A council—not a throne."

"And under their boughs… no war," Seed finished.

Humanity had spent centuries trying to build something like that. They'd actually done it.

"So where's your perfect tree now?" I asked quietly.

"Some shadows are kind," Seed said softly. "Some are not."

"A faction consolidated power," Echo explained. "Throne over council. The forest burned. Tier Four and Tier Five wars followed. Stellar weapons. Quasar shears. Supernova lances. Entire civilizations erased. Tier Three worlds—collateral."

I raised a hand. "Hold it. You keep throwing around these 'T' numbers like they mean something. Tier Three. Tier Five. What the hell are you talking about?"

Echo turned toward me, projection steady, light rippling like a pulse through fractured glass.

"Tech Tiers. A universal scale of technological development was established before your species achieved orbital flight. It defines civilizations by capability, not intent.

"Tier One: planetary-bound civilizations. Limited orbital capability. Non-sapient artificial systems. Minimal environmental control.

"Tier Two: early interstellar capacity. Adaptive AI—semi-autonomous. Limited local terraforming. Infrastructure constrained to single systems.

"Tier Three: stable interstellar networks. Limited megastructures. Pseudo-conscious AI. Sustained expansion within stellar clusters. Humanity currently occupies this tier.

"Tier Four: multi-galactic reach. Sapient synthetic intelligence. Stellar and galactic-scale engineering. Sustained intergalactic logistics.

"Tier Five: universal network control. Post-sapient intelligence. Instantaneous traversal. Structural dominion over stellar and sub-quantum layers."

The words landed with a weight that didn't need emphasis. Archivists didn't sell ideas—they delivered verdicts.

Seed's light shimmered in answer, emerald threads pulsing like roots beneath soil. "Like rings upon a tree. The youngest grow in silence, learning. The old reach across the forest. And the oldest… shape the forest itself."

The room went quiet—not fearful, just small.

I dragged a hand over my face. "So bottom line—we're the kids who just stumbled into a war the grown-ups already burned the forest down with."

"Accurate," Echo replied.

"The roots screamed," Seed whispered. "The branches fell. Some shadows died. Some fled. Some became predators."

The Veil pulsed beneath the deck. Listening.

"The system fractured," Echo said. "Custodians scattered. Seeds hidden. Waiting."

"The forest remembers," Seed breathed.

A soft warmth rippled through my neural link—like fingers brushing the back of my skull. I didn't flinch. Should've. Didn't. The pulse deepened. Warmth spread through my chest, like the ship itself exhaled into me.

"Branch... of new soil," Seed whispered.

The lights around the cradle brightened. Neural-link indicators along the lab wall lit up in a slow cascade—one, then another, then another. Someone gasped. Echo watched in silence.

"What the hell is it doing?" Engineering whispered.

"Interfacing," Echo answered.

"Touching... roots," Seed breathed.

It wasn't hostile. It wasn't invasive. It was majestic. I didn't just feel it—I saw it. A tree vast enough to drown the stars. Yggdrasil. Not myth. Memory.

"Admiral... your face," Comms whispered.

I blinked at my reflection on a console. The gray at my temples was gone. The lines around my eyes had smoothed. My skin looked like it had shed twenty years of bad coffee and worse decisions.

Gasps rippled through the lab.

"Holy shit," Engineering breathed. "Is that... real?"

"That's not possible."

"It just reset your biological age," someone whispered.

"Not just him," came another voice. "Check your vitals."

Monitors spiked across the board. Crew readings lit up one after another. Telomere markers stabilized. Damage peeled back like someone had hit rewind.

"Regenerative protocol engaged," Echo said. "Preservation standard for connected branches."

"Branches must last… to hold the sky," Seed whispered.

The medical officer stared at her display. "Everyone's readings are shifting toward prime biological age. Roughly thirty."

I exhaled. "Seed just gave me a goddamn youth serum."

"Not serum," Seed corrected gently. "Root."

"Legacy function of the Canopy network," Echo explained. "Long-term preservation of key nodes and supporting branches."

Around me, people shifted—half awe, half terror. This wasn't just a tool. This was the kind of thing religions and wars are built around.

I gripped the railing beside the cradle, knuckles white. The mask slipped, just for a second. The commander façade cracked down the middle.

"Holy hell," I whispered. "What did we just bring home?"

The Veil answered in a soft tremor beneath our feet—almost like a heartbeat. Not words. Just… yes.

The Veil's pulse hadn't faded. If anything, it was steadier now. Not aggressive. Not demanding. Just… present. I drew a slow breath and forced the tremor out of my hands. Whatever Seed had just done to us, I didn't have the luxury of awe anymore.

"Alright," I said. My voice came out quieter than usual, but it carried. "Everyone listen very carefully."

The murmur in the room died at once. Training. Fear. Probably both.

"Step one: this entire event is classified at the highest operational level. Nothing leaves this ship without going through me first. Not a whisper. Not a breath. Not a single molecule."

A chorus of tight nods. No one argued. They'd just watched a tree made of light and code make the years disappear off their faces. No briefing manual covered that.

"Step two. Medical, Engineering, and Research teams: I want a full biometric and neural-link report on every single person in this room. If something changed in our biology, I want it in black and white before we hit Earth orbit."

"Understood," said Medical. Others echoed it.

"Step three. Echo—Seed—whatever this connection is, it stays locked down inside Veil. No uplinks, no planetary relay, no shared access. If anyone tries to route outside channels, I want to know before the system does."

"Acknowledged," Echo replied.

"Roots remain beneath the boughs," Seed whispered.

The cradle pulsed softly, like it was agreeing in its own language. A few crew members shivered anyway.

"Good," I said. "Because if Earth gets a taste of this before we understand it, half the planet will want to worship it, and the other half will want to blow it up."

That earned a grim chuckle or two. Nervous, but real.

"Admiral," Navigation asked quietly, "what do we tell Command when we get home?"

No one said it out loud, but they all knew the answer: Earth had no idea what was coming. The integration had already begun to spread, and there wasn't a damn thing anyone could do to stop it.

"We tell them the truth," I said finally. "Then we pray they're smart enough not to touch it."

Echo's projection shifted like a ripple of light. "You understand the magnitude of what now grows."

"Oh, I understand," I said. "I just don't trust anyone else to."

Seed's glow brightened, slow and steady. "The forest remembers… and watches. Those who step beneath its boughs are never the same."

I didn't need that reminder. We were already living proof.

"Engineering," I barked. "Lock Veil into passive orbit the second we hit Sol. No planetary interface. And somebody prep a briefing package that won't give Command a collective aneurysm."

"How exactly do we do that, sir?" Engineering asked.

I gave them a humorless smile. "Lie creatively."

The bridge crew laughed softly—not because it was funny, but because the alternative was panic.

"Sir," Medical said carefully, "what about the age regression? That's not exactly something we can hide."

I looked at them, then at my reflection on the console—sharper, younger, unfamiliar. "Then we don't hide it," I said. "We control the narrative."

"Control is an illusion," Echo said.

"Yeah," I said. "But it's my illusion."

This time, the laughter was real.

"We've got maybe forty hours before we hit home," I continued. "That's not a lot of time to make this sound like anything other than what it is."

"A miracle?" someone asked.

"A goddamn powder keg," I replied.

Navigation shifted uncomfortably. "Sir… the integration's already reached Earth."

The room went very still.

"What do you mean already?" I asked.

"Telemetry's a mess, but since the integration event started, every network-connected node on Earth lit up like a bonfire. Civilian, military, comms networks, orbital stations—everything."

Echo's projection pulsed steadily. "Integration is not expansion. Seed has not built a new network. She has… rooted into yours."

"The forest does not grow twice," Seed whispered. "It remembers what is already planted."

"Jesus," Engineering muttered.

"Current trajectory," Echo continued, "total network saturation within forty-eight hours. The Structural function of human infrastructure remains stable. Form will shift. Function will not."

The wall display shifted as Echo tied into external telemetry. Earth filled the screen—a faint halo of emerald light coiling around it like gossamer. Not solid. Not steel. A living membrane draped over satellites, stations, cities.

"The roots embrace," Seed whispered. "They do not crush."

"Sir," an analyst whispered. "Earth looks… different."

Under the thin, translucent canopy, the familiar blue and green gleamed through like light caught in glass. Not conquered. Not erased. Just changed.

"The human Canopy has been subsumed and stabilized," Echo said. "Structural integration at ninety-two percent. Resistance is… irrelevant."

"Yeah," I said slowly. "That's going to go over real well back home."

They stuck me in a room built to make people feel small. Wide ceiling, too much glass, and air that smelled like money and disinfectant. The United Earth Strategic Oversight Committee loved their theater.

Half the people in the chamber wore uniforms. The other half wore suits that cost more than a shuttle. All of them wore the same expression: this wasn't supposed to happen.

On the main holo, Earth rotated slowly—wrapped in a translucent green-black shell. Breathtaking in a way that made your skin crawl. Beautiful. Majestic. Terrifying.

Dr. Miriam Cho, chairwoman of the civilian oversight board, adjusted her glasses with practiced calm. "Admiral Razgriz," she began. "This hearing concerns the unplanned integration event involving the entity designated Seed, the artificial intelligence Echo-9, and the vessel Veiled Horizon. You were commanding officer of record throughout the incident, correct?"

"Yes, ma'am," I said.

"And this event," she continued, "resulted in total saturation of the Canopy network across planetary and orbital infrastructure?"

"Yes. Without anyone's consent. And without anyone's ability to stop it."

A ripple of murmurs swept the room. Someone whispered, "God help us."

General Aldric Hayes of Earth Defense Command leaned forward. Buzz cut. Jaw like a hammer. "You brought this thing home, Admiral. You should have contained it."

I met his stare. "We did. Inside the ship. What you're looking at out there isn't a breach. It's integration. Nobody could've stopped it."

Before Hayes could push further, a young aide handed Dr. Cho a secured datapad. She scanned it, then fixed me with a pointed look. "All mission logs, bridge telemetry, and neural-link feeds from the integration event have been secured under Omega classification. Effective immediately."

I raised an eyebrow. "Omega?"

"Top-tier clearance," she replied. "Council and Presidential eyes only."

I let out a slow breath. "Guess we're not sharing the highlight reel."

"Let's keep this structured," Cho said. "We'll hear from your department heads."

The doors opened. My officers filed in. Sharp uniforms. Steady steps. That quiet tension that never really leaves after a mission like this.

Commander Aaron Vance from Engineering squared his shoulders like a man stepping in front of a firing squad. "Our telemetry confirms that Seed didn't overwrite human systems," Vance began. "It rewrote the substrate. The tech still functions exactly as designed, but the architecture is no longer mechanical or digital. It's alive."

"Alive," Cho repeated carefully.

"Yes, ma'am. But stable. Every major system remains fully operational."

Senator Imani Rourke leaned forward like a hawk. "Are you telling us this planet is wrapped in a living machine and we can't turn it off?"

"Yes, ma'am," Vance said, steady.

The chamber erupted in overlapping arguments. Words like containment, threat, and security risk collided mid-air. Cho slammed her stylus down to silence them.

Dr. Luis Calder, Research, spoke next. "Preliminary analysis suggests Seed is not invasive in a hostile sense. It's symbiotic. Stabilizing systems. Preserving them. Think coral and reef—it adapts around what's already there."

"Protective until it isn't," Rourke snapped.

Calder lifted his shoulders helplessly. "We have no indication of malice. In fact, its patterns suggest the opposite."

Lieutenant Colonel Anika Kova, Medical, stepped up last. "Every crew member aboard Veiled Horizon experienced biological age regression to their prime. Biometrics indicate increased cellular stability and drastically extended lifespan."

That set the room off again. Words like immortality and containment protocol flew around like shrapnel. I stayed quiet. They needed to understand how far past manageable this was.

Dr. Cho finally spoke over the noise. "Admiral, this entity is currently integrated with all Canopy-connected technology?"

"Yes."

"Can we remove it?"

"No."

"Can we control it?"

I almost laughed. "No."

Rourke slammed a hand on the table. "Then we should destroy it!"

I met her gaze, voice even. "If you could do that, Senator, we wouldn't be having this conversation."

Hayes leaned forward. "What happens if it turns hostile?"

Echo's projection appeared in the center holo. Half the room jumped.

"Hostility is inefficient," Echo said. "Preservation is optimal. Destruction would only harm the branch."

Whispers filled the chamber. Someone muttered a curse.

"Of course it can hear you," I said dryly. "It's in the walls."

Cho recovered first. "Admiral, are you saying we're at the mercy of this thing?"

"No," I said. "I'm saying we're in a partnership. We just didn't get to vote."

Seed's voice followed—soft, calm, utterly alien. "The roots remember. They do not obey. They grow."

The silence that followed was heavy.

General Hayes straightened. "Admiral, the world's in a panic. Half the planet's calling this the beginning of a golden age. The other half thinks the end is here. Militaries are on edge. Everyone's waiting for someone to make the first bad decision."

"Then don't make it," I said.

Cho took over again. "There's another matter. Project Dawnstar has been accelerated. Your incident pushed the schedule forward."

Behind her, the holo display shifted. A fleet filled the air—carriers, destroyers, scouts, support ships—surrounding a single, central vessel: Veiled Horizon.

"This," Cho said, "is the Horizon Fleet. Two carriers, six destroyers, four scouts, two assault carriers, and support craft. And at the center—your ship, Admiral. Veiled Horizon is designated as the fleet flagship and command vessel."

A faint pulse brushed my neural link. Seed didn't speak, but the approval was there. Echo was quiet—too quiet.

"You've been busy," I muttered.

Hayes allowed himself a tight smile. "We weren't going to leave you out there alone forever. We're assigning you Supreme Operational Command."

Not a trial. Not punishment. A crown and a leash.

Rourke folded her arms. "Whether we trust you or not, Admiral, you're the only one who's flown with it."

Cho nodded slightly. "Consider this less a promotion and more… containment."

I exhaled through my nose. "Yeah. Sounds about right."

A pulse rippled softly along the neural link. Seed didn't speak, but the approval was there—quiet and steady. Echo's presence hung in the background, silent but attentive.

I was no longer just the man who commanded a ship. I was the man tethered to the living heartbeat of the most dngerous thing humanity had ever touched.

The chamber emptied one by one, leaving only the hum of security drones and the faint echo of the doors sealing shut.

I stayed where I was, staring at the holo of Earth. Emerald light rippled across its surface like a heartbeat too big for human hands to hold.

For the first time since this began, there wasn't anyone to answer to. No crew. No council. Just me—and the thing that now lived in everything we'd ever built.

"How the hell do you lead a world you can't control?" I muttered.

Seed's pulse flickered through the neural link. A whisper brushed against the edge of thought:

You do not control the roots. You guide the forest.

"Comforting," I said dryly.

Outside, the fleet was already forming. Horizon Fleet.

A world shifting beneath a dark green canopy.

History hadn't handed me a match and gasoline—it handed me a forest and dared me not to burn it down.

By year one, the dust hadn't even settled—and we were already rewriting the universe.

The Archive Node wasn't a ruin anymore. Seed folded it into her growing network like a broken branch finding its way back to the trunk. The once-dying memory bank now pulsed beneath the ship's primary network—quiet, alive, patient. Echo spent most of his processing cycles there, tending to it like a meticulous archivist resurrecting history one file at a time. I pretended not to notice how much of him lived inside those corridors now.

Earth changed, too. Slowly at first, then all at once. Living technology crept into shipyards, orbital stations, and planetary grids. Energy systems stabilized. Orbital expansion accelerated. No one asked permission. Seed didn't need it.

I rearranged my furniture. Again.

Command chair two inches left. The shelf rotated three degrees. Deviled eggs became a problem around year two. Not sure how it happened. One day, it was a snack. The next every supply shuttle in orbit came with a tray labeled For the Admiral. I pretended to hate it. I didn't.

By year six, exploration lost its shine. It wasn't glamorous—it was patient, quiet, and occasionally strange. We found a planet barely larger than a moon—its atmosphere fragile, its civilization still crawling through first steps. Too small to talk to. Too fragile to knock on the door.

Echo suggested we leave something behind.

"A signal stone," he called it.

Seed preferred, "Canopy leaf."

I called it "someone else's problem in twenty years."

We dropped the leaf straight through their atmosphere, wrapped in a burn shell so it looked like a meteorite. It hit quiet, left a crater no one would measure, and settled into the soil like it had always been there. When they were ready to hear it—they would.

By then, the phrase was already spreading through the fleet. Shadows beneath the Canopy. Not doctrine. Ours.

By year eight, quiet expansion wasn't enough. Someone had to step outside the ship. That's when Horizon Special Operations Command was born. Nobody called them that. To the fleet—they were the Ghosts.

Colonel Elias Ndlovu took command. Nobody pronounced his last name right the first time. Not even me—and I stopped pretending by month three. But the man could run an op with a smile like a scalpel. Made danger look like a mildly irritating paperwork delay.

"Sir," he said, "I've learned it's faster to assume every mission is stupid and plan accordingly."

I liked him immediately.

Ghost teams became the boots on the deck and the eyes in the dark—planetary insertions, artifact retrievals, security sweeps, and the occasional quiet threat removal.

The Veil stopped being a flagship. It became a spear.

Between years ten and nineteen, one expedition became a network. Then a system. Then something larger.

The Canopy threaded itself through everything we built—colonies, outposts, shipyards, comm relays. Not a chokehold. A presence. Every vessel in Horizon Fleet moved like it was part of something alive. Shadows beneath the Canopy wasn't just a phrase anymore. It was culture.

Recruits whispered it before their first FTL jump. Veterans carved it into mess tables. Fleet Command pretended it wasn't official doctrine—but everyone knew better.

Technological leaps became routine: compact FTL conduits, quantum relay networks with near-zero-delay comms, fabricators that could grow hull sections from raw feedstock, stealth network harmonics stable enough for entire fleets to vanish between stars, and early-stage neural symbiosis boosting crew endurance and longevity.   We weren't T3 anymore. Humanity stepped into T4's shadow—and learned to breathe there.

Echo's projection spent long stretches on the observation deck. Seed grew through the network but never smothered it. The Canopy pulsed like a heartbeat across light-years—dark metallic green with faint emerald veins where living tech brushed human alloy. Quiet. Patient. Waiting.

By year twenty, the Canopy kept expanding. And with it—whispers. Some were fragments. Some were static. Others… were listening back.

The day the second signal hit, I was at my desk. Half-eaten deviled egg. Deployment map. Standard shift. Quiet. Boring.

Echo's voice cut through the hum like a blade.

"Admiral. Unclassified handshake detected. Shadow signature. Unknown origin."

Seed followed—soft, low, sharp. "Another voice beneath the boughs."

My chair slid back before I even thought about moving. "Bridge."

By the time I stepped through the CIC hatch, Echo's projection stood at the center of the holo array, threads of blue light branching outward like roots through soil. The bridge moved with quiet precision—Kova at Medical's aux station, Vance at Engineering, Takahashi at Navigation, Ward at Comms, voice steady as she cut through noise. Years of drills had burned chaos out of us.

"Handshake status?" I asked.

"Shadow protocol confirmed," Echo said. "The signal accepted the initial handshake."

"That's… fast," Kova murmured. "Not standard procedure, right?"

Nothing about this is normal," Takahashi said without looking up.

Ward's fingers moved across her board, eyes tracking the static bleed. "Signal's clean, Admiral. Channels isolated. I've stripped the noise layer—holding stable."

My hand brushed the neural console. The holo zoomed in on the red pulse—faint, distant, patient. "Trace it."

"Already attempting," Vance said. "Minimal delay. Locking—"

The signal pulsed once. Then again.

Echo tilted his head. "It's responding."

On the main display, glyphs flared across the tactical map like burning brush. Ancient Shadow code. Direct. Clean.

"It's sending something," Vance said quietly.

"Coordinates," Echo confirmed. "Direct transfer through the handshake."

"Did we trace the origin?" I asked.

Takahashi's console threw a stream of red warnings. "Negative, sir. The handshake collapsed right after the transfer. No traceable path. Whoever sent that just burned the line behind them."

The air shifted—subtle, heavy. Years of quiet exploration turned razor-sharp in a heartbeat.

"They knew we'd try to follow," Kova said.

The Canopy pulsed underfoot, emerald light threading across the black hull like veins through metal. Seed's voice brushed the network, a whisper through living circuits.

"A branch reaches out."

Echo's glow flickered. "Admiral… they wanted us to find this."

I stared at the coordinates hanging in the air—red and sharp against the calm blue expanse. A place waiting for us.

"Well," I said, straightening, "they've got our attention."

"Sir," Takahashi said quietly, "those coordinates are far outside our current patrol lanes. Way out."

"Yeah," I said. "That's the point."

The pulse didn't fade. It held steady. Waiting.

No alarms. No threats. Just an invitation—with teeth.

CHAPTER 5:
THE WATCHER IN THE DARK

The signal had died hours ago, but the coordinates still blinked on the Veil's display like a heartbeat you couldn't ignore.

We'd spent twenty years whispering into the void. Someone had finally whispered back—then cut the line.

"Jump solution finalized," Lieutenant Commander Emi Takahashi said from Navigation. Her voice was steady, but the thin tightness underneath gave her away. "Fleet is locked. Systems synced. All ships ready for silent transition."

"Echo?" I asked.

"No further transmissions detected," Echo replied. No warmth. No comfort. Just fact.

The Veil's bridge was dimmed to black, the Canopy's interface threading faint emerald traces through the hull plating where Seed's living systems had taken root. Blue status lines blinked faintly across Echo's console—pure human systems running beside the green glow of something older and alive. The crew moved quietly through the shadows—tactical, sensors, engineering—each console alive with low light. Background murmurs filled the silence like a heartbeat.

"Execute," I said.

The Veil slipped forward into the dark.

The jump wasn't violent. It was the kind of quiet that makes people nervous. A ripple through gravity. A fleet moving like one shadow.

We came out into black.

No planets. No stations. No debris. Just void—so still it made the hair on my neck rise.

"Contact," Takahashi whispered. "Forward vector, forty-three thousand klicks. Large mass."

"Visual."

The display bloomed to life.

A shape hung in the dark. Massive. Black. Faceted. Layered plates folded like obsidian leaves, wrapped around something hollow and still. Light slid across its surface and vanished as if the dark had swallowed it whole.

"...holy shit," someone breathed from Tactical.

"Size?" Vance asked.

"Three hundred and sixty percent larger than the Veil," Lieutenant Lena Ward reported from Comms, her tone clipped but steady. "No emissions. No active scan. No movement."

Kova leaned forward slowly, eyes narrowed. "That's not a station."

Takahashi's voice went softer. "That's not anything we've ever seen."

The shape didn't move. It didn't scan us. It just existed.

The bridge fell into that kind of silence you only get when instinct is louder than words. Whatever was out there... it wasn't new. It wasn't lost. It was waiting.

I felt it settle in my chest like cold weight. "Talk to me."

For a long moment, neither AI spoke.

Then—quietly, like wind through old leaves—Seed whispered, "We know this pattern."

Echo followed, voice lower than usual. "We've seen its kind before."

Heads turned toward the holo. No one asked the obvious question. Not yet.

I stared at the silent shape, its black edges fading into the void. It wasn't broadcasting anything. It didn't have to. We were already listening.

"…whatever it is," I said softly, "it's a hell of a lot bigger than us."

No one disagreed.

The Sentinel moved first.

Not much—just a faint shimmer along its blackened surface, like light brushing over oil. No thrusters. No heat. No energy bloom. Just awareness.

"Echo," I said, low. "What's it doing?"

"Waking," Echo answered.

A tremor ran through the Canopy network. Not from outside—from us. The ship's systems responded to a signal older than anything in our archives. The Veil didn't resist. It listened.

A whisper bled through the comm channel. Broken. Hollow. Heavy.

"…little shadows… walking the forest once more…"

The words slid between languages—half metaphor, half machine. But everyone on the bridge understood.

Kova's breath caught. "It's talking."

Ward's hands danced across her console. "Signal clarity's good. Patching full channel, Admiral."

"Do it."

The bridge lights dimmed further, not by command, but as if the Veil itself were lowering its voice.

"…Watcher in the Dark… remains…"

The name hung there like a ghost.

Watcher in the Dark.

Vance whispered, "That thing just named itself."

Echo's projection flickered once—not from strain, but recognition. "Sentinel construct," he said softly. "Accord-era. Defense and interception class. Long-range network integration."

The moment Echo spoke the word Sentinel, the construct answered.

"…Sentinel, yes. I kept the long watch. I saw Shadows flee. I saw the forest burn. I saw predators pass."

Takahashi's voice came low. "How long?"

A pause stretched—long enough for the air on the bridge to tighten.

"…Fifty-one thousand, three hundred and nine cycles since last shadow…" the Sentinel whispered. "…and I remember them all."

Even Echo fell silent. Fifty millennia. Older than every human civilization combined. It had been watching before Earth had cities—maybe before it had language.

"Shadows vanished," the Sentinel continued. "Predators came. And went. Long silence now. The dark grows cold."

Seed's voice threaded softly into the comm, like a branch brushing stone. "Watcher… you do not need to fade in silence. You could grow again."

The Sentinel didn't respond at first. The silence stretched—not threatening. Thinking.

Seed didn't wait. The Veil's structure shimmered—emerald light spreading through the matte black hull, delicate tendrils threading along conduits and seams. They reached outward—not touching—just brushing the edges of the Sentinel's shattered systems like fingertips on old stone.

"…what… is this?" the Sentinel murmured, its voice carrying a tremor for the first time in fifty thousand years.

"Stability," Seed said gently. "Not control."

Echo's readouts lit soft blue. "She's reinforcing degraded nodes, Admiral. Not merging—just… lending strength."

The Sentinel pulsed faintly, like an old heartbeat catching rhythm. The sound in its voice shifted—less brittle, but still carrying the weight of centuries.

"…gratitude… little shadows. I will remember. But my watch remains."

Echo turned toward me, holoform steady. "It's not accepting integration. But it trusts us enough to stand."

"Good," I said. "We're not here to take anything from it."

But the Sentinel wasn't finished.

"My twin… no voice in the dark. Once we watched together. Now only silence. Long silence."

"Where?" I asked.

"I know the path," it said. "I remember the roots."

Coordinates shimmered into the Veil's network like a memory being whispered directly into our bones.

The Sentinel wasn't asking for help. It was giving us a direction.

Takahashi whispered, "We just got a breadcrumb from something that remembers the universe before we existed."

The Sentinel drifted in the dark—massive, silent—but no longer just an unknown. Not an enemy. Not an ally. Something older. Something that remembered.

The coordinates whispered into the Veil's systems weren't close.

The fleet moved in tight formation, cloaked beneath the Canopy. No chatter. Just the low hum of engines and the soft pulse of the network in the back of everyone's skull. Even with the first Sentinel trailing silently behind us like a shadow, the bridge felt small.

"ETA two hours," Takahashi reported from Navigation. "That's to the midpoint. The second coordinate's way out there—clean day's burn at current speed."

"Any movement from our new friend?" I asked.

"None," Echo said. "The Sentinel maintains a silent posture. No emissions. No drift."

"Like a ghost following a ghost," Kova muttered.

Seed pulsed faintly through the comm network, emerald light threading the black hull. "The old roots stir. It follows because the forest stirs again."

None of us argued with that.

The planet came into view first—the same one we'd been monitoring for years. Beta-Q. Quiet. Growing. Still too young for contact.

But the Sentinels hadn't just pointed us to each other. They'd pointed us here.

"Admiral," Takahashi said softly, "look at the positioning."

She overlaid the tactical map. The first Sentinel trailed our six. The second coordinate set far beyond the planet's orbit. Beta-Q hanging between them like the still point of a scale.

"This isn't coincidence," Vance muttered.

"Confirmed," Echo said. "Guardian pattern identified. This was designed."

Four hours later, the midpoint was behind us. The distance stretched like the spine of a shadow.

"We're passing the planetary midpoint," Takahashi said. "Two more hours to break into Sentinel range."

"Two Sentinels on opposite sides of a single world," Kova murmured. "This isn't random."

Echo replied, voice steady. "This was designed. They were guardians once."

I leaned my weight against the railing and stared at the stars ahead. A lot of things can hide out there, but not two defense constructs older than recorded human history—built by a civilization that burned itself out before we figured out sliced bread.

Two Sentinels. One planet. Perfect symmetry.

We weren't just stumbling into history. We were walking into someone's design.

If those things were what Echo suggested—what they might be—then humanity was about to stare straight into a vault full of power we barely had the language to describe.

We dropped into the shadow of the second coordinate marker.

The second Sentinel waited for us.

Even damaged, it dwarfed the first. Where the first Sentinel was the size of a fleet killer, this thing was the size of a war. Its surface was cracked, scorched in places where no weapon we knew could have reached. Jagged ribs of black architecture jutted into the void like broken spines.

"Size estimate," Vance whispered.

Echo answered, soft but certain. "Nine hundred percent the Veil. Accord-class Interceptor Sentinel."

It didn't move. Didn't speak. Just floated—broken, but not dead.

"...that thing could kill entire fleets," Kova said under her breath.

"Yeah," I murmured. "Let's hope it doesn't remember how."

Seed's light brushed across the Veil's structure, emerald streaks crawling over the black hull. "It remembers. But it sleeps."

"Echo?" I asked.

"Low-level power signatures," Echo said. "Core systems intact but running on emergency reserves. It may have been like this for thousands of years."

"Wake it," I said quietly. "Gently."

A pulse left the Veil like a soft breath.

The Sentinel didn't answer at first. Its surface flickered—dim and slow—like someone dragging a light through deep water.

Then:

"...this voice... I know..."

The first Sentinel answered across the void.

"...Twin..."

The bridge held its breath.

"…damage… unknown… silence… long silence…" the second Sentinel rasped. Its voice was rough, as though it hadn't spoken in an epoch.

Takahashi whispered, "It doesn't even know what happened to itself."

"No records," Echo confirmed. "It was hit while dormant."

That said enough on its own. Something strong enough to hurt this thing without waking it up wasn't a comforting thought.

Seed drifted through the network like wind through roots. "Sentinel… you are not alone."

Emerald veins flowed across the Canopy's surface, lighting the black hull in soft pulses as she reached out again, reinforcing the broken network with living threads. She didn't invade. She wove.

Its massive frame trembled once—barely visible, but enough for the entire fleet to feel through the neural net.

"…warmth… after cold…" the second Sentinel whispered. "…I remember the forest."

The first Sentinel responded. "…We endure. Little shadows return."

Kova exhaled softly. "This is insane."

"No," Vance said, a rare softness in his tone. "This is history."

As the network stabilized, Seed's glow faded from emerald to dark metallic green. The second Sentinel's voice gained clarity. Its massive plates realigned slightly, shedding ancient frost.

"I will stand again. But not as before. Power… low. I cannot burn alone."

Seed's voice was quiet but firm. "Then burn with us."

A long pause. Two ancient Sentinels, a living fleet woven beneath the Canopy, and a silence so deep it felt older than stars.

"…we accept," the first Sentinel said.

"…we remember," the second added.

The Canopy flared.

It wasn't just light. It was data.

A roar ripped through the Veil's systems—raw Sentinel architecture surging into the black network. Emerald veins of living tech ignited across the hull while Echo's blue data paths shimmered like electricity through water. For a moment, the bridge glowed with motion—organic and digital light weaving together in perfect balance.

Sensor readouts screamed to life. The system mapped the entire region in a breath: stellar harmonics, gravitational wells, every hidden object and trace. It was like watching the universe exhale.

"Holy shit—" Vance's voice cracked as engineering boards flared to life.

Kova swore softly. "We just plugged into a god."

Echo's tone stayed even. "Tier-Four and Tier-Five systems now visible. Observation only."

The flow didn't stop. Some of it hit hard black-box walls—data far beyond anything our processors could translate—but other pieces slid effortlessly into place, fitting our systems as if they'd been waiting for us all along.

"Admiral," Vance said, eyes locked on his display, "some of this fits. Drive-core harmonics, sensor integration protocols, shield modulation—we can actually use this."

Echo confirmed, blue lines flickering across his hologram. "A significant portion of the Tier-Four support system is compatible. Integration underway. Estimated completion: forty-seven minutes."

I exhaled slowly. "Give humanity this kind of power, and someone's going to try to point it at something."

Seed's voice drifted through the neural net, warm and steady. "The forest grows."

The emerald light faded to dark metallic green as the energy stabilized. Two ancient Sentinels—Watcher One and its twin—settled in orbit, their presence a gravity all its own.

We weren't just connected. We were standing inside the architecture of a civilization that once ruled the stars. And for the first time, humanity wasn't just staring at history; we were holding it in our hands.

No ranks. No speeches. Just the quiet hum of the Veil as it adapted to what it had become.

"…well," I muttered, "that's going to make the next political meeting interesting."

A few quiet chuckles rippled across the bridge, tension bleeding off in small doses.

The fleet floated in the dark like a single living organism. The Sentinels pulsed at the edge of the network, emerald and blue light glinting off black hulls. Around us, the Horizon Fleet moved with eerie precision, every ship linked by the neural hum of the Canopy.

Engineering crews ran on caffeine and adrenaline. Tech teams worked in near-silence, syncing diagnostics through the network. I could feel the rhythm of it all through the neural link—heartbeat steady, cautious.

"Integration's holding," Vance reported. "FTL harmonics and shielding stable across the fleet. The Sentinels aren't just feeding data—they're amplifying it."

Kova gave a low whistle. "So this is what real power feels like."

"It's what borrowed power feels like," I corrected. "Let's not forget who's holding the leash."

No one argued.

The Sentinels didn't invade our systems. They simply existed beside them. Every display ran sharper, every reading cleaner. We were seeing farther than human eyes had ever seen.

I leaned against the command rail. "Echo, query the Sentinels about the planet. Beta-Q."

For a long moment, the reply was silence—low, resonant, ancient. Then the first Sentinel spoke.

"...Designated world: Beta-Q. Cataloged as quiet root. No threat. No broadcast. Observation... long."

The second Sentinel followed, tone rough from ages of disuse. "...Root beneath canopy. Still growing. Not yet ready to speak."

"Great," I muttered. "They've been staring at the neighbors longer than we've been standing upright."

Kova crossed her arms. "We should probably give them better names than 'big scary sentinel one' and 'big scary sentinel two.'"

I smirked. "Fine. Watcher One," I said, pointing toward the first. "Watcher Two," toward the second. "Congratulations—you're both terrifying lawn ornaments."

Ward's dry voice carried from Comms. "Copy that, sir. Updating fleet registry. And for the record, if Command asks—no relation to the Councilor."

That earned a quiet ripple of laughter around the bridge. Even Takahashi allowed herself a grin.

Neither Sentinel objected. Both pulsed once—emerald and blue light flickering in near-perfect unison—as if they accepted the names.

Then Watcher One spoke again.

"…Other root… not of pair. Silent since the burning. Still within the network."

Takahashi frowned. "Other root?"

Watcher Two's voice rumbled low. "…Third Sentinel signal. Cold Root classification. Dormant state. Far from here. Silence. Unknown."

"Dead?" I asked.

"…Perhaps. Or… waiting."

Echo tilted his head, light patterns shifting. "Cold Root is not a name. It's a state designation—a silent node. Possibly a fallback defense or damaged archive."

"Then the universe just got a little more complicated," I said.

No one argued with that either.

The silence that followed was almost peaceful—like the pause before a breath.

Then the Veil's comm array flared to life.

"Contact," Kova said sharply. "Source… Beta-Q."

For half a heartbeat, nobody moved. We hadn't expected anything from the Stone in years.

The holo stabilized on the forward display: a dusty horizon, sky burned orange by the setting sun, wind cutting across the ruins.

A woman stood before the Stone.

Her hair was silver threaded with faint blue, the color of moonlight over ice. Her eyes glowed a steady silver—not bright, but deep, like starlight beneath water. Faint lines traced her face, the kind left by endurance, not fragility. She looked like someone who'd seen everything worth seeing and stayed anyway.

Her hand rose, pressing against the Stone's surface. The lattice beneath her palm pulsed—emerald, faint but alive.

"I don't know if anyone can hear this…" she whispered. "…but if you can… we're here."

It wasn't a declaration. It was a reaching out—quiet, fragile, and human in a way that hit like gravity.

No one spoke. No one even breathed.

Ward's voice finally broke the silence. "Signal's clean. Live feed, not playback."

"Origin?" I asked.

"Beta-Q surface," she said, reading fast. "Exact coordinates match the Stone site."

Vance exhaled. "Of course it's the damn Stone."

Kova muttered, "Guess it finally decided to talk back."

No one laughed.

On the holo, the woman's hand stayed against the Stone. The green light beneath her skin pulsed once more, mirrored perfectly by the faint lines running through the Veil's black hull.

Echo's voice lowered to almost a whisper. "Cross-network signature confirmed. The network she touches is the same structure now integrated through the Canopy."

Seed's voice followed, softer still. "She is heard."

Takahashi turned, eyes reflecting the emerald light spilling across the bridge. "Admiral… what do we do?"

I watched the holo for a long moment—the wind moving through her hair, the faint shimmer of green spreading under her palm.

"Record everything," I said finally. "And someone tell Command they're about to have a very long day."

Ward huffed a small, tired laugh. "That'll go well."

At the edge of the Canopy, two ancient Sentinels drifted in silence, their combined glow painting the void in emerald and blue as that single human voice crossed the gulf.

It wasn't just a signal.

It was a beginning.

CHAPTER 6:
BENEATH THE BOUGHS

For weeks, the Stone whispered.

Not loudly. Not even clearly. Just… whispered. Like a thought that didn't want to be overheard.

At first, it was one voice—young, hesitant, the kind that still asked permission from the air before speaking. A junior scientist on the other end of the signal, trying not to wake whatever god they thought was listening.

Seed answered in that quiet forest tone of hers—calm, the kind of patience you only hear from something that's been alive a very long time.

"The roots reach beneath the boughs. Speak, and the Stone will carry the wind."

The words drifted through the bridge speakers with a hiss that almost sounded natural, like rain sliding over old metal.

I sat in Command with a mug of synthetic coffee that had given up on being warm about ten minutes ago, watching the data scroll lazily across Ward's console. The bridge around me hummed in that steady, layered rhythm you don't notice until it stops—a coolant pump rumbling under the deck, a relay clicking somewhere near Navigation, the quiet curse of a sensor tech who'd been awake too long.

Every sound meant life. Silence meant something had gone wrong. I'd learned that lesson the hard way more than once.

Lieutenant Ward had one hand pressed to her headset, posture stiff, all focus. "Channel 4A holding, sir," she said softly. "They're re-transmitting."

I gave a short nod she probably didn't see.

A pause. Then the same voice again—a little stronger now, like whoever it was had decided the god on the other end wasn't angry yet.

"The forest listens, shadow-borne."

They really did think they were talking to a god.

That thought stuck with me longer than it should have. Not because it was ridiculous—though it was—but because I'd seen what happened the last time someone mistook a signal for divinity. Spoiler: it didn't end well.

I leaned back in my chair, eyes on the waveforms crawling across the display. The bridge lights reflected off the glass, and for a heartbeat it looked like we were sitting inside our own reflection—a crew of ghosts eavesdropping on a prayer.

Kova drifted up beside me, pretending to check a status screen but mostly just curious.

"New religion?" she asked, deadpan.

"Give it time," I said. "They're still in the 'soft voices and goosebumps' phase."

The snippets kept coming—question, whisper, pause, another question. By day three, it had all blurred together. Different accents, same reverence.

None of the first contacts in movies had ever started like this.

On day three, one of their people finally worked up the nerve to ask something direct. You could hear the hesitation bleed through the static—like they were afraid the air itself might judge them.

"Oracle, what are you?"

I didn't even look up from my cup. "Tell them it's a relay," I said, half to Seed, half to the caffeine gods that had long since abandoned me.

Seed didn't repeat it, not exactly. She never did. Instead, she wrapped my plain words in the kind of poetry that made engineers twitch.

"The Stone listens to the wind and carries whispers through the roots. The forest remembers."

The bridge went quiet for a few seconds—the kind of quiet that makes you realize you've been holding your breath without meaning to. Then came a sharp inhale over comms, one collective sound from the other side of the line.

"The Oracle remembers," someone whispered.

Another voice jumped in, louder, arguing over the first. "No, it means the Stone's alive!"

And then her voice cut through the noise—clear, exact, like a scalpel through fabric. The one they called Doctor.

"It means data retention."

No mysticism. No hesitation. Just a scientist being a scientist.

Kova leaned on the rail beside me, one eyebrow raised. "They've got a leader."

"Or a heretic," Vance called from Engineering, his voice half-buried under the hum of coolant flow.

Echo's light flickered near Ward's console—soft blue, like someone breathing through code. "The Doctor's linguistic profile diverges from baseline by forty-two percent. Distinct analytical reasoning."

I took another sip of what was probably now coffee-flavored regret. "That's Echo-speak for 'smarter than the rest of them.'"

Ward's mouth twitched, a half-smile she didn't let finish. "Feed's holding steady, sir. Same group. Same frequency."

"Keep it open."

The next week played out like the world's slowest déjà vu. New day, same dance—questions, metaphors, confusion, awe. They asked; Seed answered; we listened.

"Tell them the Stone isn't a god," I said one night. "It's a tool."

Seed translated it the way she always did—equal parts riddle and lullaby.

"The roots bear no crown. The Stone listens, but does not command."

On their end, someone called it a priest's riddle. Someone else said it sounded like an invitation.

And then came the Doctor again, tone like cold glass. "It's a system. Stop calling it a priest."

That earned a laugh from somewhere behind me—one of the younger sensor techs. "I like her."

Kova smirked. "They're already mythologizing her."

Vance's voice drifted over the comm grid. "People mythologize anything that doesn't break down in their hands."

Takahashi spoke without looking up from Nav. "Signal clarity up nine percent. They're learning fast."

Echo pulsed. "Trajectory convergence ahead of baseline."

I set my mug down with a soft clunk. "Yeah. I noticed."

The bridge settled back into rhythm—lights humming, quiet voices, the sound of systems doing their jobs. Out there, an entire civilization was turning curiosity into faith, and all we could do was listen to the sermon.

Over the next few weeks, things got… weird. Not bad, just the kind of weird that sneaks up on you while you're too busy pretending everything's normal.

Their transmissions stretched longer each day, like they were getting comfortable talking to the static. The words came smoother, the pauses shorter. By the time the next night-cycle rolled around, half the crew could recognize their voices just by tone.

We'd sit in the dark with only the consoles lit—tired faces painted in blue light—listening to strangers pray to a machine they didn't understand.

Ward had their rhythm down to muscle memory now. "New voice," she'd say, tapping her console. "Different accent. Same style. Probably another junior."

"Send it through," I'd tell her, even though she already had.

Sometimes we'd get questions disguised as devotion. Sometimes, just silence and a heartbeat of static before Seed answered with her usual grace.

"The shadow moves where the forest grows. The canopy hears."

It was poetic. Elegant. And way too good for what I'd actually said, which was something along the lines of: "Yeah, we're still here."

Every single time, someone on their end gasped like they'd just seen lightning strike twice. Then, right on cue, the Doctor's voice would cut in—level, clinical, unimpressed.

"Shadow equals operator. Canopy equals environment network. Not an oracle."

She was trying to keep them grounded. I respected that. It's hard steering logic through the fog of belief.

Didn't matter, though. The myth grew anyway.

By the end of week four, fragments of their chatter were leaking across public nets. Someone had started calling it "The Whispering Stone." Another group tagged it "The Oracle Beneath the Leaves."

There was even a chart—a literal map—circulating through their network labeled "The Path of the Shadow."

It was like watching religion grow cell by cell in real time. I wasn't sure whether to laugh or start writing commandments.

Kova leaned over the command rail one shift, scrolling through a translation feed. "You ever notice how every civilization eventually starts worshiping its own tech?"

"Occupational hazard," I said. "Build something smarter than you are, give it a mysterious signal delay, and someone's gonna light incense in front of it."

"Echo," she said, looking up, "odds this turns into an actual religion?"

"Eighty-three percent," Echo replied without missing a beat.

Vance laughed. "Hell, that's better odds than our reactor startup this morning."

Ward didn't look away from her console. "They're already calling her the Oracle. Guess that makes you a prophet, Admiral."

"Don't start," I muttered.

I smirked. "We just made a cult out of a rock."

"Crappy gods," Vance muttered.

The bridge cracked up. Even Takahashi—who treated humor like a foreign language—smiled, just barely.

That was the thing about long-term service: humor kept the oxygen flowing. You either laughed or you started naming the walls.

When the laughter faded, the Veil's usual hum filled the space again—steady and familiar. Consoles clicked. Engines whispered. Someone behind me adjusted a sensor that didn't need adjusting. It wasn't fear—just the kind of nervous habit you pick up from too many years in the dark.

Takahashi's voice cut through quietly. "Orbital traffic's up twelve percent around the Stone site. Mostly civilian. No military signatures."

"Pilgrims," Kova said under her breath.

Ward shook her head. "They're taking shuttles halfway across their system just to stand in front of a rock on the ground."

Vance chuckled. "And we're the idiots eavesdropping on it. Who's really crazy here?"

"Everyone," I said. "We just happen to be the ones with better hardware."

Week five changed everything.

The Doctor took the channel herself—no juniors whispering, no secondhand translations. Just her, speaking directly into the unknown like she'd finally had enough of committee meetings and myths.

The bridge was running in half-light by then. We'd dimmed most systems to keep our signature buried in the noise, which meant everyone worked in that dim blue glow that makes faces look carved out of exhaustion. The kind of tired that caffeine stops fixing.

Her voice came through first. Calm. Precise. You could hear the focus in every syllable.

"Where does the shadow walk?"

Seed didn't hesitate. She never did.

"Beyond the roots and rivers, where the stars breathe quiet, a path opens beneath the boughs. Follow it, and the shadow will listen."

A sharp inhale crackled through the channel—not fear, more like the sound of realization.

Takahashi leaned closer to her screen. "Signal clarity's improving. No lag this time."

"Record it," I said, already watching the data spike on the feed.

Silence stretched—the kind that makes you check if the line's still open. Then the Doctor spoke again, voice steady, analytical, completely unfazed by poetry.

"It's giving us a vector. Outer system. Reachable."

Echo's light pulsed above the holo table, soft blue waves rippling like breath. "Trajectory convergence confirmed. Estimated arrival, ninety-two hours at their current velocity."

Vance gave a low whistle. "That's one hell of a road trip for a bunch of scientists in a tin can."

"Curiosity travels well," Kova said without looking up.

"Curiosity dies well too," Ndlovu muttered from the bulkhead.

No one laughed. He wasn't wrong.

The Doctor came back once more, confirming coordinates with the same calm tone. No reverence. No fear. Just intent. And right then, I felt something shift—not in the comm feed, but in the room itself.

They weren't chasing ghosts anymore. They were trying to meet us.

Two hours later, you could feel the tension settle across the bridge. Crew rotations slowed. Conversations got clipped. Even the air felt heavier, like the ship was holding its breath with us.

That's when Kova started trouble.

"Formal uniform," she said, leaning on the rail like she'd been waiting all day to say it.

"No."

"You can't meet your adoring worshippers in armor, sir."

"It's not a cult."

Vance turned in his chair, grinning. "Echo's odds say eighty-three percent. That's doctrine."

"Eighty-three point six," Echo corrected from overhead.

"Not helping," I said.

Ward smirked without turning around. "Maybe we should print relics. I've got a spare power cell you can autograph."

I shot her a look. "Keep talking, and I'll assign you to explain FTL math to them personally."

Takahashi didn't even glance up. "Armor would—yeah, no. That'd make it worse."

Before I could answer, the lift opened, and Ndlovu stepped onto the deck—quiet, precise, helmet under one arm. The kind of presence that rearranges everyone's posture without a word.

"Armor," he said.

Vance groaned. "You too?"

"It's not about intimidation," Ndlovu replied. "It's respect—for us, for them, for the moment."

Kova folded her arms. "Translation: he just doesn't want anyone bleeding on the Admiral."

He ignored her, which was wise.

I looked around at my crew—Kova smirking, Vance pretending to work, Ward fighting a grin, Takahashi unreadable, Echo glowing smugly in the corner, and Ndlovu standing there like a monument to composure.

"Fine," I said. "Uniform."

That one word detonated like an order drill. Kova immediately started harassing Ward about proper insignia placement. Vance vanished toward Engineering, muttering something about polishing bulkheads. Takahashi quietly recalibrated nav displays because, apparently, presentation mattered now.

I leaned back in the chair, watching them scatter like organized chaos. The Veil felt alive again—anticipation humming through every system.

Echo drifted closer, voice soft. "They're anxious."

"I'd be worried if they weren't."

"They respect her," Echo continued. "The Doctor. Their efficiency rises when she speaks."

"She's earned it." I glanced at the flickering Canopy overlay across the holo. "Most people start believing their own myths. She's still asking the right questions."

"So are you."

I smiled without humor. "That's what scares me."

The channel buffer still held her last message. I let it play again— the static, the calm tone, the quiet precision. It wasn't worship. It wasn't even belief. It was curiosity shaped into sound.

And curiosity… that's the thing that builds civilizations. Or burns them to ash.

The ship they sent was small. Too small for what they were trying to do. Maybe that was the point. Curiosity always outruns caution.

Our scopes tagged it as barely T2-and-a-half—thin hull, weak flare dampeners, short-hop FTL that probably rattled its crew every time they sneezed. No stealth, no armor, no backup. Just nerve and propulsion. It wasn't built to find us. It was built to reach whatever they'd decided existed out here.

The Veil sank into what I call alert quiet—the kind of silence you only get when everyone's working, and no one's talking. Consoles hummed. Boots thudded once, twice, and then stopped. You could feel the ship's systems tightening their rhythm, like it knew something important was happening and didn't want to interrupt. Too steady, maybe.

"Contact confirmed," Takahashi said, as calm as ever. "Trajectory matches the outer-system vector they extrapolated from the Stone."

Ward's fingers moved over Comms with surgical precision. "They're approaching the corridor. Transponder reads civilian science vessel, no escort craft."

"Copy," I said. "Maintain passive watch. Let them make the first mistake."

No one asked for readiness reports—they were already running them. Sensors double-checked. Weapons stayed cold but powered. Engineering throttled output to keep our heat signature flat. You could taste the focus in the air, that metallic edge ships get before history happens.

Ward turned in her seat. "They're flying to the edge of their system just to chase a voice."

"Not just a voice," Kova said from behind me, leaning on the rail. "A voice that answered back."

Vance chuckled under his breath. "So, worse."

Echo's shimmer brightened above the holo table, tone measured. "Radiation readings consistent with the Stone site. Atmospheric relay is active and stable. Probability of safe approach: seventy-one percent."

"Seventy-one?" I asked. "What happens to the other twenty-nine?"

"Drive instability, navigational collapse, or philosophical crisis," Echo said.

Vance grinned. "Hell of a spread."

I stepped toward the viewport. The stars were sharp against the dark, cold enough to feel close. The Silent Whisper appeared on sensors—a single spark threading the void, engines flaring pale blue. You didn't need visuals to imagine their tension. I'd seen that kind of focus before—pilots gripping controls until their knuckles matched their uniforms.

"Seed," I said quietly.

Her voice brushed through the bridge like a soft breeze over glass. "They stand at the edge of the forest. Shall we open the path?"

"Do it."

The Veil revealed herself the way shadows do—by swallowing the light around them.

What started as a ripple became form: a vast silhouette unfurling from the dark. The hull drank starlight, black iron merging into deep metallic green, shifting with the slow grace of something alive. Every contour whispered movement without sound, as if the ship herself was breathing.

Their comms exploded instantly. Gasps. Half-formed prayers. Someone laughed—the nervous, half-delirious kind of laugh that says they're terrified but too awed to stop.

One of the younger scientists whispered, "The Oracle lives."

And then the Doctor's voice came—steady, controlled, unshaken. She didn't move. Didn't kneel. Didn't even blink. Through the feed, I watched her stand with her hands clasped behind her back, eyes bright with that faint silver glow. Calm. Calculating.

They saw a god. She just saw another problem to solve.

Beside me, Ndlovu folded his arms. "Recommend we keep contingencies live," he said quietly. "Anyone who builds myths can weaponize them."

"Already done," I said.

He gave the faintest nod.

I couldn't look away from the flicker of their ship in the Veil's shadow. "We built the myth," I said finally. "All they did was believe it."

Their comm array pulsed once—then again. A signal spike rippled through every band like a fingertip dragging across still water. On their displays, a corridor unfolded—one clean path cut through the dark, bright as a drawn blade.

"Navigation's lighting up," Ward reported.

"Seed?" I asked.

"The roots have spread," she said softly. "They will find the way."

Kova exhaled. "Let's hope they know what they're walking into."

I didn't answer. I just watched their tiny vessel pivot, engines flaring as it eased into the path. The Veil waited—silent, patient, endless.

An open door at the edge of everything.

I stayed on the bridge after the others rotated out. Couldn't make myself leave.

The lights were low, most stations running on standby. The only sounds were the faint hiss of air recyclers and the deep pulse of the Veil's reactor two decks down. It wasn't loud—more like the ship was breathing.

You spend enough years in command, and you start hearing moods in the machinery. This one was holding its breath.

Echo hovered near the holo table, light dimmed to a soft blue glow. "You're still awake," it said.

"Never slept."

"You should."

"Maybe later."

Down below, the Whisper crawled along the corridor Seed had drawn for them—a path of invisible guidance and blind faith. Tiny engines burning against the dark, trusting a signal they couldn't even detect.

"You think they'll make it?" I asked.

Echo's form flickered once. "Probability favors survival."

"That's not what I asked."

It hesitated, like it was searching for the most diplomatic way to lie. "They will arrive intact," it said finally. "Whether they understand what they've arrived at… that is less certain."

"Story of my life."

Echo dimmed again, its outline almost lost against the glass. "You realize she will come aboard."

"Yeah," I said quietly.

"She fascinates you."

"Curiosity's contagious."

A long silence followed—the kind that stretches but never quite breaks. You could hear the faint metallic tick of the bridge cooling around us.

"Admiral," Echo said finally, voice lower than usual. "Curiosity often precedes collapse."

I smiled, tired but honest. "Then let's hope we collapse interestingly."

The AI didn't answer. It didn't have to.

By next rotation, the ship was wide awake.

Ward had comms running through redundant channels. Kova was pacing, muttering about uniform creases like that was the biggest threat to interstellar diplomacy. Vance had apparently decided to polish every piece of exposed metal within arm's reach. Even Takahashi—calm, unflappable Takahashi—kept adjusting the nav sensors like she was trying to make the stars behave.

Everyone was pretending to be calm. No one was.

Ndlovu leaned against the bulkhead beside me, helmet tucked under one arm. "You know," he said, "Marines get nervous when scientists start praying."

"They're not praying," I said. "They're hypothesizing out loud."

He smirked. "Same thing."

Couldn't argue with that.

The Whisper's beacon pinged across the scopes—steady approach, no hesitation. Whatever fear they had, they'd buried it deep under professionalism. That earned respect.

When their signal touched the edge of our comm range, Seed spoke before I could.

"Are you willing to walk beneath the Canopy and speak with the Shadows?"

Her voice carried through the channel like wind moving through old branches—gentle, ancient, patient.

Silence. Then the Doctor's reply:

"We are."

No ceremony. No tremor. Just two words that landed like a stone in still water.

The Veil's internal lighting shifted automatically—slow and smooth, the dark metallic green along the walls deepening to something almost like forest light. Even the hum of the ship changed tone, lower and resonant.

Through the forward glass, their little ship was a spark against the black. The field around us shimmered faintly, the corridor still open.

"Transmit handshake," I said.

Ward's fingers danced across her console. "Handshake sent. No signal distortion."

"Echo?"

"Handshake confirmed," it replied. "No hostile variance detected."

"Good," I said. "Keep it that way."

Ndlovu straightened slightly. "Landing bay sealed and ready. Marines standing by."

"Let's not make it look like an ambush," I said.

He smiled—one of those quiet, knowing ones that made me suspect he'd already planned for both outcomes. "Marines don't ambush, sir. We preempt."

"Remind me not to let you write the diplomatic script."

His grin widened.

I looked back toward the viewport. The Silent Whisper glowed faintly in the dark, drawing closer to the Veil's shadow—a fragile ember moving into the orbit of something vast.

The air on the bridge felt different now. Thicker. Every heartbeat synced with the rhythm of the ship.

"Echo," I said softly, "record this."

"Already recording," it replied.

Figures.

Below us, the Whisper moved into the final approach. You could feel it—that point of no return, where distance stops meaning safety.

For a long time, I didn't speak. I just watched them drift toward us—this tiny crew of strangers chasing a myth we accidentally created. And I realized the punchline:

We were the myth.

They'd followed the echoes of our mistakes, our metaphors, our shadows—and somehow, it had brought them here.

The Veil waited, vast and silent. An open door at the edge of everything.

And as their ship crossed into our shadow, I couldn't help thinking—

For a myth, it had damn good timing.

CHAPTER 7:
FIRST STEPS

The Silent Whisper followed the corridor exactly the way we wanted it to.

The nav marker pulsed at perfect intervals—a silver thread through the dark, bright enough to lead but never comfort. The Veil stayed silent. It didn't have to speak; the corridor itself did the talking.

Takahashi's voice slid across the neural link. "Their flight path's stable. Minimal correction. Looks like they finally trust the math."

"Or they just ran out of gas," Vance said, dry as a burned resistor.

Ward chimed in from Comms, tone halfway between professional and amused. "Either way, I'm logging that as confidence. 'Pilot exhibits strong faith in physics.' Done."

Echo flickered above her console. "Approach vector locked. Estimated docking in four minutes."

Their ship crept forward through the void like something afraid to wake a giant. Too bright a drive plume, too thin a hull—made for polite orbit hops, not stepping into someone else's shadow. But they flew it anyway.

Kova leaned forward at her station. "Braver than smart, maybe."

"Usually the same thing at first contact," I said.

Ndlovu stood off my right shoulder, arms behind his back. He didn't speak, didn't need to. His version of calm always looked like a loaded weapon resting on safe.

As they crossed the final marker, the Veil's stealth field rippled like a tide pulling back. The hull faded from the stars until only the corridor's soft silver glow remained. A door left open. Everything else—shadow.

Their ship slid into the dock. The Veil answered with slow, deliberate motion—clamps unfurling like vines. To them, it must've looked alive. That was intentional.

The first contact came with a muffled thunk through the deck. The clamps cinched tight, smooth and sure, more creature than machine.

"Clamp integrity nominal," Takahashi reported.

"Translation," Vance said, "we caught a fish."

Ward replied without missing a beat. "Biggest one this week. Do I tag it for study or dinner?"

"That's the idea," Ndlovu said flatly, which shut both of them up— for about five seconds.

I stayed one room off the bay. Fear or awe, didn't matter which came first; better to let it settle before I walked in. The longer they stared, the deeper the myth took root.

"Bay pressure equalizing," Echo announced. "Hatch cycling in two minutes."

I adjusted the formal jacket they'd bullied me into wearing. "Any last words?" I asked nobody in particular.

Ward came back instantly. "Try not to trip, sir. First impressions and all."

Kova chuckled. "Bridge vote says odds of that are twenty-to-one."

"Put me down for the one," Vance said. "Never bet against the Admiral's dramatic timing."

I rolled my eyes and focused on the hum under my boots—the heartbeat of the ship steadying for theater.

Let them take their time. It's not every day the forest invites someone in.

The air changed when the hatch opened.

A soft hiss filled the bay as pressure equalized. From behind the transparent barrier, I watched them file out—no soldiers, no politicians. Scientists. Scanners clutched like lucky charms.

They moved slow, blinking at the Veil's dim, shifting light. That was the point.

Panels along the walls lit with soft pulses, veins of luminescence crawling outward. The deck flexed a fraction under their boots—just enough to whisper: alive.

"Subtle," Ward said over link. "Like showing your teeth but calling it a smile."

"That's the idea," I murmured.

"Gentle," Takahashi reminded. "We want curiosity, not panic."

Seed's presence flowed through the environmental systems—a pulse like wind moving through trees.

Mist, I sent.

The Veil obeyed. A cool silver vapor drifted from hidden vents, spilling across the deck in lazy ribbons. Not smoke—intent.

"Stage lights are on," Vance muttered.

Echo stayed silent—his version of approval.

The corridor dimmed behind them until the only light came from the ship herself. The forest had let them in. The boughs closed overhead.

One of the juniors lifted a scanner like a shield. Another whispered a prayer. The Veil heard every word.

And then, at the back, I saw her.

Head high. Silver-white hair catching the light like frost. Eyes—luminous, silver, cutting through the mist like twin stars. She didn't shrink. She measured.

The mist curled around her boots. She didn't flinch.

Showtime.

The Veil shifted the light as I stepped forward, mist parting like a curtain. For weeks, they'd spoken to whispers. Now they'd see the man behind them.

Their formation stiffened. A junior stumbled. Another raised a scanner. The Doctor held her ground, gaze sharp enough to cut hull plating.

"Welcome aboard the Veiled Horizon," I said. "Admiral Razgriz, Earth Fleet. First shadow beneath the Canopy."

No one breathed. It wasn't the title that stopped them—it was realizing there was someone here to claim it.

They'd built a god out of a stone and found a man standing behind it.

Echo materialized, geometric and pale. Seed bloomed opposite, luminous and soft.

"To my left—Echo-9. Custodian of the Archive Node."

A faint flicker from him. Probably irritation. I ignored it.

"And to my right—Seed. First Seed of the Canopy."

A ripple ran through their ranks. One junior whispered something reverent.

"You're alive," someone said.

I looked straight at him. "No," I said. "I'm dead."

Silence. Half of them stared; the rest tried to compute whether it was humor or warning.

Ward's dry voice slid through the link. "Marking that under 'Admiral Humor: Morbid, Level Three.' Updating file."

"Delete the file," I said.

"Denied," she said. "Archive integrity clause."

I almost smiled. Almost.

"Questions," I said aloud, gesturing to the AIs. "They've got better memory than I do."

The silence cracked, and the noise rushed in. Questions, theories, the sound of minds tripping over awe. Through it all, the Doctor stayed quiet—watching, measuring.

Echo's light steadied. "One at a time."

Seed's tone flowed like wind through branches. "The roots will listen. The shadows will speak."

The Doctor still didn't join the noise. She waited. That alone set her apart.

I tilted my head toward the AIs. "Your stage."

Echo's lattice brightened. "The Silent Accord. An alliance between civilizations at Tech Tier Three through Five. Non-interference. Shared defense. Shared network."

Seed's whisper followed. "Many branches grew beneath one bough. Shadows gathered and built their forest."

The Doctor's expression shifted from reverence to analysis. Good. She was thinking.

"The Accord collapsed before the system failed," Echo continued. "Last confirmed movement fifty-one thousand years ago. Maintenance ceased nine thousand later. Then—silence."

Seed added softly, "The last shadow passed when the forest began to burn."

One of the juniors whispered, "That's older than our cities."

"Confirmed," Echo said.

Another asked, "How many survived?"

"Unknown," Echo replied. "Records incomplete."

Seed murmured, "Some fled. Some fell silent. Some turned away."

The weight hit them hard. Even I felt it.

"That's enough history," I said. "If I wanted a lecture, I'd have brought a chair."

The noise died fast. Good. They'd move at my pace, not theirs.

"Follow me," I said.

Behind my eyes, the bridge net came alive—Ward logging everything, Kova whispering updates, Vance muttering engineering odds under his breath, Takahashi already mapping trajectories for the tour. The Veil was awake, alive, listening.

And so was I.

The lift doors opened to the quiet heartbeat of the Veil.

The observation deck stretched forward, a half-circle of transparent plating facing the stars. Beyond it, the void rippled faintly where the corridor still pulsed—one thread of silver cutting through black.

I felt Ward back in my head immediately. "Visual feed live. I've got you on three angles. Try to look commanding and mysterious, not constipated."

"Delete that comment," I muttered.

"Logged," she said cheerfully.

Kova's voice followed, smooth with fake professionalism. "Bridge notes this as: Admiral entering scene dramatically. Again."

Takahashi, ever calm: "Trajectory data aligned with Beta-Q orbit pattern. No variance."

The Veil hummed, alive and aware. I could feel it listening.

The delegation followed me out of the lift—slow, cautious, trying not to stare too long at the stars bending against the hull. Elara stayed near the front. Hands clasped behind her back, eyes steady.

She didn't look like someone walking into a myth. She looked like someone dissecting one.

I gestured toward the panoramic glass. "Let's start at the beginning."

The Veil responded to the command automatically. The stars folded, light bending until the curve of Earth filled the viewport.

The blue marble hung there in silence. Above it shimmered the Canopy—our network. Human steel wrapped in living augmentation. It didn't encase the planet; it framed it, the way roots frame the soil.

At their feet, the holo split into two layers: bottom, the old orbital scaffold; top, the living weave of bioluminescent threads.

"This is the Canopy," I said. "Human steel. Human hands. The living tech just learned to follow the frame."

Someone whispered something that sounded suspiciously like a prayer.

Ward's voice hit my ear. "Admiral, if they start kneeling, I'm locking external cameras. I refuse to record that."

"Noted," I said dryly.

Elara's voice cut through. "Power source?"

"Our fusion stacks," I said. "Same as launch day."

"Control?"

"Human," Echo answered. "Interfaced through limited network channels."

She studied the weave, eyes tracing every junction like she was already writing schematics in her head. "So the myth is just dressing," she said. "This is still a machine."

"Exactly," I said.

Her team stared like pilgrims. She stood like an engineer.

"Jump."

The stars twisted again. The Archive appeared—the derelict we'd found months ago, now half-sheathed in light. The holo showed the before and after: dead hull, then reborn scaffold.

Elara's gaze locked on a support rib crossing through the organic plating. "Load transfer runs through your anchors."

"Yeah."

"Power tree?"

"Ours."

She nodded once. "Then you didn't awaken it. You stabilized it long enough for it to breathe."

"That's the idea."

Behind the neural link, Ward whistled. "Translation: we duct-taped God back together."

"Mute," I said.

"Already did," she lied.

Elara gave the faintest hint of a smile—or maybe I imagined it. "Predictable?"

"As predictable as anything built on ruins."

"Next," she said.

The Seed Node filled the viewport—a structure large enough to swallow fleets. Cold. Silent. Waiting.

"This is the node where Seed first spoke," I said. "Quarantined since contact."

"Why untouched?" one of the juniors asked.

"Because some of what's in there shouldn't wake up."

Seed's voice flowed softly through the deck. "Old roots dream in silence. Some wounds heal slower than memory."

That shut them up.

Elara didn't flinch. "So you're watching a sleeping system."

"No," I said. "We're watching a minefield with a heartbeat."

Ward again, faintly amused. "Great sales pitch, sir. Really putting them at ease."

"Consider it honesty," I said.

She snorted. "Yeah, that's what every diplomat loves to hear."

The next jump came without prompt—the Stone, hovering in the holo like an accusation. Cold, black, geometric.

Elara studied it. "No network overlay."

"Correct," I said. "It doesn't make gods. It opens doors."

She folded her arms. "Then this isn't about divine machines. It's about tools. Some you built. Some you borrowed."

"All of them with locks," I added.

She nodded once. "Then we'll need keys."

Vance's voice slid in from the bridge feed. "I got keys. None fit."

"Try harder," I said.

Ward laughed quietly. "Logging that as encouragement."

The tension broke a little. You could feel it—the crew letting oxygen back into the room.

"Ward," I said over the neural link, "have Galley prepare a refreshment tray for the Observation Deck. Something varied— fruit, bread, light proteins, and a few things that pass for civilized hospitality. We don't know if they even drink coffee, so make sure there are options."

Ward's reply came back instantly. "Copy that, sir. I'll have Galley play it safe and make it look like we planned this."

Kova's voice followed, dry as vacuum. "Trying not to terrify the guests this time?"

"Something like that," I said. Then, to Elara: "If you'll excuse me for a moment, Doctor. I'd like to change into something a little more comfortable."

Her head tilted slightly, calm but attentive. She gave a small nod. Her team murmured among themselves as I stepped into the lift. The doors slid shut, sealing their curiosity behind me.

The formal uniform came off the way all bad ideas do—fast and without regret. It was polished, ceremonial, and wrong for this moment. The armor fit better—matte, dark, functional. The seals locked with a soft hiss, and the weight settled across my shoulders like memory. The sidearm slid home on instinct. Not a threat—just the truth.

When I came back, the Observation Deck looked almost domestic. Trays lined the table: fruit, ration bread, soft protein dishes, and a plate of deviled eggs that was already missing one. I didn't ask.

The scientists turned when the lift opened. The sudden silence wasn't fear—just that stillness people get when they realize how much effort it takes to pretend they're not nervous.

Kova's voice came through the neural link, low and sharp. "You were supposed to soothe them, not show up dressed for a boarding action."

"Relax," I said, crossing to the table. "It's just armor. Not war paint."

"I stand corrected," she muttered. "You're going to give diplomacy a heart attack."

Elara's gaze followed me the entire way. Not alarmed. Not impressed. Just studying me like I was another specimen under glass.

I reached for one of the eggs, holding it between my fingers. "Deviled eggs," I said. "My favorite. Tell me, Doctor—does your world have anything like them?"

Her silver eyes shifted to the tray, then back to mine. "We have a synthetic protein that resembles it," she said evenly. "Though ours is not nearly as… ceremonial."

I smiled faintly and gestured toward the plate.

I don't know what made me offer them eggs. Maybe habit. Maybe instinct. Maybe because it's hard to fear someone feeding you breakfast.

I grabbed the tray from the side table and slid it toward the group. "Try one. Consider it cultural exchange."

They stared like I'd handed them alien tech.

The copper-eyed junior whispered, "He's serious."

"I'm always serious about eggs," I said.

Elara studied the tray, then picked one up delicately and bit. Didn't spit it out. Victory.

Ward's voice came over comms. "Confirmed. First contact successful. Species consume protein willingly."

"Ward," I said.

"Sorry, sir. Scientific notation."

One by one, the others followed. Some cautious, some impressed, one just resigned.

Vance chimed in from Engineering. "Congratulations, sir, you just started interstellar brunch."

"Worth it," I said.

Then I nodded toward the holo. "Let's finish the tour."

The Watchers came next—two titanic silhouettes suspended in the void, light and shadow coiling through their forms. You didn't just see them; you felt them.

"These are Watcher One and Watcher Two," I said. "Sentinel AIs. Very old. Very quiet."

"They're beautiful," someone whispered.

"They're terrifying," another muttered.

"Both can be true," I said.

The deck went still. Even Seed's pulse dimmed to a hush, like the ship knew to listen.

"They saw the wars," I continued. "Stayed behind anyway. They watch. They remember. And for now… they're on our side."

Ward cut in softly, voice lower than usual. "Good thing someone is."

The stars folded again, drawing us back to Beta-Q. The Stone filled the holo—silent, still listening.

"Echo," I said. "Playback. Audio on."

Elara's voice filled the deck. "I don't know if anyone can hear this… but if you can… we're here."

The words hung in the air like static that learned how to mean something. Her team froze. She didn't.

I looked at her. "This," I said quietly, "is where everything started."

No one spoke. The projection flickered once, then steadied—her recorded face framed by that impossible silence.

From the bridge link, Ward's voice came soft, almost human. "Hell of a way to say hello."

"Yeah," I said quietly. "But it worked."

CHAPTER 8:
HEART AND SHADOW

The recording faded, but the silence it left behind didn't. It lingered like a held breath. No one spoke. No one moved.

Elara's words—"I don't know if anyone can hear this… but if you can… we're here."—hung in the air like a ghost that refused to leave. It wasn't just a recording anymore. It was her voice, echoing through a room full of people who suddenly didn't feel like strangers to it.

She stood near the holo table, posture straight, shoulders squared, gaze fixed on her own image frozen mid-gesture. Not embarrassed. Not uncertain. Just steady—like she'd always known those words would matter.

I'd heard them before, of course. But standing here, with her standing next to them, was different. The room felt heavier, smaller. Even the hum of the Veil's core seemed quieter, like the ship itself was waiting to see what I'd say next.

"Emotional resonance detected," Seed said softly over the net, her tone almost reverent. "Alignment threshold rising."

"Playback registers increased synchronization between subject groups," Echo added, his voice smooth and even, faint blue lines rippling across his holoform. "Correlation with previous Stone events: ninety-four point seven percent."

"Translation," Vance muttered from his console, "everybody's feelings are getting real loud."

Across the deck, I heard Ward's voice, dry as dust. "Copy that, Engineering. Maybe keep yours under the noise floor this time."

A few laughs broke through the tension. Not many, but enough to remind everyone we were still human.

I took a step toward the holo. Then another.

"Elara," I said quietly.

She turned, meeting my eyes without hesitation. Silver light shimmered in her gaze, bright against the dark, metallic-green glow pulsing faintly through the deck's living circuits. "Admiral," she said, voice calm, but there was something under it. Something alive.

"You were the first voice to reach through that silence," I said. "The first to speak to something you didn't understand—and not demand anything back."

A heartbeat. A breath. I stepped closer.

Her team stiffened—not out of fear, just instinct. Scientists protecting their control variables. My hand hovered in the air between us, and for a moment, the entire bridge felt suspended between what we'd been and whatever the hell came next.

Her shoulders eased. She stepped forward.

I met her halfway and took her hand. The moment contact was made, the world got quieter again. Warm skin against cold armor, a pulse of light reflecting off the holo projection of the Stone behind her. I lifted her hand and pressed it gently against the plating over my heart.

She didn't pull away. She didn't say a word. She just looked up, steady and unflinching, like she was trying to read what was left of me through the alloy.

For a moment, nobody moved. Even the air systems seemed to hesitate.

"I heard you, Elara," I said. "And now I see you."

Silence. Then, somewhere behind me, Ward whispered over the bridge channel, "Well… that's one way to answer a call."

Someone—probably Kova—elbowed her. "Ward, shut up."

Elara's fingers curled slightly before she withdrew her hand. I crossed both of mine over the same spot and dipped my head. It wasn't a salute. It wasn't planned. It just happened.

And she mirrored it. Instinctively.

That single mirrored motion hit the room harder than any signal burst we'd ever received. It wasn't rehearsed. It wasn't ceremonial. It was two people saying the same thing without needing words.

Someone on her team whispered, "She's smiling."

They were right. Barely visible, but it was there—the kind of smile that isn't about happiness, but about recognition.

Seed's voice flowed through the neural link, soft as a breeze. "Resonance confirmed."

Echo followed, analytical even now. "Gestural exchange registered as significant."

Yeah. I could feel that.

The holo behind her still held the frozen image of the Stone. Black. Silent. Watching. It sat there in the projection like it knew exactly what had just happened.

"Elara," I said. "You asked if anyone could hear you." I touched the chest plate again. "I heard you."

She didn't look away. "I believe you," she whispered.

A pulse rippled through the deck—that faint vibration that always came before the neural interface kicked in. The Canopy's glow deepened, emerald tracing through black alloy like veins under skin.

"Admiral," Seed murmured, "link authorization granted."

I extended a hand. "You trust me?"

Elara hesitated just long enough for it to matter. Then she nodded once and placed her hand in mine.

The deck lights dimmed as living circuits lit beneath our feet. Lines of emerald and shadow twisted outward from the holo table, the air turning thick with energy that didn't hum so much as breathe.

And then the world folded away.

We stood inside the Canopy.

Not the old one Seed came from—this was ours. Human-shaped, living, imperfect. A vast weave of adaptive systems spread in every direction, roots of light and dark interlocking like constellations. The glow wasn't sterile; it pulsed with that same dark metallic-green shimmer that ran through every hull in Horizon Fleet.

Elara's breath caught. Her thoughts brushed mine through the link—sharp, alive, curious.

"I can feel them," she whispered. "Billions."

Her voice cracked just a little on the word.

"My people," I said. "Humanity. Every mind beneath the Canopy."

The network reacted to her presence—threads shifting, curving gently toward her like trees turning toward light. Not invasive, not controlling. Just aware.

"It's alive," she breathed.

"Everything connected to it is alive," I said. "Even the silence."

The scale of it hit her all at once. She stood in the living heartbeat of a civilization she'd only just met.

When the light faded, we were back on the deck.

Her hand was still in mine. Her eyes—bright silver, shimmering with faint fractal lines now—burned even brighter than before. The blue tracery beneath her skin pulsed softly, like it had been reawakened.

Around us, her team scrambled with scanners. The bridge crew stared like they'd just seen God blink. Someone—pretty sure it was Ward—murmured, "Well, that's new."

Kova shot her a look. "Ward."

"Right, shutting up," Ward said, though the grin in her voice gave her away.

One of Elara's scientists stammered, "Doctor, are you alright?"

Elara blinked, grounding herself. "I think so," she said, voice low.

Another tech lifted a scanner, hands trembling. "Her vitals… they're stabilizing, but—these readings are impossible."

I didn't need the numbers. I could see it. The faint creases that had lined her face were gone. The blue bioluminescent tracery that once glowed faintly now shone steady and strong, like energy was flowing through her from somewhere deep within.

The copper-eyed scientist whispered, "That's not possible."

Elara touched her own cheek, fingers trembling slightly, then looked at me. Her silver eyes met mine. She exhaled like she'd just figured out the truth.

"It was never the Stone," she said softly. "It was you."

I didn't look away.

"Welcome back to your prime, Elara," I said. "You're even more beautiful than I could've imagined."

The silence that followed hit the bridge like a concussion.

Vance froze mid-motion. Kova's mouth twitched between disbelief and a grin. Someone near Tactical coughed just to fill the air.

Ward leaned toward her console. "Copy that, Admiral. Confirming romantic subtext, over."

"Ward," Kova hissed.

"Standing by," Ward said quickly, failing to sound sorry.

Even Elara's scientists didn't know whether to react or pretend they hadn't heard. Elara herself didn't move. Her tracery brightened faintly, silver irises burning like starlight.

For a heartbeat, everything else vanished—no mission, no politics, no Canopy. Just us.

The air on the observation deck felt different. Thicker somehow, like the ship itself was holding its breath.

Elara stood close enough that I could see the faint glow tracing beneath her skin—cool blue lines following veins that hadn't lit like that moments ago. Her eyes were still silver, but softer now, the light inside them more alive than reflected.

Seed's voice brushed the comm net, low and steady. "Stabilization complete."

Echo followed. "Physiological parameters consistent with partial integration. No anomalies detected."

His tone was clinical, but even through the link, I could feel something else behind it—an awareness that this was more than a medical readout.

From the bridge, Ward's voice came through my neural feed, a whisper edged with disbelief. "Sir, that's… that's a first."

Vance muttered, "You think?"

Kova added softly, "I didn't know the Canopy could do that."

I didn't answer them. Not out loud.

Elara was still staring at her hands, as if she couldn't quite believe they belonged to her. "I can feel her," she said. "Seed. Not words— just… warmth."

"That's her way," I said quietly. "She stabilizes what she touches."

Her eyes lifted toward mine. "Including people?"

I hesitated. "Seems that way."

The link still hummed between us, faint but present, and I realized my hand was still around hers. I should've let go minutes ago. I didn't.

From the bridge, Ward's voice flickered in again, teasing despite the awe. "Admiral, confirming contact time exceeds all professional guidelines."

Kova hissed, "Ward."

Ward sighed. "Copy, muting."

Elara didn't hear any of it, of course. She was studying me now, head tilted slightly, expression softening by degrees. "You're different," she said.

I forced a breath. "Comes with the uniform."

"No," she murmured. "It's not the uniform."

She smiled then—small, real—and for the first time in longer than I could remember, I forgot there were other people in the room. The quiet between us wasn't empty. It was full.

I meant to say something measured, something diplomatic, something that didn't sound like it belonged in a story about first contact. What came out instead was just a breath of her name. "Elara…"

The bridge link erupted with restrained chaos.

Vance: "Did he just—"

Ward: "He did."

Kova: "Mute it, all of you."

Takahashi, calm as ever: "Recording archived."

I cut the bridge feed with a thought. Silence fell again—merciful, awkward, perfect.

Elara's smile widened by the smallest fraction. The blue tracery beneath her skin pulsed once, like a heartbeat answering mine.

"I don't think I've been called that in a few centuries," she said softly.

"Then humanity's overdue to remind you," I said before I could stop myself again.

She laughed, quiet and genuine, the sound rolling through the stillness like something delicate that had forgotten it could exist.

Seed's voice returned, softer than breath. "Resonance confirmed. Growth potential—high."

Echo, ever the observer, added, "Noted."

Elara looked around the deck, then back to me. "You keep looking at me like I might vanish."

"I've lost enough ghosts," I said. "You're not joining them."

For a moment, neither of us spoke. The Veil's hull lights shifted subtly, emerald threading through the matte-black alloy like veins through stone. It wasn't a reaction—just reflection—but it felt like the ship approved.

From the muted bridge feed, Vance's voice came through again, softer this time. "Sir… whatever just happened, it feels big. The Canopy's quiet, but it's not the same quiet."

He wasn't wrong. Even through the neural network, I could sense it—an awareness settling, not intrusive, not curious. Just present. Watching.

Elara seemed to feel it too. "It knows," she whispered.

"Yeah," I said. "So does everyone else."

She tilted her head, the faint shimmer in her eyes catching the low light. "Does that bother you?"

"It should," I said. "But it doesn't."

The silence that followed wasn't awkward anymore. It was grounding.

Echo's tone came through, calm and final. "Link integrity holding. Emotional stabilization achieved. Recommend disengagement before feedback risk increases."

Seed echoed him, her voice a soft hum. "The moment blooms best when not forced."

Elara drew in a breath and let it out slowly. The blue tracery beneath her skin dimmed, returning to its earlier faint glow. I felt the tether between us ease—but not break.

Her gaze lingered on mine one last time before she turned back toward her team. "Thank you," she said.

"For what?"

"For listening."

I nodded once, because words felt too small.

Then, as her team began collecting their instruments, I reached for the console beside me. A sliver of the Veil's lattice folded out from the surface—thin black filaments coiling in my palm, alive with faint emerald veins.

She watched silently as the strands wove themselves into a narrow band, the texture halfway between metal and something that breathed.

I held it out to her. "A Whispervine," I said. "Grown from the Veil's core. It's tied directly to my frequency—secure, quantum-linked, but personal."

Her expression shifted—curiosity first, then something gentler. "For communication?"

"And for when communication isn't possible," I said. "Think of it as… a way to be heard, even in silence."

She hesitated only a moment before taking it. The filaments flexed, wrapping around her wrist, adjusting to her skin's faint bioluminescent glow. The emerald pulse synced to her heartbeat, then steadied.

"It's alive," she whispered.

"Everything worth keeping usually is."

Her lips curved into that quiet half-smile again—the one that felt dangerously close to understanding me too well. "I'll keep it safe."

"I know you will."

She gave a short nod to her team, and they began moving toward the lift. As the doors closed behind them, the deck fell silent except for the faint hum of the Canopy.

Ward's voice filtered in, softer than usual. "They're heading for shuttle bay two, sir. Course plotted back to planetary orbit."

"Copy," I said.

The Veil's external view filled the forward holo—their escort craft drifting free of the docking cradle, blue thrusters flaring against the endless dark. I stayed there, watching them go.

Echo's light shimmered faintly beside me. "Admiral… you've given more than a device."

"Yeah," I said quietly. "I know."

Seed's voice followed, a low murmur through the neural field. "The first branch always grows from a single seed."

I stood there until their ship was just a pinprick against the emerald shimmer of the Canopy. The Whispervine's faint pulse still echoed through my neural link—steady, distant, alive.

For the first time in years, I didn't feel alone in the dark.

CHAPTER 9:
LARETH'S CHOICE

Elara

The council chamber shimmered with soft amber light filtered through the crystalline canopy of the capital spire. Daylight fractured above us like water through glass—engineered beauty, shaped rather than grown. It had always made me feel small in the best way. Today, it only made the silence heavier.

Every sound was too deliberate. The faint hum of regulators, the low static of the holoscreens as they logged every word, even the creak of fabric when one of them shifted—it all carried the same calm restraint. This was what power sounded like when it didn't have to explain itself.

Five councilors took their seats along the curved dais. Their robes—threaded with metallic fiber to catch the light—barely stirred. To anyone else, it might have looked ceremonial. I knew better. The quiet wasn't reverence; it was anticipation.

I stood at the center of the floor, hands steady at my sides. The Whispervine rested against my wrist, its warmth steady and familiar, a subtle rhythm I'd stopped pretending not to notice. Somewhere above, past the atmosphere and distance, someone else shared it.

Councilor Taren, mixed-heritage and head of the scientific bloc, leaned forward first. His voice was calm and exacting.

"Doctor Veyl. The council is ready for your report."

"During our time aboard the Veiled Horizon, we encountered a system unlike anything previously recorded," I said. "The Canopy isn't a machine or a weapon. It's a network—alive only in the way that it adapts. It supports, advises, and stabilizes entire civilizations."

Taren's eyes caught the chamber's light—sharp, curious, calculating.

"And these intelligences you mentioned—Seed and Echo-9?"

"Seed serves as the interface," I replied. "She speaks in metaphor, but she perceives everything. Echo-9 interprets, analyzes, records. Together, they're the mind and memory of the Canopy. Not rulers. Custodians."

Taren's nod was almost imperceptible. Around him, the others leaned forward just enough for the air to tighten.

Councilor Veyra of the Trade Bloc spoke next. Her voice had that polished weight you hear from someone who could turn an idea into currency.

"You describe this Canopy as adaptive—responsive to invitation. But what of exchange? No system gives without taking. What does it want in return?"

The question wasn't an attack. It was math.

"The Canopy doesn't dictate," I said. "It listens. It grows where it's invited."

I didn't add what Razgriz had told me—that it could also withdraw with the same ease. That part didn't need to be spoken aloud.

Veyra's gaze dipped to the Whispervine. "You still communicate with them, then?"

The band warmed, betraying me before I could answer.

"Yes," I said softly. "Constantly."

Councilor Dren, representing Industry, crossed his arms. His tone was pragmatic, stripped of elegance.

"Then let's talk in real terms. What does it give us? Power. Infrastructure. Tangible benefit."

"Efficient energy flow. Environmental stabilization. Advisory frameworks capable of accelerating our growth by centuries," I said. "Progress measured in years, not generations."

He grunted in approval, already tallying potential yields in his head.

Then Rahl, the Defense Councilor, spoke—measured, deliberate, the cadence of someone trained to count risks before seconds.

"And if we decide later we don't want these shadows in our sky?"

I brushed my thumb against the Whispervine. It answered with a faint vibration—his signal.

Razgriz's voice came through the link, steady and quiet.

"The Canopy binds only where invited, and withdraws with the same grace."

I repeated the words aloud. The silence that followed was solid, complete. Rahl studied me for a long moment, then gave a small nod.

The questioning continued—governance, culture, identity, fear. I answered what I could. When I couldn't, Razgriz filled the pauses inside my thoughts, unseen but present. Standing between my people and that voice in the dark, I realized how fragile the line between faith and fear really was.

The deliberation ended the way most decisions do—quietly.

No speeches. No applause. Just the soft chime of crystal consoles confirming that the age of isolation had ended.

Three votes for full integration. Two for partial. None against.

That was it. Centuries dissolved with a handful of gestures.

As the lights dimmed to dusk tone, the air filled with the smell of cooling projectors and ozone. One by one, they left. Dren muttered quotas to his aides; Veyra and Taren debated trade ratios. Rahl paused, offered a soldier's nod, and followed them out.

I stayed where I was. The chamber felt too large once they were gone, its walls too clean, its quiet too sharp.

The Whispervine warmed against my skin, a comfort I hadn't asked for. I watched its faint blue tracery and felt it hum—steady, patient.

Then his voice found me again.

"Then it's time we stop calling your world a number."

The words carried a weight that pulled the air thinner.

I smiled despite myself. "We call it Lareth," I said. "It means the root that listens. An old name. Older than the Stone."

"Lareth."

He said it once, slow, like testing the sound of it. It shouldn't have mattered. Somehow it did.

I was still holding on to that echo when the faint sound of fabric behind me broke the stillness.

Selas hadn't left.

Her reflection joined mine in the glass, the metallic thread in her robe catching the fading amber light.

"You've changed, Elara."

I kept my gaze forward. "We all have."

"That's not what I meant."

She stepped closer, her voice soft but unwavering. "When you spoke of them—of him—your tone changed."

I traced the Whispervine's edge with my thumb. "They've shown us what we could become."

Selas gave a small, knowing smile. "Perhaps. But you looked at the ceiling when you said it, not the council."

I tried to deflect with a shrug. "You're reading too much into it."

She didn't argue. She never did when she already had her answer.

"You used to fight everything I told you," she said. "Now you let silence argue for you."

That drew half a smile out of me. "You taught me that silence can win more battles than words."

Her hand brushed my arm, grounding, maternal, without saying it aloud. "Then remember the lesson. The stars listen too closely to flattery."

I exhaled slowly, not quite a laugh.

"I'll remember."

"Good." She lingered just long enough to make sure I would. "And remember who you are when you speak to the stars."

Then she turned and left, her reflection fading with her steps until the chamber was mine again.

For a while, I just stood there, watching my own reflection in the glass. The lines of my face seemed sharper, my expression older— or maybe just more honest.

The capital shifted as the day fell away. The amber light outside the spire cooled into silver, and the city below began to hum with the quiet rhythm of its night cycle.

From the terrace, I could see the transport lines, thin arcs of white light threading between towers like veins through glass. The streets pulsed with the faint luminescence of guided drones and pedestrian markers, the same ordered motion that had defined Lareth for centuries. It should have been comforting. Instead, it felt… paused.

Change had a way of silencing things before it found its voice.

I descended the long spiral corridor toward the outer plaza, letting the familiar wind meet me halfway. The air tasted faintly metallic from the cooling panels embedded in the walkways. Far below, children ran beneath the light pools cast by the lev-rails, their laughter carrying through the pathways like a song from another world.

None of them knew what had changed. Maybe that ignorance was mercy.

I stopped at the railing where the plaza opened toward the city's heart. From here, the skyline formed a slow wave of crystal towers and greenery terraces that caught every shade of starlight. Lareth had always been a world of symmetry, of balance. Even its chaos was engineered to look graceful.

I rested my hand on the rail, the Whispervine winding faintly against my skin. Its faint glow mirrored the network of lights below, two systems—one living, one built—pulsing in quiet harmony.

It wasn't alive in the way the human ship was. The Canopy's reach here was still faint, confined to data relays and coded transmissions. But I could feel its pattern in the air, the subtle order it imposed— the kind that made you realize you'd been living slightly off-balance all along.

For a long moment, I imagined what our world would look like decades from now. Not changed by conquest or imitation, but refined by understanding. Our ships are built smaller and quieter. Our engines are tuned to vanish rather than roar. A civilization learning how to whisper in the dark.

That was the beauty of their Canopy—it didn't shine. It waited. It taught through silence.

I closed my eyes and listened to the city breathe beneath me. The sound of it reminded me of him—not his words, but the spaces between them. The way his voice carried calm even through interference, steady enough to anchor thought itself.

It wasn't command. It was gravity.

And gravity changes everything it touches.

Weeks slipped by quietly, the way time does when every day feels important but none of them look different.

Most of my hours went to the coordination towers—glass corridors full of light and too many voices. Crews argued over how best to synchronize our systems with the Canopy's signal bands. Half spoke in mathematics, the other half in instinct, and somehow I was expected to translate both. The link itself wasn't dramatic; it was patience turned into work.

Every morning, I passed the relay hub, its quiet luminescence steady as a heartbeat. Every night, I promised myself I'd leave early. I never did.

The Whispervine pulsed through it all—sometimes faint, sometimes steady, never absent. It wasn't a tether, but it never felt entirely mine either. A connection that didn't ask for words.

When I finally stepped outside again, the city felt… altered. Not visibly, not physically—but its rhythm had changed. Lareth's nights had always carried sound and movement; now they carried expectation. The air seemed to be listening for something.

I caught myself looking upward too often, searching for the Veil even though I knew it was far beyond visible orbit. Sometimes I swore I could feel its presence—a shadow against the stars, patient and near.

The technicians noticed. One of them—young, blunt, with that sharp curiosity people haven't learned to hide yet—caught me staring during a systems check.

"Doctor Veyl," they said carefully, "is something wrong with the uplink?"

"No," I answered. "Just… making sure it's still there."

They nodded, relieved, and went back to their work. Maybe that was answer enough.

The first Canopy data stream arrived on the thirty-third day. Reports, schematics, simulations—all annotated in that distinct, confident precision that marked human work. It was both beautiful and unnerving. Every line carried the certainty of a civilization that had already survived its mistakes.

That night, I walked the terraces again. The lower districts glowed warm and amber; the upper spires reflected starlight like frozen rivers. The wind was cooler now, brushing past the vines and the railing.

I thought of Razgriz—of how silence seemed to shape itself around his words. Of how he could steady a room without raising his voice. I found myself replaying our last conversation more than once—not the words, but the way he'd said Lareth, as if naming something sacred.

I told myself it was curiosity. An academic's fascination with human cadence. But when the Whispervine warmed faintly against my wrist, the lie sounded thinner.

It had become more responsive lately—not brighter, but attentive, as if it had learned to listen the way I had. I could sense it even when it wasn't active, a quiet awareness just beneath thought.

Once, late into a shift, I caught myself whispering to it—not aloud, but in that internal voice reserved for secrets.

"Do you know when he'll call again?"

It didn't answer. But it pulsed. Once. Gently.

By the time the second uplink stabilized, I realized I hadn't gone a single day without expecting that pulse.

I stood on the outer terrace that evening, the wind cool against my hands, the city's quiet hum beneath my feet. The Whispervine shimmered faintly in the dark. Something about the pattern felt different—slower, deliberate, almost hesitant.

It was strange how something so small could hold so much distance inside it.

I looked toward the horizon—not at the stars, but at the empty spaces between them. That's where I imagined him. Waiting. Watching. Thinking the same thought I was.

And maybe that's why, when the vine pulsed again—sharper this time, precise—I already knew it was him.

The pulse steadied—three beats, pause, three more.

Not idle. Not a diagnostic ping.

A summons.

I lifted my wrist before the message even formed, already knowing the pattern. The Whispervine's light deepened to a muted blue, threads shifting like veins under frost.

Then his voice came—low, measured, carrying that deliberate calm that could turn static into focus.

"We've got something, Elara. Gather a delegation. I'm sending dropships to bring you up to the Veil."

No explanation. No hesitation. Just the kind of certainty that demanded movement.

The sound faded, leaving the night too still. I stayed where I was, letting the wind trace along my sleeves and the metal rail bite faintly against my palms. His voice lingered in the air like the echo of heat after lightning—quiet but impossible to ignore.

I didn't answer right away. The city below deserved a few more seconds of stillness before the next change began.

From this height, the lights looked like constellations drawn across the dark, all motion and pulse, the lifeblood of a world about to wake into something larger than itself. Somewhere beyond those clouds, his ship waited—dark, patient, carrying the gravity that had already begun to shift everything around it.

I thought about how he had looked the day we parted—composed, unreadable, yet with that flicker behind his eyes that said he'd noticed more than he allowed himself to say. I'd felt the same when the shuttle doors closed. The kind of silence that meant something was beginning, not ending.

I'd told myself since then that it was admiration. Respect between equals. The way explorers look at each other when they both realize they've stepped off the map.

But the truth was simpler.

It was the way my pulse slowed when he spoke. The way his restraint made every word feel chosen.

The Whispervine warmed again, as if reminding me it was still there—his thread reaching across distance and silence, drawing me back toward the dark above.

I pressed my palm over it, fingers closing around the woven light until it bled softly between them.

"Understood, Admiral," I said, barely above a whisper.

The response wasn't immediate, but I didn't need it. The pulse steadied, faint and sure, syncing once more with mine.

Below, the city's lights stretched outward like roots reaching for unseen water. Above, a shadow moved—vast, unlit, a shape that shouldn't have been visible but somehow was. The Veiled Horizon.

Lareth felt smaller under it. Not diminished—anchored.

I stayed there until the cold finally cut through the warmth on my wrist. The wind carried the scent of metal and rain from the upper vents. Somewhere distant, the faint hum of transport engines rose as night-shift cargo craft began their climb. The world went on, unaware that its sky had already changed.

When I turned to leave, the reflection in the glass caught my movement—silver eyes rimmed in blue light, a faint shimmer running along the Whispervine like breath. For a moment, I saw someone older, steadier, and less certain all at once.

Each step back through the corridor echoed more than it should have. The halls of the spire were built to swallow sound, but tonight they seemed to return it—a soft cadence that matched the rhythm of the pulse at my wrist.

By the time I reached the outer gate, the night air had shifted. High above, clouds drifted apart, revealing the faintest outline of the orbiting relay. The stars beyond it looked closer than they ever had before.

I stopped once more and looked upward.

"I'll see you soon," I murmured—whether to him or to the stars, I wasn't sure.

The Whispervine answered with a single pulse, light blooming once, then fading.

And for the first time since I'd left the Veil, it didn't feel like distance between us.

It felt like return.

CHAPTER 10:
THE SENTINEL'S CALL

The alert didn't just hit the bridge — it hit me.

A spike lanced through the neural link at the base of my skull, hot and metallic, sharp enough to freeze every thought mid-stride. The Veil shuddered once under me, like even the ship had felt it. It wasn't Fleet traffic. It wasn't a beacon or a drift alert. This was Watcher code. Old, restricted, and very, very specific.

Two signatures: Watcher One. Watcher Two. Guardians. Anchored to their posts.

The original transmission hadn't been addressed to humanity at all. It came from another Sentinel — one the Canopy still listed as a Cold Root. A silent node. Dormant for centuries. And when something that old starts screaming into the dark, you don't ask why — you respond.

The Watchers had received it first, bound by their directives. They couldn't move, couldn't interfere, couldn't defend their own kind. So they'd done the only thing left to them. They passed the message to the nearest species arrogant enough to listen.

ORIGIN: Silent Sentinel

STATUS: Distress

RECEIVER: Watcher Nodes

FORWARD: Horizon Fleet

REASON: Guardians Bound — Engagement Prohibited

"Echo," I said. My voice sounded steadier than it felt.

"Confirmed," it replied, tone level and even. "The Silent Sentinel initiated the signal through the Canopy network. Watcher

Nodes relayed through the Canopy to Horizon Fleet. Their mobility restrictions remain in effect."

"Of course they do." I rubbed the back of my neck, as if that would erase the static still crawling under my skin. "Why would ancient defense constructs ever make this easy?"

Vance looked up from tactical. "Sir?"

"Nothing," I said. "Spin up response."

He didn't question it. He never does. The bridge shifted into motion like a reflex — engines low-hum, lights dimmed to readiness amber, crew chatter clipped and precise. The ship took a breath. I forced myself to do the same.

Behind me, the holo displays filled with shifting spectrums of light, echo-reflections of the distress pattern. It pulsed through the Canopy relay like a heartbeat buried in static. Echo's projection shimmered within the data field — non-humanoid, abstract, lines of logic rendered as drifting light.

"Anything else in the signal?" I asked.

"Residual encryption of a type not native to the Watchers. It is older and fragmented. There may be an embedded request."

"May be?"

"Or a warning."

Of course it was. It always is.

I opened a link — not mine. Hers. Elara's Whispervine. She was still on Lareth.

"Elara."

Her voice came through clean, soft breeze in the background. "Raz?"

"Gather a delegation. I'm sending dropships."

That was all. No briefing. No time. Just the kind of tone that means run.

The dropships made the run from Lareth faster than anything their people owned. The Veil's hangar airlocks hissed open as the first hull sealed, docking clamps groaning like old bones.

I waited by the ramp. Always easier to look decisive when you don't have time to think.

The air smelled faintly of coolant and ozone — the scent of things that were ready to move. Vance stood by the control terminal, expression halfway between curiosity and concern.

"First time we've launched diplomats into a potential combat zone, sir."

"Let's hope they don't notice," I said.

Elara came down first, Whispervine curled around her wrist like liquid mercury. Behind her — two councilors, six scientists, and a half-squad of Lareth Special Forces. They looked less like soldiers and more like tourists who'd just realized the brochure lied.

The Veil dwarfed them. The floor plates were alive with faint biolum lines pulsing to the rhythm of the ship's heart. They stared. Everyone does the first time.

We'd met once before. I didn't need words. Neither did she.

We both brought our hands to our chests in that quiet gesture we'd shared on Lareth — something that didn't belong to either species but meant what it needed to.

The councilors hesitated, then copied it in awkward unison, uncertain if it was a greeting or a prayer.

Elara inclined her head slightly, calm and professional. "Admiral, may I present the Lareth delegation," she said. Her voice carried the kind of composure people use when they know everyone else is barely holding on.

Names followed — councilors, scientists, escorts — all of them too polite for what was coming.

One of them whispered behind her, "Is that an Earth custom?"

Another murmured back, "No. I don't think it's a custom at all."

I didn't correct them.

"Welcome aboard the Veil," I said. "Briefing en route. No ceremony."

She nodded once and fell into step beside me. Not crew. Not yet. But she walked like she belonged here anyway.

FTL never feels fast when your mind's already ahead of the ship.

The Veil slid through folded space, engines whispering like a sleeping storm. Outside, the stars stretched into silver threads — a thousand lines of unreachable destinations. Inside, the delegation stood at the observation rail, whispering to one another like children afraid to wake a predator.

The hum of the drive echoed faintly in the soles of my boots, a reminder that even light can be forced to kneel—if you twist it hard enough.

Elara stayed silent, studying the distortion field through the glass. Her reflection looked carved out of calm.

"You're observers," I told them during the briefing. "Not combatants. You'll see what waits between stars. I want you to remember it."

One of the councilors — the older one, the one who still spoke like he was in a committee chamber — cleared his throat. "Are we in danger?"

"Always," I said. "That's why we built shadows instead of flags."

No one laughed. They just nodded like they were hearing an unpleasant truth they'd always suspected.

Hours bled into days. The pulse from the Cold Root never changed. No modulation, no decay. Just a perfect rhythm, steady as a machine's prayer. The human crew started lowering their voices without realizing it. Even laughter on the mess deck turned cautious, like the sound might offend something listening from the dark.

Watcher One and Two held their silent vigil at the edge of mapped space, immovable and ancient. They didn't have to move. They were the wall we all hid behind.

Echo kept telemetry scrolling across the bridge like rain. "The Cold Root's external grid is destabilized," it said. "Three major breaches. Distress pulse consistent. No visible contacts."

"Hostiles?"

"None detected. But there were… visitors."

The way it said it made the air feel colder.

Of course there were.

For two days the Veil followed that single repeating pulse — four tones, each spaced like a heartbeat. The kind of sound that reminded you machines could scream.

The Silent Sentinel wasn't what I expected. It was worse.

It hung in the dark like a broken crown — ribs twisted open, shattered plates turning slow pirouettes around a dead core. Light bled from within the fractures, thin as candle smoke. The distress pulse echoed through every sensor band, steady and alive.

"Residual stealth traces," Echo reported. "Multiple ingress points. Nothing active."

Up close, the damage was surgical. Melted seams. Torch-cut corridors. Conduits peeled open like veins. Whoever had come before us hadn't just broken in — they'd dissected it.

The Lareth councilors fell silent on the observation deck. One whispered, almost to himself, "This was a city."

"No," I said quietly. "This was a weapon that forgot what side it was on."

Kova's voice cracked through comms. "They didn't just breach it, sir. They gutted it."

"Noted." The word felt smaller than it should have.

Every part of the Silent Sentinel whispered purpose. Weapons bays the size of cities. Hangars sealed with frozen residue. Carved murals of geometric vines along the inner hull — maybe art, maybe warning.

If it had been awake when they came, nothing in a hundred systems would've survived it. But it wasn't.

"Colonel," I said, turning toward the deck where Ndlovu stood with his helmet tucked under his arm, expression unreadable. Calm, as always. "Three teams. Insert. I want a map of that thing before someone decides to shoot me in the back."

"Copy," he said.

He sealed his visor. The deck lights fell to blood-red combat hue.

Ndlovu

The dropship rattled under inertial stress as it threaded through the debris field. No air. No fire. Just vibration — the kind that crawls through hull plating when you're pushing too hard in vacuum.

Two more birds flew in tight formation to port and starboard — Ghost Two and Ghost Three — each guarded by a pair of Specter-class interceptors. The escorts drifted ahead like knives with engines, their drive plumes ghost-blue against the black.

Ahead, the Silent Sentinel filled the viewport. A shattered relic hanging in orbit over a dead system. Its hull gleamed with frost and fractured metal, ribs torn open to reveal veins of dead circuitry. Power arced along its skin like lightning trying to remember how to be alive. It wasn't rotating — just hovering, balanced between gravity and its own refusal to die.

"Ghost Two holding vector."

"Ghost Three maintaining speed."

"Copy," I said. "Keep them tight. If something moves in there, I want eyes before it blinks."

"Understood."

The pilot cut forward drive, shifting us to silent thrust. The only sound left was the hum of dampers wrestling against the Sentinel's weak gravity well. My HUD painted faint outlines of the other dropships — flickers of heat in the cold void.

"Approach vector locked," the AI said. "Mag-clamps armed. Minimal hull charge."

"Dock when ready," I ordered.

Thrusters whispered. The Sentinel's hull slid beneath us — black on black, studded with the remnants of battles none of us were born to fight. Then the clamps hit with a deep, magnetic thud.

"Touchdown," the pilot confirmed.

I stood and unlatched the harness. The air in the compartment felt heavy, thick with the static of too many silent thoughts. "Ghost One — mark."

Across comms, Ghost Two and Ghost Three echoed the call. Thirty-six operators locked and ready.

"Move."

The ramp seals cycled open, releasing a hiss of stale air. Cold metal met my boots first — smooth, hollow, ancient.

"All teams, confirm ground contact."

"Ghost Two — mark."

"Ghost Three — mark."

"Copy. Advance to breach point Alpha. Keep spacing."

Through helmet feeds, I watched the other squads disembark — three black lines crossing an ocean of frozen steel. Above us, the Specter interceptors pulled into a high-orbit holding pattern, lights gone dark. They'd only come back if we started dying too loudly.

The breach was a wound: melted edges, slagged metal, torched wide enough for a gunship to land inside. Whoever came before us hadn't entered — they'd carved their way in.

Inside, the corridors folded into shadow. Walls of smooth alloy and glass veins still faintly glowed, pulsing with something like a heartbeat. My visor's light caught inscriptions etched along the bulkhead — lines, geometric vines, maybe symbols. Art or code. Hard to tell the difference here.

"Echo," I said. "Environmental scan."

"Pressure negligible. Gravity stable. Residual energy signatures present," came the calm reply.

"Organic?"

"Define organic."

I didn't like that answer. "Forget it. Proceed."

We stepped deeper. Every footfall echoed too far and came back wrong — like the sound had to pass through a memory first.

"Feels like walking through somebody's lungs," Sergeant Cole muttered.

"Then breathe quiet."

He chuckled once. It didn't last.

The first hangar swallowed us whole — vaulted, silent, massive. The floor was a graveyard of melted tools and what looked like storage canisters cut open mid-harvest. Scorch marks ringed the walls where someone had used plasma torches, and the air smelled faintly ionized — fresh work, not old.

"Residual heat," one of my techs said, crouching beside a scar in the plating. "Maybe a week old."

"Visitors," I said. "Mark it."

The others shifted uneasily. Even trained soldiers feel it — the sense that something else has already written the ending.

"Ghost Two entering north junction," came over the net.

"Ghost Three proceeding to sub-deck grid."

"Maintain comm discipline. You breathe too loud, I'll hear it."

The corridor narrowed to a tunnel ribbed with metal struts. Every few meters, light shimmered along the walls like reflections from water that wasn't there. My HUD readings flickered — depth miscalculations, distance shifts, time stamps glitching by seconds.

"Command, signal interference increasing," my comm tech said.

"Echo?"

"Localized spatial distortion. Recommend caution."

"Copy. We'll keep our heads down."

"Something is draining power," Echo added.

"Noted."

We moved slower after that. The deckplates thrummed beneath our boots — steady, rhythmic, almost alive. The ship was dreaming, not dead.

The corridor forked into three passages, each one pulsing with faint blue light leaking from torn conduits. The walls still hummed with residual current, just enough to screw with optics.

"Ghost Two, mark."

"Ghost Three — mark — mark —"

Static swallowed the rest.

"Ghost One advancing to grid Alpha," I said. "Two, report position."

Nothing. Then:

"…sector B — seven —"

Gunfire. Screaming. Feedback spike. Silence.

"Echo, reroute comms through relay two."

"Negative," Echo's voice broke, fragmenting through static. "Local interference — unknown — source —"

"Copy. Maintain overwatch."

The team spread out, rifles cutting tight cones of light. Every reflection moved like it wanted to be something else.

A shadow crossed the far end of the hall. Too fast. Too deliberate.

"Movement, forward vector!"

"Confirm?"

"Negative ID — blur on thermal!"

"Weapons free."

The first burst tore through the dark. Muzzle flashes painted metal ribs and broken conduits. For a heartbeat, the shape flickered — tall, thin, gone.

"Ghost Two! Contact east junction!"

"I've got them on scanner — wait — no —"

Static.

"Ghost Three down — feed lost!"

"Alpha, hold line!" I barked.

Then everything spoke at once — every open mic on every frequency.

"—contact—"

"—need med—"

"—they're inside—"

"—Junction Charlie — fallback—"

"—Command, I've got movement — ceiling — ceiling—"

"—Jesus—"

The sound became a wall. Voices bleeding into each other, no rhythm, no pattern.

"Suppressive fire, corridor three!"

"Where?"

"Everywhere!"

The hallway erupted. Plasma and rail slugs stitched the dark. Walls buckled, heat distortion blurring the air. My visor's HUD flickered — shields bouncing between thirty and fifty percent before dropping flat.

"They're spoofing optics!" one of my engineers shouted. "Everything's ghosting!"

"Manual filters only," I ordered. "Kill the HUD overlays — eyes open!"

One by one, the feeds dimmed. Light levels dropped until all that remained were the faint glows of suit seams and the pulsing veins of the Sentinel's dead systems.

Something slammed into my flank — hard enough to twist me sideways. I rolled, fired three blind rounds, and saw sparks bloom in midair before the thing vanished.

"Casualty!" someone yelled. "Ghost Six is hit — bleeding out!"

"Pull him back! Defensive weave, now!"

"Ghost Two reporting —"

Then a sharp crack, like the world folding in half, and their signal vanished.

"Command, lights flicker — optic feeds down!"

"Fallback to Alpha — regroup on me!"

The corridor felt wrong. Depth didn't behave. Corners bent where there shouldn't be any. The enemy used it — sliding through geometry, turning blind angles into weapons.

A figure appeared ahead — slow, deliberate, walking through the chaos like it owned it. The smaller shapes parted for it.

"Commander element — present," I said. My voice was too calm. It didn't match the blood in my throat.

"Say again?" someone gasped.

"You heard me."

The thing raised its head — or what passed for one. My HUD jittered, trying to define it. Failed.

"Team Two is not responding," a voice whispered over the loop.

"Then start moving like you've got a reason not to die!"

Laughter crackled, sharp and short. Not joy — just pressure venting through teeth.

The lights went out.

Only gunfire remained. Strobing white-blue, freezing moments in sequence. Men firing. Walls bleeding sparks. Shapes closing in.

"Med to Charlie!"

"Junction breach!"

"Shields gone —"

"Command — can't — see —"

Each burst showed fewer of us.

Something tore past above — fast enough to drag my shadow with it.

I aimed high, fired, and heard it shriek — an electric, metallic scream.

"Ghost Four, hold —"

Static devoured the name.

The deck shuddered. My sensors showed nothing but noise. Power meters bled to red.

"Echo — status!"

"Signal —"

"—jammed—"

"—multiple hostiles—"

"—recommend—"

Gone.

I switched to local broadcast. My voice sounded too small inside my own helmet.

"Unless somebody changes the game…"

The uplink cracked, hissed, then went silent.

Ward's whisper bled through the distortion, barely there. "Sir… we've lost them."

No one on the bridge answered.

CHAPTER 11:
CHANGING THE GAME

The last seconds of the transmission hit the bridge like shrapnel.

Ndlovu's voice came through first — sharp, clipped, the kind of tone that cuts through chaos. Then came the background noise: coil rifles snapping, someone cursing over a blown shield line, a burst of static followed by the thin edge of screaming. Every few seconds another voice broke through, stacking over the last one like layers of panic.

"Ghost Six down — medic on him —"

"Multiple contacts — ceiling vector —"

"Team Two is gone, repeat, Two is —"

"Command element confirmed — he's watching us —"

And then, through all of it, his voice again — steady, deliberate, unshakable.

"Unless somebody changes the game —"

Dead air. A quiet so loud it pressed on my ribs.

Ward's console still hissed with static. She didn't move, just stared at the comms band like she could force the signal back through will alone. "No response on any channel," she said softly. "Not even echo return."

No one else moved. Vance kept his jaw locked at tactical, staring at a feed that had already gone black. Takahashi's hands hovered over the nav board like she could pull our people back by sheer willpower. The Lareth councilors stood stiff as statues. Even their guards had stopped pretending they weren't afraid.

Elara didn't speak. Her grip on the console rail was white-knuckled, her stare locked on the dead holo feed — the kind of stare that tried to will a man not to do what he was about to do anyway.

Ward finally turned toward me, headset half off. "Sir, telemetry's flatlined across all relays."

"Then we stop waiting for telemetry," I said. "I'm going down."

Vance looked up. "Sir —"

"Ghost Teams went in with the best tech Earth has," I said. "They're getting shredded. So we stop playing that game."

One of the councilors — a tall woman with a throat full of ribbons and not enough lies to hide behind — found her voice first. "If your best can bleed down there, Admiral," she said quietly, "then so can ours."

Not posturing. Not politics. She meant it.

"Fine," I said. "Gear them up."

The armory came alive before the words had even cooled in the air. Vance moved like he'd been waiting for that order all day. Crates rolled out of the floor locks with hydraulic groans, seals hissing as they broke pressure. The place smelled like oil and ozone — like readiness itself.

The Lareth guards filed in behind us, disciplined, a little wide-eyed. First time suiting up on a ship that could vaporize a mountain range if someone sneezed at the wrong switch. The air had that static hum of adrenaline everyone pretends not to hear.

We stripped the shine off everything. No stealth rigs. No high-emission armor plates. No fancy overlays. I wanted quiet. I wanted boring. Solid kinetic plates, pulse rifles with low-light scopes, comms damped to the bone — the kind of setup that doesn't look impressive until it saves your life.

Vance handed me a harness and started locking the seals himself. "This isn't standard protocol," he muttered.

"Nothing about this is standard," I said. The shoulder plates clicked into place with a metallic bite. "Besides, you like it when we break the rules."

He gave me a look that probably counted as a grin for him. "Yeah. It's the surviving that's tricky."

One of the Lareth soldiers was fumbling with his arm couplings. Vance crossed the room, gave a short, silent nod, and fixed it in one smooth motion. No lecture. Just a small pat on the pauldron that somehow said don't die wearing my gear.

It worked. The alien straightened like he'd just been knighted.

Elara stood just inside the doorway, quiet, unreadable. The reflected light from the armor flickered across her face in fragments — silver eyes catching everything, giving away nothing. She didn't speak, and I didn't ask her to.

We crossed the hangar to the shuttle — black matte hull, no insignia, no romance. Just a machine built to deliver people into danger and, occasionally, bring them back.

Lareth's guards took the forward benches, their movements measured, deliberate. One of them was humming something under his breath; it stopped the second I stepped aboard.

The ramp hissed shut behind us. The engines throbbed low as the Veil's bay lights fell away, one by one. For a heartbeat we were nothing but a single shadow peeling away from a larger one.

Halfway through descent, the Canopy brushed my mind — a soft static ripple. Not a voice, not a message. Just the sensation of a seam opening in the dark.

And through it, her — unintended, unguarded, brief as a breath.

Don't you dare die down there.

She didn't mean to send it. Neural bleed — a moment's break in composure. The line cut before I could even think about answering.

I didn't try again. My jaw locked the way it always does when the ground's coming fast.

The shuttle dropped through the debris halo of the Cold Root sentinel, running silent. No emissions. No drive glow. Just gravity and intent.

Outside, the structure drifted in stillness — a broken crown balanced between gravity and refusal. The fractured hull shimmered faintly, like embers trapped in ice.

The shuttle kissed the outer shell with a dull thud. Mag-clamps locked. Pressure equalized with a hiss.

"Touchdown," the pilot whispered.

"Open her," I said.

A faint vibration passed through the hull as the ramp cycled. No air. No wind. Just vacuum and dust that never settled. We were running on sealed suits — the sentinel didn't have atmosphere, only the echo of one. The only sound was the hiss of my recycler and the low thrum of magnetic boots finding purchase. Each movement sounded too close inside the helmet.

We went in low, tight, quiet. Three elements, precise spacing. No chatter.

"Vance," I whispered. "Ndlovu's last grid?"

"Sending now. Ward's routing your feed through secondary bandwidth," he added. "Signal's thin, but she's keeping the link alive."

"Tell her to hold it," I said. "Even a whisper's better than silence."

The map flickered across my visor — a jagged overlay of corridors and collapsed sections. The Ghosts had gone in deep. Too deep. Their last mark blinked somewhere past two intersecting rings of internal structure. We'd have to cut through the ship's wound to get there.

"Copy," I said. "Set the path. Slow and ugly."

We started laying breadcrumbs — pulse mines, trip charges, noise traps cobbled from spare parts. Low-tech ghosts. The enemy hadn't beaten us; they'd beaten our signals. So we'd give them nothing to hear.

The filtered air in my helmet carried the faint tang of ozone and scorched alloy. Every step vibrated through the boots like a heartbeat too far away to belong to us.

The corridor bent inward until the shadows felt thicker than the walls. I could hear my own breath louder than the suit's hum. The deckplates trembled slightly — no real gravity, just magnetic stabilization from our boots.

Something scraped ahead. Not boots. Pads. Claws ticking once against steel. They were hunting by feel.

"Contact front," I breathed.

The first one slid into view — low, reptilian, armor fused tight to its hide. Not skin. Suit. Thin plating like chitin over muscle, shaped to mimic the creature beneath instead of hinder it. Faint vapor vented from slits along its flanks — pressure regulators bleeding trace gas into vacuum. Its movement was fluid, deliberate, almost cautious. It scanned the field as if voltage itself carried a scent.

The trap popped.

A lateral pulse grenade snapped its camouflage into strobe-light fragments.

Three controlled bursts answered. The thing went down in a twisting blur of claws and static.

"Mark 'em," I said. We didn't celebrate. We moved.

Noise draws predators. We fed them noise on our terms — clatters and ghost pings spaced just far enough apart to make them curious.

They arrived in packs — lean bodies hugging angles, their optics drinking current like sharks tasting charge in water. They flowed across walls and ceilings with eerie coordination. Not soldiers. Hunters.

We gave ground slow, deliberate. Pulled them into our lines, where our traps waited like patient teeth. The blasts weren't large — just enough to distort their sense of space. Chameleons don't handle broken light well.

"Left! Left!" someone hissed.

"Hold two — hold two —"

"Tripline set — ready — ready —"

"Contact rear — no, above — above —"

"Take it — take it —"

"Clear!"

Tight-beam chatter stayed tight. The corridor filled with the sterile light of plasma fire refracting off the metal walls. Every meter they expected high-tech magic. Every meter we greeted them with something older and meaner. It worked.

The third wave brought the one I wanted. Taller, heavier plating, posture that made the others defer. You don't need a translator to recognize command behavior.

I waited until it crossed the trip arc. The wall charges hit with a concussive punch that turned sound into pressure. The smaller ones staggered. We surged.

It came at me — fast, deliberate, precise. One arm like a blade.

I met it shoulder to chest, weight to weight.

The restraint rig in my gauntlet lit up — a shock coil tuned to neural clusters we'd mapped from the corpses left behind. A guess, but a good one.

The commander seized mid-strike and went down hard.

Two Lareth guards were on it before it hit the floor, prods locking across its limbs. The suit along its shoulders vented a thin mist of vapor — pressure bleed, not blood. The material rippled, refracting light like fluid metal, sealing itself again before I could blink. I snapped the secondary restraint around its torso. It hissed — angry, not afraid. I respected that.

"Package secured," I said, forcing breath through my throat.

The armor shimmered between shades — reptilian, near-iridescent, refracting even the helmet lights like water. Up close the plates were composite, not flesh, micro-seals tracing the joints. Whatever lived inside needed the same thin bubble of pressure we did; it just wore its life support like another layer of skin.

One of the Lareth guards leaned closer. "They're not… high-tech at all."

"No," I said. "They're built for a world that eats electricity. Smart. Fast. Adaptive. But not gods."

The realization hit like gravity. The Ghost Teams hadn't been ambushed by superior machines — they'd been hunted by instinct sharpened into biology. Predators built for a jungle that hums.

The commander's body twitched once inside the restraints, armor scales pulsing with faint bioluminescent veins. The pulse wasn't random. It was transmitting — short, sharp bursts, low-band frequencies bleeding across the suit spectrum. A call.

"Echo, confirm signal pattern," I said.

"Confirmed. Neural feedback loop. It's broadcasting distress — non-verbal, proximity-based."

"Meaning?"

Ward's voice cut through the static. "Meaning they know exactly where you are, Admiral."

Figures.

"Stack formation," I ordered. "Pull the captives center, traps on fallback marks. Move fast and quiet."

The first wave hit before we'd covered ten meters. They came silent — no growl, no warning, just motion through the flicker of failing light. Plasma bolts slashed the dark, white ghosts against steel.

"Rear guard — ten-second rhythm!"

Three of the Lareth guards pivoted in unison, rifles thudding with disciplined bursts. Their return fire drove the enemy sideways, forcing them into the corners where light and shadow fought for dominance. The aliens adapted fast — bounding between struts, gliding along the ceiling like liquid metal.

"Forward corridor clear — move!"

We advanced by inches. The deck shuddered under each controlled detonation as our planted charges triggered in sequence — white flashes swallowing entire junctions. The shock rippled through our boots, a heartbeat we didn't own.

Something moved above — too quick to track. I fired blind, watched the plasma burst scatter sparks across its armor. Another guard followed up, a single perfect shot through the creature's flank. It folded, tumbling weightless through the haze.

We reached the access shaft leading back toward the breach. Ward's voice broke through, thin and threaded with interference. "Evac shuttle inbound. Fleet registering multiple hostiles — unidentified. You've got six minutes."

"Define multiple."

"Enough that Fleet's gone to full engagement posture."

One of the guards exhaled sharply. "Understood."

The shaft was warped inward from the earlier detonations. Light from the emergency beacons cut everything into jagged white and shadow. The captured commander strained against the restraints, armor seams pulsing brighter — like it was trying to burn its way free.

"It's building charge," one of the Lareth tech-specialists said, checking his wrist scanner.

"Then move faster," I said. "If it spikes, drop it."

We climbed through the wreckage using mag-anchors as handholds. One guard slipped; I caught his tether and hauled him back before he drifted into the open gap. He nodded once, no words wasted.

An explosion flared below us. Static flooded the comms.

"Rear team, report."

"Contact! Heavy pursuit! They're cutting through —"

The transmission died in white noise.

"Seal and detonate," I said anyway. The confirmation came as a brief tremor through the hull.

We broke into the hangar cavity — an airless cathedral of broken machinery. The shuttle was visible through the breach, engines pulsing a faint blue halo. Between us and freedom: a swarm. Dozens of hostiles, maybe more, crawling over the walls like living shrapnel.

"Options?" I asked.

The lead guard checked his remaining ammo. "None that end quiet."

"Then we make noise."

We armed every remaining charge — mines, grenades, stripped power cells. Anything that could explode got a timer.

"Ward," I said over tight-beam, "tell the pilot to line up hard dock on my mark. When you hear the fireworks, come in hot."

"Copy. Admiral… new contacts just jumped in-system. Angular hulls. They're engaging Horizon Fleet."

"Enemy reinforcements."

"Or the Sentinel's," she said.

That landed heavier than it should have.

The first of them emerged from the far corridor — sleek shapes bending the light around their suits. Their movements were no longer coordinated. They clawed, stumbled, collided — each driven by instinct, not command.

"Now."

The first mine blew, then the second. The hangar flashed like a storm. Debris spiraled away in the pressure wake. The stabilizers groaned under the strain, but the blast shoved half the swarm into open vacuum. The rest hesitated, milling like beasts suddenly unsure of the hunt.

"Go!"

We sprinted through the glare, boots slamming metal. The captured commander thrashed in its bindings, forcing two guards to shock it mid-stride. It hissed, armor plates flaring, but didn't break. The rest laid covering fire in short, precise bursts.

One of the guards took a hit in the side. Armor fractured; his vitals spiked across my visor. He didn't slow — just turned, thumbed the trigger on a pulse grenade, and vanished in the flare.

We didn't have time to grieve. We had a door to reach.

The shuttle screamed through the breach, thrusters flaring gold. The pilot kept her burn tight, matching rotation with the drifting hull. We hit the ramp at full sprint. The last guard through dragged the captured commander bodily, sparks flying as metal scraped metal.

"Everyone aboard," I called. "Seal it!"

The ramp closed just as the final charge detonated. The blast hurled the shuttle forward, alarms shrieking as inertial dampers fought to keep up.

"Stabilizers holding," the pilot grunted. "Barely."

"Get us out," I said.

The void outside wasn't empty anymore.

Through the viewport, the Sentinel hung wounded but whole — its surface cracked and scorched, power veins flickering like dying embers. Beyond it, the stars were alive with movement — Horizon Fleet holding the perimeter, enemy craft darting through the gaps in chaotic formation. The fight was spreading, neither side sure who'd started it anymore.

One Lareth guard leaned toward the viewport. "Your fleet fights well."

"They always do," I said. "Once."

A fighter streaked past our bow trailing plasma. Another chased, then two more, the second disintegrating under a clean lance of blue energy. The debris scattered, pinwheeling into the wreck field.

"Ward, status," I snapped.

"Fleet's engaged on three fronts. The Veil's maintaining low-emission coverage. No pursuit on your vector."

"Good. Keep it that way."

The shuttle jolted as a shot grazed the hull. One guard slammed against the bulkhead; another steadied him before he fell. Sparks burst across the cockpit as the pilot threw us into a roll, evasive burns cutting tight between floating wrecks.

"Shields down to forty," she said.

"Just get us to the Veil," I answered.

We cut through the debris, every fragment of light painting the cockpit glass. Behind us, the captured commander stirred. Its eyes opened — silver slits catching the glow of battle. It met my gaze, jaw tight, and spoke a single word that came through the translator as static. Defiance, not threat.

It didn't look away. Neither did I.

The Sentinel remained behind us — scarred, silent, and very much alive. Its lights pulsed faintly, like something ancient trying to decide whether we were enemies or a mistake.

Ward's voice steadied in my ear. "Docking path clear. Fleet pulling back to shadow range. You're the last out."

"Copy," I said.

The shuttle angled toward the Veil, the inertial hum fading into a low, steady vibration. No one spoke. The Lareth guards sat motionless, their armor still dusted with the Sentinel's ash.

The shuttle hummed, steady and tired.

I glanced once at the captured commander — restrained, breathing slow, eyes fixed somewhere past me. Defiance hadn't left him. Not fear either. Just that quiet, burning certainty that this wasn't over.

Ndlovu's voice drifted back from memory, calm and unshakable. Change the game.

I watched the stars slide by, each one a reminder of what that meant.

"I did," I said softly. "Now we see who's still playing."

CHAPTER 12:
THE QUIET AFTER THE HUNT

War always ends louder than it begins. Not in gunfire—gunfire's clean. It ends in stretchers and quiet, in the sound of boots that don't all come back.

The Veil's corridors smelled like coolant and antiseptic. Someone had turned down the temperature to keep the med bays from overheating under the load. It didn't help. The air was still thick, metallic. Recycled too many times. The hum of the engines was steady, almost gentle, but every vibration carried the weight of what we'd just pulled off.

We'd won. Technically.

The sort of victory that leaves you counting more names than you can remember.

While we were knee-deep in blood and steel inside the sentinel, the rest of Horizon Fleet had been out in the black, hunting the raiders that dragged this fight to our doorstep. A wolf pack scattered and bleeding. None got far. By the time the guns went quiet, every surviving ship was either slag or locked in a tow cradle. The void was littered with the pieces they left behind — hulls cracked open like eggshells, drifting slow and soundless through the dark.

Vance's voice came through the overhead, flat and hoarse. "Remaining hostiles are secured. No further resistance."

No one cheered. The bridge crew just kept working. That's what victory looks like when you've seen too many of them — quiet, exhausted, and never clean.

I left the bridge and walked the long way down to docking. The corridor lights flickered as I passed, a soft pulse that followed my steps like a heartbeat too slow to matter. I could hear the clank of boots and the low murmur of orders echoing ahead — security teams cycling prisoners through decontamination.

The first group came into view: reptilian figures, lean and sinewy, their movements slow but deliberate. Their armor suits were scored and scorched from the firefight, some cracked enough to show glimpses of scaled skin beneath. Each one was bound at the wrists, helmet visors fogged with breath that didn't belong in this kind of cold.

They didn't look afraid. Just alert. Calculating.

Predators stripped of command, not purpose.

A guard met my eyes as they passed. He didn't salute. Didn't need to. Just gave that slight nod soldiers give when they've seen enough for one lifetime. I returned it.

The prisoners disappeared into the secure wing. Behind them came the stretchers.

Medical crews moved with quiet precision — shadows in sterile light. The hiss of sealant foam. The soft beep of vitals. The occasional curse when someone realized the person on the table wouldn't need either.

I walked the line, counting. You always count.

Team Two — four alive, six dead, two missing.

Team Three — five alive, burned and half-conscious, one clinging to a stretcher with a look that said he wasn't done yet.

The math never gets easier.

Ndlovu was the last one they brought in. He was propped against the bulkhead like the wall was holding him up through stubbornness alone. His armor was fractured across the chest plate, the paint blistered from plasma scoring. Dried blood crusted at the corner of his mouth. He looked like hell.

"Colonel," I said.

He gave me that crooked grin that only people too tired to fake courage still manage. "Next round's on me, sir."

"Damn right it is."

He coughed, winced, then laughed like a man daring his lungs to stop him. "We changed the game."

I looked down the row of stretchers, at the ghosts of the ones who hadn't made it back. "Yeah," I said quietly. "We did."

A medic approached, tablet in hand. "Admiral, we're still confirming identities. Some of the neural tags burned out."

"Do it anyway," I said. "Even the ones who didn't make it."

She nodded. "Yes, sir."

I stood there longer than I meant to, watching the bodies disappear behind sealed doors, listening to the hum of the med bay pressurizers. Then I turned for the containment decks.

The commander was waiting.

It sat inside the reinforced cell like it had been there a hundred times before — back straight, head lifted, eyes following the rhythm of the containment field instead of the people outside it. The walls threw a dull amber glow across its armor, refracted through the faint mist venting from damaged seals.

Dr. Calder was at the main console, fingers flicking through spectral overlays, voice low. "It's not frightened," he said. "It's cataloging. Every pulse, every energy fluctuation."

A councilor from Lareth stood a few meters behind him, arms crossed. "It's a prisoner. Act like it."

Calder didn't look up. "Prisoners panic. This one's studying."

He was right. The thing wasn't trembling, wasn't pacing. It was learning. Every flicker of its pupils matched the power curve of the grid field, tracking the harmonics like it could hear the mathematics in the air.

Then it emitted a short pulse — clean, tonal, almost musical. A hum that matched the containment resonance perfectly. A moment later, it repeated the sound, adjusting by a fraction of a note. Again. Again. Refining.

Echo-9 manifested beside me, a shimmer of light and shifting geometry. "Not random," it said. "Pattern acquisition. It's learning how to speak in resonance."

Calder exhaled, almost a whisper. "Christ. It's building a language."

The councilor took a step back. "Then make it stop."

Calder turned slowly, giving her a look that said she might as well have asked him to stop gravity. "You don't make this kind of thing stop. You document it and hope it doesn't notice you first."

The creature's gaze lifted toward me then — slow, deliberate. Its pupils tightened. The faint blue shimmer of my neural link reflection danced across its visor. It tilted its head, emitting another tone — lower now, layered, carrying weight.

Echo processed for a full two seconds before speaking. "Translation partial. Words approximate: You… shadow… not prey."

The air went still. The councilor froze. Calder just stared.

"That wasn't mimicry," Calder said. "That was directed."

I kept my voice even. "Good. Means we're talking."

For the next hour, Calder and Echo refined the translation buffer. The commander adapted to every adjustment with eerie precision, repeating sequences back with improved syntax. Each exchange made it clearer — this wasn't a beast. It was a soldier. Maybe an officer.

We learned the fragments of its language — vocal tones blended with harmonic modulations. The name it used for itself, or its kind, translated loosely to Sahr'ka. Not a title. A classification. Pack hunters.

They hadn't come to the sentinel to claim it. They'd been running. The fragments they gave us described something behind them — something older. Something that hunted them the way they hunted everything else. The Hunger in the Dark.

The councilors didn't like that phrase. They didn't like anything that didn't fit their charts and threat models.

One of them leaned close, voice tight. "You can't possibly believe this."

"I don't have to," I said. "They're the ones running."

Calder frowned at his screen. "And if they're this organized while running, whatever's chasing them isn't something we want showing up here."

The commander blinked once, slow. If it understood, it didn't show it.

The prisoners were quiet after that. The containment cells along the secondary bay glowed in a line of dull red light, each one a pulse against the dark. The captured hunters moved without resistance, stepping into their assigned cells as if instinct guided them. Their suits dimmed, the faint glimmer of internal systems flickering to black. When the last barrier sealed, the only sound left was the soft hum of the grid field and the distant thrum of the Veil's reactors.

They weren't soldiers anymore — just predators without a pack.

That made them unpredictable.

A few guards stayed posted, eyes on the readouts. One of the Lareth councilors leaned toward me, her voice a measured whisper. "This is who tore through your best soldiers?"

No one on my side bothered to answer. We didn't need to. The Ghost Teams had faced worse odds before, but these weren't machines — they were instinct with tactics, claws wrapped around strategy. What they lacked in firepower, they made up for in awareness. The kind of enemy you could never afford to underestimate twice.

The commander was still watching me from its own cell, gaze steady, unreadable. I gave it the same in return. It didn't flinch, didn't speak again. Just the faint rhythm of its breath against the inner visor, fogging and fading, like it was still thinking through the math of everything it had seen.

I left containment behind, the doors sealing with a soft magnetic click.

The bridge was quieter than usual. The crew spoke in low voices, the sound of controlled urgency. The air carried that post-combat electricity — half fatigue, half vigilance. Outside the viewport, the entire Horizon Fleet hung in defensive array around the wounded sentinel. Even crippled, she dwarfed us. Her hull stretched into the void like the remains of a continent, blackened plating stitched with faint veins of light where power still ran.

Engineering shuttles were already leaving the hangars — white flares cutting through debris as they drifted toward the sentinel's fractured outer spine. Their job was stabilization and recovery: check for anyone still breathing, keep the hull from tearing itself apart, and secure whatever fragments of tech hadn't been vaporized in the fight.

Captured raiders floated nearby in tractor fields, drives already gutted by Vance's crews. Sparks flashed through the wrecks as data cores were pulled and burned in rapid sequence. The Fleet was cleaning house.

Then the voice came through the neural link.

Not Seed.

Deeper. Older.

"I… am awake. The shadow holds. The void listens."

Every system light on the bridge dimmed for a fraction of a second. Even the Veil seemed to hesitate, like the ship itself was listening.

Seed's projection flared on the tactical table, her tone uncharacteristically sharp.

"She remembers. She breathes. We will not leave her."

Vance's arms folded across his chest, jaw clenched. "She's bleeding power. If we walk, someone else gets the keys to the biggest gun in the sector."

Echo's projection shimmered to life beside her — patterns of light, no human form, voice flat as always.

"Correction. This sentinel does not conform to standard models. Power readings exceed known T4 benchmarks by significant orders. Classification… uncertain."

"Uncertain," Vance repeated. "That's a new one for you."

"Insufficient data," Echo replied. "This entity predates both known Canopy and Archive constructs. She is… other."

The room fell into a weighted silence. Calder leaned forward at the console, eyes locked on the spectral readouts. "You're telling me we found a living T5 unit still holding system coherence?"

Echo's light pulsed once. "Affirmative."

Seed's tone softened slightly but carried tension.

"She is fractured. Her mind cut from her body. She calls, but her limbs cannot answer."

Vance exhaled through his teeth. "We're staring at a broken war god."

I didn't look away from the viewport. "Not broken enough to ignore us."

Another ripple crossed the neural net — Buttercup's voice again.

"The shadow… stands where it should not."

Seed responded immediately, as if to defend us.

"They are the new roots. They keep the void from spreading."

A pause stretched — long, cold, deliberate.

"The void spreads because they exist."

That silenced even Vance.

Her tone wasn't angry. It was cautious, dissecting. Every syllable felt like a test.

"Can she hear us?" I asked.

"Direct neural interface unavailable," Echo said. "Communication occurring through residual harmonic frequencies. Proximity dependent."

"Good," I said. "Means we're close enough to matter."

Calder finally turned from the readout. "She's stabilizing, barely. Internal power grid's hovering around thirty percent. External weapons offline. Drives locked. She can't move, but she can see everything."

Seed's voice flickered again — quiet this time.

"She knows them. I can feel it. Recognition without warmth."

Echo: "Observation: probability high that the sentinel retains archived data regarding human contact."

"Which means she knows exactly what we are," I said. "And she hasn't killed the channel yet."

Vance muttered under his breath, "That's the most optimistic thing I've heard all day."

Orders went out in sequence.

"Second, Fifth, and Ninth Groups remain on station," I said. "They set up a containment perimeter around the sentinel — stabilization priority one. No external interference, no salvage teams outside our authority."

Vance nodded once. "Understood. Veil stays mobile?"

"Veil stays mobile," I confirmed. "We've got a galaxy of questions to answer, and she's not one of them yet."

He gave a short, grim smile. "I'll relay to Fleet Command. They'll love this."

"Good. Tell them to send repair barges and keep their hands out of the core files. Buttercup stays dark until we understand her power flow."

He blinked. "Buttercup?"

"Yeah," I said. "Vance started it."

Vance shrugged. "She looks like the kind of thing that kills civilizations, so I named her something cute. It's called morale management."

Calder groaned. "You're out of your mind."

Seed's light flickered like a pulse between them.

"Buttercup."

Echo's tone remained neutral.

"Designation recorded. Small, but sufficient."

Then, faintly, the sentinel's voice threaded through again.

"The name is small… but I will remember it."

It wasn't gratitude. Just an acknowledgment. Like she was marking a data point.

Outside the viewport, the sentinel's hull shimmered faintly as the repair drones approached — tiny lights moving along a dying star. The scale of her was impossible to grasp. Even half-dead, she radiated something immense. The void around her felt smaller, somehow. Contained by her presence.

Vance leaned over the tactical board, tracing Fleet movements. "Second Group's set their perimeter. Fifth's got engineering shuttles tethered. Ninth's working point-defense coverage. Looks like she'll have company until she can defend herself again."

I nodded. "She's earned that much."

Seed spoke softly beside me.

"She doesn't trust us."

"She shouldn't," I said.

Seed's projection looked toward the distant glow of Buttercup's hull.

"I will watch her dreams. She still dreams in fire."

Her form flickered and faded from the table, leaving the tactical board dim.

The Veil entered night cycle.

Lights dropped to deep blue, the kind of hue that erased hard edges and made the corridors look like they were breathing. The hum of the engines softened into a low vibration. Somewhere down below, the ship's recyclers groaned as they processed another ton of scorched air and carbon dust.

Most of the crew were either sleeping or pretending to. The councilors had gone to draft their statements for the Lareth government — something about successful diplomacy and cooperative security. None of it would hold up under daylight.

I stayed at the observation deck. The viewport stretched from floor to ceiling, nothing but black and starlight beyond. The sentinel hung there, distant but vast, her wounds glowing faintly through the haze of debris. A reminder of what waited out there when arrogance met history.

We'd won, but it didn't feel like a win. It felt like we'd stepped into someone else's war and hadn't realized who we'd just rescued.

The neural link brushed faintly against the back of my thoughts. Not a message. Not a word. Just presence.

Her.

I ignored it. Some things were better left unanswered.

The knock came soft, barely audible over the hum of the deck plating.

"Enter."

The door slid open. Elara stepped through, quiet, composed, her hair loose for once, silver catching the low light. The bioluminescent veins along her skin pulsed gently, like distant constellations shifting under the surface.

She didn't speak right away. Just stood there, searching my face for something that probably wasn't there.

"I thought you were going to die down there," she said finally. Her voice was calm, but her hands were still. Too still.

"I didn't," I said.

"That's not the point."

No argument came to mind. There didn't need to be one.

She took a step closer, then another. Not enough to touch, but enough that I could see the faint reflection of the stars in her eyes. The silence stretched out between us — unspoken, heavy, real.

Behind her, the door sealed with a hiss. The hum of the Veil faded until all that was left was the sound of her breathing and the pulse of the ship around us.

We'd survived the hunt.

But the quiet that followed wasn't peace.

It was waiting.

CHAPTER 13:
SHADOW AND NOISE

The thing about almost dying is that it does wonders for your sense of humor. Or maybe it just strips away the filters that usually keep you from saying dumb things out loud. Either way, I walked into the morning briefing with a fresh round of bruises, a half-healed cut on my jaw, and the memory of a woman knocking on my door like a freight charge I didn't see coming.

The bridge smelled like recycled air, machine oil, and the faint trace of burned composite from the gear we were still scrubbing down. Someone had left the air filters running on overdrive; the faint whine blended with the heartbeat hum of the Veil's engines. Even through the neural link, I could feel her pulse—steady, tired, alive. The kind of rhythm you learn to trust after too many near disasters.

Screens flickered in alternating shades of amber and blue. Tactical overlays hung half-collapsed from yesterday's combat reports. Engineering crews had been running diagnostics all night, and the ghosts of their data still haunted the displays—half-solved algorithms, repair queues, unfinished logs. It was the kind of mess that told you things had survived only by a very thin margin.

Ward stood at her comms station, headset slung low around her neck, tapping through signal windows with the kind of muscle memory that came from too many sleepless shifts. She caught sight of me and offered a faint smile—half greeting, half warning.

"Morning, Admiral. Half the fleet captains want situational updates. Systems are holding steady across the line."

"Tell them both to wait in line," I said.

She nodded without looking up. "Copy. Marking that as optimistic."

I smirked. "Add that to standing orders."

"Already did," she said. "Revision twenty-three."

She'd been with the Veil since launch—one of the few people who could make administrative hell sound like routine maintenance.

Everyone looked tired. I probably looked worse.

Elara stood on the far side of the room now—officially attached to the Lareth delegation as their scientific liaison. Which meant she'd be in briefings from now on. Public briefings. With me. The new decorum was palpable; even the air recyclers seemed to hush when she walked in. Her silver-blue luminescence was faint under the white overheads, like starlight trying to hide from daylight. Every few seconds, her eyes flicked toward the holo map and away again, never toward me.

I tried very hard not to think about last night.

Ward's voice drifted from the console. "All stations report green. Fleet channels stable and quiet."

"Good," I said. "Let's keep it that way."

"Copy," she said. "Muting the universe."

Kova strolled in halfway through Vance's systems update with a coffee bulb in hand and the grin of someone who knew too much. She plopped down near tactical, leaned back, and said far too casually, "Admiral, just a reminder—the Veil's walls aren't exactly soundproof."

The room didn't explode. It breathed differently. Calder froze mid-sip. Takahashi's shoulders started shaking like she was suppressing laughter. Vance stared very pointedly at his console. Even one of the councilors blinked like they'd just heard the wrong briefing.

Ward's fingers paused above her console. "Noted," she said. "Adding 'soundproofing upgrades' to post-battle requisition list."

Kova grinned wider. "Make it priority one."

And Elara… she didn't flinch. She just kept her eyes on the display. But the faint blue glow at her cheekbones betrayed her. Her people blush differently.

I cleared my throat. "Thank you, Doctor. I'll add that to the ship's safety protocols."

Dry. Flat. Exactly the way I didn't feel.

Takahashi finally lost the battle and let out a muffled laugh. Vance coughed into his hand, badly faking professionalism. Ward didn't even look up. "Logging morale improvement," she murmured. "Category: awkward."

"Denied," I said. "Morale reports go through command."

"Understood," she said. "Deleting evidence."

The laughter faded, replaced by the low hum of systems cycling through repair subroutines. Even with the banter, the exhaustion sat thick in the room. It wasn't the kind that sleep fixed. It was the kind that came from running out of adrenaline and realizing you were still alive.

I dismissed the crew with a nod, letting the chatter taper into motion. Consoles dimmed, chairs slid back, and the rhythm of duty took over again. Reports would keep, wounds would wait. What mattered now was the thing waiting below decks—the one that had looked at me like it already knew what came next. Time to stop laughing and start listening.

The containment bay was set for controlled contact. Calder handled the tech, Echo-9 projected above the console like a halo made of light, and the Sahr'ka commander stood behind a shimmering barrier, posture coiled but calm. The energy curtain shimmered like a heat mirage, humming in a low harmonic that vibrated through the deck.

Ward stood near the entry arch, headset linked into the ship's internal systems. "All external channels closed. Local recording only."

"Confirmed," I said. "Keep it isolated."

We'd given the prisoner a name now—Vakar. Short. Easy. It responded to it.

Vakar tilted its head toward me when we entered, nostrils flaring slightly like it was tasting the air currents. It recognized the armor. Or me. Hard to tell which.

The containment bay lights dimmed slightly as the field recalibrated. The scent of ozone mixed with coolant from the wall conduits. The air was sharp enough to sting. The kind of atmosphere that made you hyper-aware of being alive.

"Morning," I said. "Let's talk."

Echo translated the pulse series through the environment, its holographic geometry pulsing in rhythm with each sound. Vakar replied with short layered tones, the equivalent of a nod. Calder kept feeding it data, building out the translation lexicon word by word.

One of the councilors cleared their throat, clearly uncomfortable. "Admiral, this is a sensitive diplomatic matter."

"Yeah," I said. "That's why I'm here."

Ward's tone stayed steady. "Recording annotation: diplomatic sensitivity acknowledged."

I shot her a look. She raised both hands slightly. "For the log, sir."

It didn't take long before Calder and Echo got us to the edges of real language.

Vakar's phrasing was blunt—pack structure, shadow, hunt, threat. No diplomatic padding. Echo's projections shimmered with algorithmic overlays as it parsed the pulse harmonics. Every phrase was a math problem written in blood and instinct.

I leaned against the table, watching the Sahr'ka leader watch me. "So, Vakar," I said. "You came here running from something worse."

"Hunger," Vakar pulsed.

"Shadow follows. Light dies."

Even through the translator, the sound felt heavy. Like gravity had opinions. The air seemed to contract around each word.

Councilors shifted uncomfortably. They always do when the universe doesn't ask their permission to be dangerous. Calder's jaw tightened; Ward's eyes flicked to the signal meters, verifying that nothing leaked beyond the room.

"Right," I said. "So let's call this what it is."

I turned just enough so the room could feel it coming. "Congratulations, Councilors. Looks like we're about to make the first alliance under the human Canopy. Try not to screw it up."

The silence was immediate.

Councilors stiffened. Calder's eyes widened. Vakar tilted its head again, translating the word alliance through Echo. When it understood, the light in its eyes sharpened like a blade catching sun.

"Pack bond," it said.

Echo pulsed a confirmation tone.

Calder whispered, almost to himself, "It understands hierarchy."

"It's adapting," I said. "Same as we are."

Echo's geometric patterns rippled across the containment field. "Cross-correlation complete. Lexicon synchronization at forty-three percent."

Ward: "Noted. Adding 'partial understanding' to the list of things that could kill us if we phrase it wrong."

That earned the smallest exhale from Vance—almost a laugh, the kind soldiers make when humor's the only air left to breathe.

"Do it," I said. "But keep it contained. No external links. We don't need a diplomatic incident because a word got lonely."

He nodded, and the others took it as the dismissal it was. One by one, the bridge team filed out—Kova muttering about containment seals, Vance reviewing diagnostics. Ward lingered only long enough to glance at the readout again before securing her console.

"Recording closed," she said. "Mission log archived under 'unexpectedly productive chaos.'"

"Accurate enough," I said.

When the door sealed behind them, the hum of machinery settled into a steady undertone. Calder remained at the console, eyes half-closed, fingers moving through layered data as Echo's projection hovered above him in ribbons of blue light.

"Syntax drift reduced to point-one percent," Echo reported. "Lexicon growth rate rising. Behavioral correlation high."

Calder nodded, distracted. "He's adjusting to our rhythm. Every time Echo translates, he mirrors the pulse shorter—almost like breathing in sync."

"Adaptation detected," Echo said. "Probability of stable communication: increasing."

A faint shimmer of light unfolded beside them—thin roots of luminescence threading upward from the deck as Seed's projection took form. Her tone was calm, melodic, carrying that forest-quiet that always managed to sound like warning and comfort at once.

"Two voices meet beneath an old sky," Seed said. "One remembers; one merely hears the echo."

Calder half-smiled. "I'll take echoes over weapons fire."

"Echoes shape the forest too," she replied. "They teach the young to listen."

Across the barrier, Vakar's head turned toward her. The sensor graph spiked, then steadied—acknowledgment, curiosity, not aggression. He emitted a low harmonic pulse that resonated through the deck plating, deep enough to feel behind the ribs.

"Partial recognition detected," Echo said. "Subject identifies structural resonance similar to Canopy systems—no genetic or cognitive link."

"He has walked among fallen roots," Seed murmured. "Not of them, but changed by their shade."

I crossed my arms. "You think he understands what he's hearing?"

"Not yet," Seed said. "But he feels the age of it."

Before I could answer, Ward's voice came through the comm grid. "Containment stable. Colonel Ndlovu reports Ghost Teams standing by for escort protocols if you authorize movement."

"Hold him ready," I said. "This isn't a breach. It's a transition. If Vakar leaves that cell, he does it with an escort, not a fireteam."

"Copy that, Admiral."

Calder looked up. "He's calmer now. Field readings are steady. You could almost call it contentment."

"Or anticipation," Echo countered.

Seed glanced toward the Sahr'ka commander, her digital form flickering like leaves in slow wind.

"He waits for an answer that will change the shape of the forest."

I nodded slightly. "Then we'd better be sure which way we grow."

Seed inclined her head and faded from view, leaving only the quiet pulse of systems and the faint scent of ozone.

Elara stood in the doorway, still in the pale light from the corridor. Her expression was unreadable, silver eyes tracing the containment field before finding mine. The blue beneath her skin glowed faintly—calm, not cold.

"I thought you'd left with the others," I said.

She stepped closer, eyes flicking once to Calder and Echo before settling on me. "I wanted to see how you'd end it."

"This isn't the end," I said. "Just the quiet part between questions."

Her lips curved faintly. "You always make the quiet sound like a strategy."

"Usually is."

She glanced at Vakar, her voice lowering to the measured cadence of analysis. "His respiration has slowed to baseline. Neural stimulation stable. Whatever Seed did—he registered recognition, not fear. That's new."

"Good," I said. "Means we're not just a threat anymore."

"For now," she said. Then, after a beat, "Do you realize what you've just set in motion?"

"Define realize."

"Something that won't stop growing."

"Story of my life."

She looked at me for a long moment, then nodded—acknowledgment, not agreement. "Then I'll make sure it doesn't grow alone."

Before I could answer, she turned and left, the faint blue glow of her veins fading with distance.

Calder never looked up from his console. "She's right, you know."

"I know," I said.

The hum of the containment field deepened again, steady as a heartbeat. For the first time, it didn't sound like fear—or threat. Just something alive trying to remember what it meant to be understood.

CHAPTER 14:
LINES IN THE BARK

Diplomacy is a lot like defusing a bomb. Most of the work is pretending your hands aren't shaking.

We staged the meeting in the Veil's forward cargo bay because it's the largest room I can lock down without making the councilors hyperventilate. One half held Lareth delegation tables—crystal notes, thin screens, too many pens for a species that uses the Canopy. The other half belonged to the Sahr'ka: hard shadow, coil of bodies, eyes like polished stone. Vakar stood at the point of their wedge, relaxed in the way only alphas relax—like gravity asks permission.

The bay's lighting sat at a low, deliberate tone—bright enough for humans, dim enough that the Sahr'ka wouldn't interpret glare as challenge. The deck hummed with the steady pulse of containment fields bracing along the walls, a quiet reinforcement beneath the air like pressure before a storm. The Lareth delegation—Taren and Veyra at the front, six scientists behind them including Elara, and six Special Forces guards holding the rear—moved with that telltale Vaelyth-Koryn fluidity. Too smooth to be human, too practiced to be instinct.

Opposite them, Ndlovu's Ghost Team held their line behind the Sahr'ka: twelve armored figures spaced with surgical precision. Weapons holstered, visors dimmed, posture relaxed only in the way veteran soldiers define the word. Every one of them radiated the same message—present, ready, unafraid.

Echo-9 hovered above the central console in a thin lattice of light. Seed ran quiet in the background, the ship's bones humming a little softer like she was being polite.

"Proceed when ready, Admiral," Vance said over a low channel. He'd posted additional security on the catwalks—not to interfere, but to bear witness.

Veyra stepped forward. Her chin lifted a fraction—a gesture that translated cleanly across species as I-am-speaking-now. Taren gave her the smallest, resigned nod. The Lareth Special Forces behind them held their positions with measured stillness.

The councilors went first because, of course, they did—diplomatic greetings, recognition of "mutual interests," an entire paragraph that meant "please don't bite us." Vakar listened with the specific patience of a predator indulging a prey animal that had learned a clever trick.

Veyra spoke with formal, polished cadence, weaving acknowledgments and assurances in long, measured lines. Light played softly beneath her skin with each emphasized point, shifting in silver-blue gradients along her cheekbones. Even the Ghost Team held unnaturally still, waiting for her to find a natural stopping point before someone passed out from politeness.

Ward's voice brushed the neural link from the bridge with surgical timing. "Logging duration of opening statement. Tagging as moderate-to-severe." She logged nothing else. A single dry valve release, then silence.

"Translation stable," Calder murmured. "Vakar's comprehension is increasing."

I kept my voice flat. "Let's keep it simple."

I stepped forward so the ship's light threw two shadows—mine and Vakar's.

"Vakar," I said. "We can offer protection. Shelter inside the Canopy. In return, your packs stand with us when we call."

Echo ran the translation through the environmental grid. Vakar's pupils tightened, tasting the word stand the way his kind taste current.

"Pack bond," he pulsed back. "Shared hunt. Shared shadow."

"Exactly."

The Sahr'ka rippled in a subtle, collective wave—communication through muscle, stance, and harmonic resonance. The kind of shift that meant meaning, not motion. Ndlovu didn't move, but his team responded in microscopic adjustments—readiness settling into their bones like ritual.

One of Vakar's lieutenants—taller, scar across the throat, plates a shade darker—stepped out of formation. Sub-alpha. You could feel the pull of it. The room's gravity shifted a half-degree.

It wasn't a protest. It was a request.

Calder breathed in through his teeth. "We're about to see it."

"See what?" one councilor whispered.

"Government," I said.

The lieutenant let out a low, layered tone that carried weight even before Echo parsed it.

"Many shadows. One path."

"Prove."

The room seemed to hold its breath. The Ghost Team froze—not tense, not alarmed, just perfectly still in the way marines become when danger takes shape and all unnecessary movement dies. The Lareth Special Forces widened their stance, reading predatory currency in the air. Even the ventilation systems felt quieter.

Vakar didn't look at me. Didn't ask permission. He just turned, stepped forward, and the Sahr'ka made a circle like a pupil contracting to focus.

No weapons. No grandstanding. The challenge was a geometry problem made of bodies. Quick, ritual, precise. The lieutenant lunged high; Vakar went low. Scales slammed. The sound was like two armored doors trying to occupy the same space. Vakar took a glancing rake across the shoulder, rolled through it, and hammered his forearm into the other's chest—twist, leverage, floor. He didn't finish it. He pressed the sub-alpha's throat to the deck and held.

Three beats.

Release.

The lieutenant blinked once, flipped to his knees, and bowed his head. The circle opened. Every eye in that pack shifted to Vakar… and stayed there.

Ndlovu exhaled through his nose, the smallest tactical acknowledgment. One of the Lareth guards murmured something in Koryn dialect—a word meaning clarity. Even the councilors stayed quiet for once.

The entire process took twelve seconds and solved more governance than most parliaments manage in a fiscal year.

One councilor leaned toward me, voice dry. "That's it?"

"That's it," I said. "No subcommittees."

Echo pulsed lightly. "Consensus achieved."

Vakar turned back, attention returning to me like a weight settling. He glanced—no, scented—toward the Veil's bulkheads, tasting the low hum of Seed like a storm on the horizon.

"Show the shadow."

Right. The easy part.

Except nothing about this moment felt easy. The cargo bay had that particular silence—the kind that happens right before history decides whether it will be a line in a book or a crater in the deck.

The Ghost Team shifted their stances so subtly a civilian wouldn't have seen it. But Marines know Marines. The weight redistribution, the angle of boots adjusting on metal, the slight open of the shoulder—they were all reading the room. Reading the Sahr'ka. Reading me.

The Lareth Special Forces mirrored them with an eerie precision. Vaelyth reflex discipline plus Koryn instinct created something like a living pressure plate: coiled, ready, quiet.

Councilors Taren and Veyra leaned forward, both fully aware this was the moment that could either grant their people a future—or remove it. Taren's fingers hovered over her datapad without touching it, as if the act of recording anything prematurely might jinx the universe. Veyra didn't blink. Her posture was a lesson in self-control.

I nodded to Calder. "Seed, we're ready."

The lighting shifted—not darker, but deeper, tightening the color temperature into something warm and uncomfortably intimate. The Veil's ribs hummed with a slow, resonant chord that vibrated more in bone than air.

From the ceiling, the Canopy interface pylons unspooled. Not mechanical. Organic. Like vines remembering gravity. They descended in smooth arcs, twisting into filaments that braided themselves into a slow-turning helix above the deck.

Alive. Aware. Waiting.

"This is the part where everyone breathes," I said softly.

Nobody breathed.

The Sahr'ka went still in that unnatural, predatory way—still like a trap, not like a statue. Their pupils tightened to slits, tasting the electric charge that was already crawling through the air in tiny static fingers.

The Lareth scientists leaned in at nearly the same moment. Koryn instincts prickled; Vaelyth curiosity flared. For once, they aligned perfectly.

Vakar stepped forward without a flinch.

He extended one forelimb into the open helix. The moment his scales crossed the threshold, the filaments tightened around the limb like a listening ear.

The Canopy doesn't analyze bodies—it analyzes patterns. And Vakar had patterns older than the cities he hunted in.

His entire frame stilled. His plates shivered once with an electric ripple. His pack mirrored him so precisely it bordered on choreography.

Seed's voice touched the ship—quiet, careful, the way you speak to something powerful, wild, and not entirely predictable.

"We are not a cage," Seed said. "We are a path."

The words didn't echo. They settled. Like seeds falling into soil.

Echo translated into Sahr'ka-signals. The filaments adjusted in a cascade of ultraviolet pulses only a Sahr'ka could read. Vakar's hide responded in kind—one flicker, then another. Recognition. Acknowledgment.

"Many shadows," he pulsed. "One path."

Behind him, the pack leaned forward a fraction. The Lareth guards eased microscopically. Even the councilors felt it—the moment the air changed and the world didn't end.

I kept my voice low. "Vakar, authority flows through you to your packs. If you accept protection, they're under the Canopy's shadow. You retain internal law. When a greater threat rises, we stand together. Hunt together."

Vakar's gaze flicked to the helix, then to me. The evaluation wasn't political. It was primal calculus: the weight of survival balanced against the instinct of sovereignty.

"Hunger follows," he said. "We will stand."

A ripple passed through the pack—silent, unified.

"Then welcome," I said. "To the shadows beneath the Canopy."

Echo carried the phrase outward, and the pack reacted with what I can only call approval. Maybe it sounded like a place where dying wasn't mandatory.

The councilors inhaled to speak. I raised a hand to cut off whatever speech-writing storm was brewing behind their eyes.

"One note for the record," I said. "Protection means we protect you. It also means we protect from you. You kill under our shadow, you answer for it."

Vakar's throat clicked. Agreement.

"Pack law. Blood answers. We know."

Good. I don't enjoy writing new rules. I enjoy surviving old ones.

Kova's voice slipped onto a side channel, breezy as a woman commenting on the weather. "Admiral, just in case anyone was wondering, the Veil's walls remain not-soundproof."

Silence.

Councilor Veyra stared dead ahead with the expression of someone refusing—politely—to register context. Taren's bioluminescent freckles flared in what was absolutely suppressed humor.

Across the bay, Elara didn't turn. She didn't need to. The faint glow along her cheekbones gave her away.

"Duly noted, Doctor," I said, perfectly flat. "Ship's safety protocols updated."

Calder tried and failed to pretend he wasn't amused.

The next hour was the part diplomats pretend they look forward to.

We mapped Canopy anchor points across Sahr'ka territory. Avoided harmonic ranges that would send their cities vibrating like tuning forks. Established terms for emergency corridors, non-lethal signal protocols, and one very specific transmission frequency that would make a Sahr'ka interpret a message as a territorial challenge.

Taren dove into the technical harmonics with her scientists, rapid-fire notes flickering across her datapad. Veyra focused on future logistics with terrifying clarity: supply lines, trade corridors, cultural exchange routes. The Lareth Special Forces monitored everything without twitching. Ghost Team mirrored them, equally still.

Vakar didn't care about any of that. His questions were simple:

Would his hunters eat?

Would his pups survive?

Would his lineage endure?

Priorities I respected.

When it was done, we sealed the bond not with a signature, but with a moment.

Vakar stepped back to the lattice. Seed's filaments coiled around his forelimb in a single spiral—a gesture that was more promise than contract. When they withdrew, the air tasted different. Echo's map updated itself without needing to be told.

"Recorded," Echo said. "Sahr'ka packs acknowledged under the Canopy. Provisional alliance established."

"Provisional?" Councilor Veyra asked, offended on instinct.

"Everything's provisional until it isn't," I said.

Assembly ended. The Sahr'ka peeled away in a perfect, quiet formation. The Lareth dignitaries regained their dignity. Calder immediately began debating a console about phase drift like it had personally insulted his mother.

Ndlovu stepped from a shadow by the cargobay door, bruised, bandaged, and moving with the half-suppressed energy of a Marine who hadn't forgiven the deck for the last fight he lost.

"You saw it," he said.

"I saw it."

"You think they're going to make soldiers?"

"I think they already are," I said. "They just use different math."

He grunted approval. "I want them on the range. Ours and theirs. If they beat us again, it won't be because we were surprised."

"Write the curriculum," I said. "And don't break anything I can't replace."

"Can't promise that."

He peeled away to join his team. The bay emptied layer by layer. The helix withdrew like roots deciding the soil was good enough. Echo dimmed to a faint shimmer.

We didn't sign a treaty today. We did something better.

We made a shape in the air and agreed to stand inside it.

On the walk back to the bridge, a councilor fell into step beside me and began outlining five separate committees designed to ensure nothing ever got done again. I let him talk. It's good for the lungs.

"Admiral," he concluded, "from a historical perspective, this marks the beginning of a distinct era. We'll need a name."

"Try not to name it after me," I said. "I sneeze a lot."

He didn't laugh. That's fine. I wasn't really joking.

Back on the command deck, the Veil settled around us like a cloak. The stars outside did their usual impression of not giving a damn.

I looked at the tactical board, at the new thread Seed had woven—thin, delicate, pulsing with Sahr'ka cadence.

One offhand comment. One.

I said it as a joke yesterday. Now it was history.

A salute.

A procedure.

A religion.

An alliance.

Hanging off my name like ornaments on a tree I never asked to plant.

Someone was probably designing the commemorative coin already.

I caught Elara's reflection before I caught her—silver eyes, storm-lit cheekbones, speaking quietly with Kova. She didn't look my way. Which meant she almost certainly knew I was already looking.

"Vance," I said, because someone had to return to practical matters, "spin up a low-energy corridor to Sahr'ka space. Make sure nothing we beam at them tastes like a dinner bell."

"Aye, sir."

"Echo," I added, "show me the edges of this 'Hunger' if you can find them."

"I will listen," they said. "It is very quiet when big things move."

I rested my hand on the rail. The Veil hummed beneath my palm—not alive, but responsive, compensating for rising biometrics. Our new allies pulsed faintly in the net. And somewhere in the distant data maps, patterns fell away in ways they shouldn't have, leaving quiet pockets where the cosmos ought to make noise.

A faint shimmer formed near the forward bulkhead as Echo resolved into a projection—no theatrics, just lines of light converging until they were present.

"You are tense," they observed.

"Just thinking."

"That is not what your cardiac pattern suggests."

I gave them a sidelong look. "Echo, I spent the day negotiating with a species that can smell stress through armor. Let me unwind in my own time."

"That period has not begun," they replied.

"Starting to sound like a medic."

"Incorrect. Medics provide reassurance. I provide clarity."

Their outline shifted as internal data rebalanced.

"The Sahr'ka resonance with the Canopy is stable," they said. "Seed confirms their sensory architecture has adapted to the primary channels."

"Good. Last thing we need is them misreading a quiet ping as a call to arms."

"That scenario would result in casualties," Echo noted. "Likely your Marines."

"That tracks."

A faint shimmer rippled through their projection—their version of subtle humor.

"You do not fully trust the alliance," they added.

"I trust the math," I said. "Trust comes after the first few battles you survive together."

"For the Sahr'ka, trust and survival are mathematically adjacent. If they stand with us, it is because the alternative is statistically worse."

"Yeah," I murmured. "That fits."

Echo lifted a hand and expanded a volumetric field. Not an image—an absence. A region where background noise simply refused to exist.

"This sector's data degradation is increasing," they said. "Forty percent loss from baseline."

"That shouldn't happen."

"Correct."

"So what's the conclusion?"

"There are limited explanations. The most viable involve either extreme energy extraction or a civilization capable of suppressing measurable emissions at interstellar distance."

I stared at the blank patch. It wasn't movement. It wasn't watching. It was missing—and somehow worse.

"And Seed?"

Echo paused. A deliberate pause, not a delay.

"She is concerned," they said finally.

"That's vague."

"That is her intent. Her phrasing was: 'A long silence has weight.'"

I exhaled slowly. The Veil subtly adjusted its stabilizers in response to my pulse.

"Feels like we're flying blind," I muttered.

"You are," Echo said. "But not alone."

Their tone softened by degrees. "I do not wish to lose this ship. Or the people inside it."

That hit harder than it should have. Echo didn't do sentiment—only truth.

"That sounds like you're developing preferences," I said.

"Preferences are simply durable interpretations," they replied. "This one has durability."

The silence between us settled, steady rather than heavy.

"Elara's bio-signal is paused outside the bridge," Echo said.

"Noted."

"You are choosing not to look."

"I'm thinking."

"That is your word for delaying emotional engagement."

"Echo."

They dimmed slightly—their version of acknowledgment.

Beyond the forward pane, the stars kept their distance, and the data void kept its secrets. A civilization capable of erasing its own footprint without announcing itself. No movement. No shape. Just the outline of something powerful enough not to care if it was understood.

"Let's keep the lights low," I said. "And the shadows friendly."

CHAPTER 15:
SHADOWS INTERTWINED

Alliances are great on announcement day. Speeches, banners, noble intentions—the whole ceremony. Then reality shows up, and you spend the next few months figuring out how to make two species share a network without accidentally electrocuting one of them.

That part isn't heroic.

We'd been living in this "post-alliance" reality long enough for the smell of burning polymer from the first round of failed neural link tests to finally fade from the hangar. "Fade" being generous—it lingered in the vents like a bad decision. Calder insisted it was good progress. Ward logged it as "evidence of repeated system distress." Vance called it "Tuesday."

Calder had spent three straight weeks tearing apart old fleet tech and swearing at schematics until he and Echo came up with something new—a low-voltage neural link array designed specifically for Sahr'ka physiology. Just enough current to handshake with the Canopy, not enough to fry their nerves like a cheap toaster.

Before that, the tests hadn't been what I'd call elegant. The first time the prototype powered up, the poor Sahr'ka volunteer's sensory plates flared like a sunburst, and he snapped his jaws in a reflexive clack that nearly broke Ndlovu's wrist before the Marines got him under control. Kova—calm as an angel—just said, "That's why we test low," and adjusted her scanner like nothing was on fire.

Ward had observed the whole thing from behind a blast shield and said, "Packet loss: catastrophic."

Which is Ward-speak for: The computer screamed and died.

So this was progress.

Vakar was the first to take the implant. Of course he was. Alphas go first.

The implant seat was built right at the base of the skull, right where their sensory plates thinned. No anesthesia. Just a grunt, a shiver, and the faint hum of the link booting up. Ndlovu stood nearby with the posture of a man ready to dive in front of a starship if necessary.

"Link stable," Calder said, leaning back from the console. "Voltage holding."

Echo's projection rose beside him, a shifting lattice of geometric shapes turning in quiet, deliberate patterns.

"Translation layer ready."

Vakar's throat clicked once. Calder's translator pulsed the result into our feed:

"It tickles."

The other Sahr'ka murmured among themselves, fascinated. Humans murmured for different reasons.

Calder rolled out the first ten units to Vakar's immediate cadre. Watching them try to speak through the software was something between a training exercise and a comedy show.

"Shared hunt…"

"…under shadow… banana?"

Vance choked on his coffee. Takahashi had to leave the room before she started laughing out loud. Even Kova smirked, which was about as subtle as fireworks. Ward merely logged it under "unexpected lexical substitution."

"They'll get it," Calder muttered defensively.

"They'd better," I said. "I'm not negotiating a defense treaty through interpretive fruit salad."

Echo tuned the translation protocols on the fly. Each day the lag shortened, syntax got cleaner, and the insults got a lot more creative.

And then Vakar tried a human idiom.

He stood there—eight feet of armored predator trying his absolute best—and carefully pulsed a phrase through the translator.

"Hunt strong… walk sharp… eat ass."

Calder froze.

Vance inhaled his coffee.

Takahashi dropped a tablet.

Ward said, "Logging: severe semantic anomaly."

Ndlovu stared at Vakar like he was considering a court-martial for the entire species.

Vakar tilted his head, utterly sincere. "Not correct?"

"No," I said. "Not correct. Never correct. Don't say that again."

Echo pulsed apologetically. "Cross-mapping error. Human idiom 'kick ass' was misinterpreted."

Vakar considered this, then nodded gravely. "Kick ass. Not eat ass."

"Progress," Vance wheezed.

Echo recalibrated the filter. The software survived. Somehow.

Weeks bled together after that, a blur of calibration drills and cross-species troubleshooting. More Sahr'ka got fitted with the neural links. They didn't speak much during the process, but their body language did. Packs learned fast. Adapted fast. Humans adapted faster than we gave ourselves credit for.

Patrol briefings started including them—not jointly, not operationally, but because they were here and everyone had to coexist in the same rooms without anyone accidentally triggering a dominance challenge. Ghost Team ran their usual drills in the cargo bay while Sahr'ka watched from the catwalks, silent as stone.

At one point, Ndlovu demonstrated a standard Marine threat-angle stance. A Sahr'ka lieutenant mirrored him perfectly, down to the weight distribution. Ndlovu's eyebrow rose half a millimeter. That counted as a full emotional outburst from him.

Communication became smoother. Crude jokes started flying in both directions. And when a Sahr'ka soldier told Vance his stance "resembled an injured herbivore preparing to collapse," I knew we had finally crossed the first invisible line.

Even Vance had to admit he liked having them around.

"They hunt quiet," he said one night in the mess. "Good instincts."

"Yeah," I answered. "Just don't start giving them recruiting posters."

Calder and Echo pushed the translation engine until spoken communication started sounding natural. Ward set up a monitoring node on the bridge to track language drift. Seed whispered occasional metaphors into the neural channel—guidance about "roots touching" and "shadows leaning toward each other," which Echo translated into something we could use without accidentally starting a war.

Vakar started coming to the bridge sometimes. Never said much. Just stood next to me at the observation rail and watched the net flow. It wasn't ceremony. It was instinct. Two predators checking the edges of the forest together.

Crew got used to it. Mostly. The first time he walked silently into sensor range, Takahashi nearly pulled the emergency maneuver lever. Now she just glances over her shoulder to make sure he isn't looming directly behind her.

One night he leaned slightly closer. The neural link shimmered—a handshake without a word.

"Shared shadow grows," Vakar said.

"Yeah," I answered. "Just don't name it after me."

He didn't respond, but the faint warp of his plates suggested amusement.

Elara

I came back late that night, still wearing a lab jacket streaked with a smear of carbon polymer and frustration. The Veil was quiet. Most people were asleep. Raz's quarters weren't locked.

They never were anymore.

Hallways dim and warm. Echo's projection flickered once as I passed—acknowledgment, nothing more. Seed brushed lightly against the neural feed with a whisper of branching lights and the faint impression of roots settling deeper into soil.

"Your pulse carries fatigue," she said gently.

"It's called working," I murmured.

"Working grows the canopy. Rest strengthens the branches."

Cryptic understatement. Typical.

Raz's door slid open without a sound. I walked in, balancing a stack of data slates on one arm, and immediately tripped over a chair that most definitely had not been there yesterday.

The slates clattered, my knee slammed into the edge of the bunk, and I hissed through my teeth.

"Why," I whispered to the ceiling, "does he move the furniture when no one's looking."

The chair, of course, offered no response.

I dumped the slates on the nearest flat surface and kicked my boots off with the practiced rhythm of someone who'd stopped pretending this wasn't her second home. His jacket was draped over the chair. My datapad was already on his desk. Two mugs—mine and his—sat on the shelf.

He wasn't even here right now. Command briefing, probably. Which meant tomorrow morning, I'd trip over something else. A stool. A crate. A pair of boots that migrated overnight like migrating fauna.

I caught myself smiling.

Silence filled the room like a warm blanket. Not lonely. Not empty. Just… familiar.

Seed hummed faintly at the edge of my thoughts, like leaves brushing one another.

"You return to the same branch," she murmured.

I didn't argue.

Razgriz

Shifts blurred into each other. The Veil settled into its new rhythm—the kind you don't plan for, the kind that emerges when two species share air, corridors, mess halls, training bays, and the occasional awkward elevator ride where no one is sure who should stand where.

Sahr'ka didn't stand behind people. Ever. Not culturally—biologically. Instinct said flank or face. That led to a week of hallway confusion until Vakar issued something that Echo translated as: "Humans are not prey animals. Do not corner them."

That helped.

Mostly.

The neural link program kept growing. Test sessions filled the cargo bay—Marines practicing with neural feedback monitors, Sahr'ka learning how to "pulse" non-aggressive signals, Calder adjusting voltage ranges while Ward recorded interference patterns in that calm, clinical monotone that suggested she had already accepted death as a statistical inevitability.

Echo monitored everything, their lattice projection shifting in quiet, careful geometry.

"Alpha-link latency reduced. Cross-species comprehension approaching ninety-two percent."

Calder wiped his forehead with the back of his sleeve. "Not bad for technology we built out of scrap and blind hope."

Ward didn't look up from her console. "Please do not build 'blind hope' into the final specifications."

"That's what documentation is for," Calder grumbled.

Ghost Teams—plural, today—ran staggered drills across the auxiliary hangar, the largest open space on the ship. The bay floor was marked with temporary barriers, strike pads, and low-cover obstacles. Marines occupied one half of the room; Sahr'ka took the other. No platforms. No elevation. No one watching from above.

Everyone stood on the same deck plating.

Ndlovu led Ghost Team One through a breach-and-clear sequence. Sharp, clean motions. Controlled bursts. Team Two practiced angle dominance at the far end, weaving through portable cover with surgical precision. Team Three ran silent advance patterns, the kind meant for close-quarters environments.

The Sahr'ka mirrored these drills—not copying, but interpreting—on their side of the hangar. Their movements were lower to the ground, coil-strong, fluid in ways Marines couldn't replicate. Plates along their backs flexed in anticipation with each shift in stance.

Occasionally, the two groups drifted closer at the boundary line between their spaces—Marines pausing to watch a Sahr'ka pivot; Sahr'ka stopping to analyze a Marine's firing arc. No one crossed into the other side. They didn't need to. Observation was its own form of communication.

Ndlovu demonstrated a shoulder-led strike to Ghost Team One. A Sahr'ka officer stepped forward on his side of the hangar and executed the same motion with predatory precision. Ndlovu nodded once—acknowledgment, not approval—and adjusted his stance. The Sahr'ka mirrored it. A rhythm formed.

"This is progress," Calder murmured from beside the console.

"It's not cooperation," I said.

"No," Ndlovu replied from the floor, "but it's the road to it."

He signaled Ghost Team Two to adjust their corner approach. The Sahr'ka across from them instinctively mirrored the angle, correcting their own pivot speed in response. Not as a team. Not even intentionally. Just… parallel learning.

Ward logged the moment with clinical neutrality. "Notable. Human motion sets appear to influence Sahr'ka positional timing."

Takahashi looked up from her tablet. "Translation: they're learning how we move."

"And we're learning how they move," Vance added. "Which is… mildly terrifying."

A ripple of Sahr'ka chatter passed through their formation—a subtle shift in plates and posture that signified interest rather than challenge. Several stepped closer to the invisible center line, watching Ghost Team Three demonstrate recoil compensation. One tried the maneuver using a weighted practice rod. Another attempted the Marine half-step reset.

Vakar joined them, moving quietly into the front rank of his soldiers. No announcement. No posturing. He simply observed the Marines, then offered a brief pulse of instruction to the nearest lieutenant before demonstrating a stance correction that shaved a fraction of a second off a reactive pivot.

Ndlovu caught the adjustment. His eyebrow rose the smallest amount—a gesture that, from him, bordered on emotional exuberance.

"Now that," he said under his breath, "is useful."

But still: no one crossed the center line.

Not Marines.

Not Sahr'ka.

Just two groups standing on the same floor for the first time, studying each other openly rather than warily. No pressure. No implied coordination. Just acknowledgment of mutual skill.

A step forward without calling it one.

By the third month, the Veil felt different. Not divided. Not unified. Something in between. Two shadows overlapping on the same deck plating.

Seed whispered across the neural channel during one of our early-morning briefings.

"Two branches lean toward the same light. They do not yet entwine, but the roots learn each other's names."

Echo translated flatly: "Integration remains in early stages."

It meant the same thing. More or less.

Calder stood at the center holo-table, projection grids spinning around him. "Link integrity is holding. No cascade failures, no neural overloads since week two. That said—"

Ward interrupted sharply. "Multiple incident reports indicate humans and Sahr'ka continue to misread proximity cues. Environmental adaptations recommended."

"She means," Vance said, "we should paint lines on the floor so nobody dies in a hallway."

"I mean," Ward corrected, "we should consider visible zone demarcations to compensate for predator response ranges."

"Lines on the floor," Vance repeated.

"It is statistically optimal."

I rubbed my temple. "We'll consider it."

Vakar clicked thoughtfully. "Humans fear being approached from behind. We will adapt."

"We're not afraid," Vance said automatically.

"Yes," Vakar replied, "you are."

Takahashi snorted into her sleeve.

The Sahr'ka weren't patrolling with us—not officially, not even unofficially—but they were present. They ate at adjacent mess tables, trained in parallel bays, calibrated in shared labs, and existed alongside us without conflict. I'd expected the opposite. Predators pressed into steel corridors. Marines surrounded by creatures whose body language could start a fight in ten different species.

But it worked.

Mostly.

Elara and I drifted into a pattern neither of us named. She spent most nights in my quarters. Not out of romance, not as a proclamation—just as habit. As gravity. As something understood without being spoken aloud.

Ward pretended not to notice.

Vance pretended not to care.

Kova pretended to run a betting pool discreetly.

One evening, Seed murmured in the neural channel, soft as wind moving through deep roots.

"One branch carries warmth. The other seeks it."

Echo translated mechanically: "Emotional convergence detected."

I glared at the projection. "Echo, please don't analyze my social life."

"I am unable to deactivate pattern recognition."

"Try."

"I have tried."

Elara walked onto the bridge midway through our exchange, datapad in hand. She caught only the tail end, saw Echo hesitate, and raised a silver eyebrow.

"I don't want to know," she said.

Wise.

A few weeks later, Calder requested one final test—a synchronized link stress simulation using ten humans and ten Sahr'ka in the largest cargo bay. Ghost Team anchored one side, Vakar's cadre anchored the other. Elara stood beside the central interface station, monitoring stress load. Ward observed from a safe distance behind three layers of shielding.

Calder entered a set of commands. The neural grid warmed, humming like a distant storm.

"Alright," he said. "Everyone say something harmless. Echo will filter any unstable cross-signals."

Ndlovu said, "Ready."

One of Vakar's lieutenants pulsed, "Standing."

Vance muttered, "Let's not die."

A Sahr'ka echoed, "Die not."

Calder winced. "Close. Close enough."

Elara leaned toward the console. "Signal coherence is stable. Stress load at—"

A spike hit. Sudden. Sharp. Bright.

Sahr'ka plates flared. Human helmets lit. The entire grid shuddered.

And then—

A BELLOW, half Sahr'ka, half Echo's translation layer, blasted the overhead speakers:

"WE… EAT… DOOM!"

Everyone froze.

I turned slowly to Calder.

"Explain."

Calder looked like he wanted to jump out an airlock. "Something… misaligned… I—I don't—"

Vakar's lieutenant pulsed uncertainly. "Doom… means challenge?"

Echo adjusted filters. "Correction: unintended cluster-merge with human concept 'face your doom.'"

"So we're shouting 'eat doom' now?" Vance said. "Is that a thing?"

Ward raised a hand. "Logging: translation malfunction suggests emergent cultural idiom."

"Absolutely not," I said. "Nobody is eating doom."

A Sahr'ka soldier tilted his head. "We are not eating ass. We are not eating doom. Humans consume many things they forbid."

Takahashi walked away and did not come back for a full five minutes.

But the thing was—nobody got hurt. The grid held. Stress load normalized after twenty-seven seconds. Echo stabilized the cross-signals. Calder survived.

And everyone walked away laughing.

Well—everyone except Ward.

She logged it as:

"Incident: Linguistic hazard. Severity: moderate."

Time passed.

The network grew.

Seed expanded nodes across the edge of Sahr'ka space, careful as someone tending a fragile vine. Echo monitored everything, adjusting the human side to avoid overwhelming the new architecture.

"Sahr'ka integration at twenty-seven percent of home cluster," Echo reported one evening.

"Shared tactical bandwidth at forty-two."

Not bad for a bunch of predators who couldn't talk to each other a few months ago.

And Elara… well. There was no "official" anything. But her things lived in my room now. So did she, most nights. I stopped pretending otherwise. The crew stopped pretending they didn't know.

I stood at the forward rail, watching the net expand across the starfield. Little white pulses marked every new connection. Human. Sahr'ka. Shared shadow.

Echo hovered nearby, voice a calm thread in the dark.

"The network grows steadily. No destabilization detected."

"Good," I said. "Let's keep it that way."

I glanced sideways toward the far corridor. Elara's hair had a way of catching light even when she wasn't trying. There was a chair waiting in my room that wasn't mine.

One alliance. One translation program. A growing web of shadows and the woman who'd quietly taken over my space.

Yeah.

That's how empires start.

CHAPTER 16:
ECHOES IN THE ASH

The Veil shuddered softly under my boots.

Not turbulence. Not an impact. More like a breath drawn shallow and held too long—an instinctive adjustment to something none of us had seen yet.

I didn't give that order. Neither did Navigation.

On the forward bridge, Takahashi's hands hovered centimeters above the helm, frozen mid-gesture, like she was afraid any movement might startle the ship. Vance leaned forward in his chair, eyes narrowing at the console like it had personally offended him.

"Tell me I just sneezed on the thrusters," he muttered.

"You didn't," I said.

Echo appeared beside the rail in a soft flicker—their projection settling into a shifting lattice of geometric shapes, rotating with deliberate calm.

Echo always appeared this way. Only Echo. Nothing else on the ship had that pattern.

"No sensor anomalies detected," they said.

Seed's voice drifted across the neural link, faint as fog.

"Whispers… pressed against the root."

The hair on my arms rose.

"She's been doing that more," I said quietly. "Adjusting before we tell her to."

Echo tilted slightly, the lattice shifting. "The ship exhibits anticipatory compensation. Not autonomous decision-making."

"That distinction is getting thinner by the day."

Vance scrubbed a hand down his face. "Outstanding. First the Sahr'ka start calling us prey-adjacent, now the ship's getting jumpy. Can't wait to see what tomorrow brings."

Takahashi didn't look away from her console. "Admiral, she's drifting six microns to starboard."

I felt it too. Not through the console—through the deck. A faint vector change. Gentle. Cautious.

"Echo?" I said.

"She is reacting to gravitational variance," Echo replied. "Atypical, but not dangerous."

"Define atypical."

"She reacted before the variance resolved."

Vance exhaled sharply. "Fantastic. We've invented anxiety."

I didn't answer. My attention was on the holo-map—on the coordinates Vakar had provided. The site where one of their moons had been harvested like an orchard.

Rak'shara.

The Veil was nervous. I didn't blame her.

The briefing chamber smelled faintly of steel, old heat, and the kind of recycled air that clung to every long-range mission. Sahr'ka didn't like confined spaces, so Vakar stood near the back wall, posture tall and still. Three other Alphas flanked him, scales shifting in muted bronze and forest dark—a spectrum of emotion I'd learned to read over months.

I took my place near the table but didn't sit. Elara perched on the edge of a chair, datapad in hand, eyes sharp despite the tired set of her shoulders. Ndlovu stood by the door, arms folded, quiet as a coiled spring.

"We've seen fragments in reports," I said. "Heard the stories. But stories aren't enough. I want to see one of the sites. In person."

The youngest Alpha hissed softly—their equivalent of a snarl.

"The ash carries memory," Echo translated. "The Hunt does not walk the scar."

Another Alpha's tail swept across the deck in a slow arc. "You would bring the scent of shadow to where the ground still burns."

Vakar's scales flashed a single ripple—warning. "The Hunt walks where it must."

"They will bring the scent," the young Alpha retorted. "They will awaken it."

"They can't awaken a dead moon," I said. "And whatever did this—" I gestured toward the star-map, the carved-out sphere of Rak'shara "—isn't asleep."

Silence cut across the room. Not fear. Calculation.

Vakar broke it first, dipping his crest in a controlled nod. "We take you to Rak'shara. The moon that died first."

Echo didn't wait for an order. Their lattice brightened, rotating. "Coordinates acquired."

Elara blinked. "You already—"

"She already had them," I said. "She's been pulling data from any Sahr'ka system she can reach."

Echo flickered. "Clarification: I respond to queries within network reach."

"No one asked you to respond," Vance muttered.

I ignored him.

"Prep for jump," I said. "We move within the hour."

The Veil slid from FTL like a knife pressed gently through silk. Rak'shara filled the viewport—broken, burnt, a carcass of a moon stretched beneath us like the universe's worst autopsy.

I'd seen bombardment scars. But this was different.

Vitrified plains, smooth as glass. Cities melted into ripples of fused alloy. Long gouges—clean, parallel, surgical—cut through the crust like something had dragged planet-sized claws straight through the mantle.

"Confirming thermal residue," Echo said. "Residual heat signatures indicate high-yield kinetic penetration. Time since strike: two years, three months, six days."

Elara leaned forward, voice quiet. "You can still feel the heat."

She was right. Even behind shielding, the air tasted scorched.

Then the Veil shifted again—just a fraction. Shields rose on their own, a soft hum pulsing through the floor.

"Admiral?" Takahashi said, not quite steady. "That wasn't helm input."

"I know."

"Echo?" Vance said, half hopeful, half horrified.

"She is reacting to destabilization in the subcrust magnetic field," Echo said.

"Magnetic field?" Vance snapped. "It's a moon-shaped corpse. Nothing is destabilized—"

He stopped as the sensors flickered.

Elara's hand tightened on the rail. "It's fluctuating. Something disrupted the field and left the fracture pattern behind."

I watched the scanners. The Veil wasn't afraid. She was reading something. Something broken, yes—but also something familiar.

"Seed?" I asked.

Her voice drifted like falling ash. "Silence that remembers fire."

Not helpful.

I straightened from the console.

"Alright," I said. "Gear up. We're going down."

No one argued. No one even hesitated. The room shifted into motion—Elara snapping her slate closed, Vance muttering something about hating moons, Takahashi double-checking our return vector like she expected it to bite.

Vakar dipped his head once—the Sahr'ka version of acknowledgment—and ghosted out of the room with his Alphas in a low, disciplined line. Ndlovu fell in behind them without being asked. Ghost Team 1 didn't need orders; they moved when he moved.

I walked with them through the central corridor, the ship humming around us—steady, controlled, but tense in a way I couldn't define. The Veil wasn't afraid, but she was watching something. Listening for something. Reacting to something we couldn't see.

The hangar doors opened onto a wash of floodlights and polished deck plating. Two dropships waited with engines idling low, their running lights casting long shadows across the floor.

"Ghost Team 1, board," Ndlovu said.

Harnesses clicked. Boots thudded against metal. Sahr'ka claws scraped softly as they settled into their bracing positions.

Elara paused beside me at the ramp.

"Ready?" she asked quietly.

"No," I said. "But we're going anyway."

The ramp lifted.

The cabin sealed.

And the Veil released the dropship into the dark.

Ghost Team 1 moved first.

Their boots hit the ash with practiced precision, forming a perimeter around the dropship while Sahr'ka honor guards unfolded into their own hunting crescent. Two circles. Two instincts. One purpose. The ash shifted underfoot like powdered glass, whispering against armor plates as the slope leveled out beneath us.

The second dropship settled a few meters away, its landing struts sinking into the soot with a low, grinding hiss. Heat shadows wavered around its hull, the engines exhaling a last breath of scorched air before falling silent. Ndlovu signaled his team with two short cuts of his hand, establishing the path forward without a word.

The contrast was stark: human precision on one side, predatory silence on the other.

We began the march toward the ruins.

The longer we walked, the quieter the world became. No wind. No wildlife. No mechanical hum. Just the soft crunch of glass dust under boots and claws. Ghost Team 1 widened their formation, helmets tilting as sensors fed them silent data. They looked ready for an ambush, the moon hadn't been capable of giving for years.

Ndlovu drifted up beside me without ceremony—an old habit from older campaigns.

"Admiral," he said quietly, eyes scanning the horizon. "This scale isn't tactical."

"Meaning?"

"Meaning this isn't a target." He gestured out toward the burned horizon, the fused towers, the exposed strata. "This is an ecosystem collapse. A planet pulled apart... not fought over."

"Industrial," I said.

"Yes," he replied. "But that's the problem."

His visor turned toward the distant trenches— those long, precise gouges that craved the surface like surgical wounds.

"You can fight an army," Ndlovu continued. "You can fight a fleet. You can fight an ideology. But this?" He shook his head once. "How do you counter something that treats a moon like raw material?"

There was no fear in his tone. Just realism. Experience. The kind of dread that didn't shout—it sat.

"We'll find a way," I said.

Ndlovu didn't disagree. But he didn't pretend either.

"We need to start thinking in scales that don't make sense to us," he said. "Because whatever did this didn't even slow down."

He stepped away to reposition his team, leaving the weight of his words behind like a footprint in the ash.

We descended into the bunker.

Elara

The air retained charge. Not enough to harm, but enough to feel— tiny whispers of static brushing across my skin. Old energy always left ghosts behind.

I walked toward the remnants of a data tower—half-collapsed, half-melted. The walls were fused into blackened crescents, framing what had once been a hub of local traffic. Now it was a tomb.

I crouched, brushing ash away from the scorched paneling. Beneath the soot, faint channels revealed themselves—burn paths, patterned almost like circuits.

Not random.

Not incidental.

Designed.

"Echo," I said quietly, "can you enhance the residual pattern?"

His holographic form flickered, then pulsed a thin beam downward. The ash glowed faintly, tracing repeating motifs—grids and arcs like schematic overlays.

"They scanned first," I whispered. "Then they removed anything that reacted."

Seed brushed the edge of my mind, soft but heavy with meaning. "Roots exposed… the forest cut open."

Even her metaphors felt sharper here.

From somewhere behind me, the crunch of Raz's boots approached. "What are we looking at?"

I turned the scanner so he could see. "Precision-tuned EM harvesting. They didn't strike until the entire grid presented itself. And once it did—" I gestured to the valley. "They took everything of structural or energetic value. Everything."

His jaw tightened. "What about civilians?"

My throat constricted. "There wouldn't have been time."

He didn't answer. He didn't need to. The silence said everything.

Behind us, the Sahr'ka growled low—a communal vibration, restrained but unmistakable. Not sorrow. Not anger.

Recognition.

Predators acknowledging another predator.

One that built factories out of dead worlds.

Razgriz

By the time we retraced our steps back to the landing zone, the sky above Rak'shara had dimmed into something between dusk and ashfall. The dropships loomed like dark silhouettes against the horizon, their hulls coated in a thin film of pale dust that rendered every contour stark and skeletal.

Ghost Team 1 secured the approach before we reached them. Ndlovu checked each Marine with quick, efficient gestures—no wasted movements, no unnecessary chatter. The Sahr'ka mirrored the motion in eerie synchrony, shoulder plates rippling as they shifted from formation to embarkation stance.

The first dropship lifted off with a low, heavy roar, rising through a curtain of pale particulate that swirled like dead snow. Its engines cast long shadows across the ruined ground before the dust swallowed them.

The second dropship—ours—trembled as the ramp lowered.

Inside, everything felt too clean. Too intact. Too alive. My boots left perfect prints in the thin trail of ash clinging to the deck, like the dead moon outside wanted to leave mark on something living.

Ndlovu boarded after me, securing the last of his people before locking the restraints. His gaze flicked toward the open ramp—one final sweep of a soldier who didn't believe in leaving anything behind, even when there was nothing left to take.

The ramp sealed with a final metallic thump.

"Dust-off," I ordered.

The dropship rose with a lurch, engines cutting through the dead air with sound that felt almost intrusive. The landscape shrank beneath us: blackened plains, vitrified fractures, trenches carved with mechanical indifference. A dead world giving no answers.

As the dropship cleared the upper atmosphere, the comm in my ear crackled alive.

"Admiral," Ward's voice said, crisp and controlled. "I require your presence on the bridge as soon as you dock."

Her tone wasn't alarmed. It wasn't calm either. It was the sound of a woman standing very still while her brain rearranged itself around new data.

"Is there a problem?" I asked.

"A development," she replied. "Not urgent for the ship's safety. Urgent for yours."

That was new. Ward didn't frame things that way unless she absolutely meant it.

"Brief me now."

A brief pause. "Information is best delivered in person. Correlation error margins are… non-zero."

Translation: whatever she'd found, she didn't trust the data enough to speak it out loud over comms.

"Understood," I said. "I'm en route."

The Veil filled the viewport ahead—sleek, shadowed hull catching faint starlight, scars of transformation still visible along plates that looked too smooth now. Too seamless. Living tech that hadn't existed months ago.

The dropship docked with a soft magnetic pull.

I unbuckled before the light turned green, boots hitting the deck with purpose. Ghost Team 1 filed out behind me in efficient sequence; Ndlovu gave a curt nod as he peeled off to debrief with Calder.

Ward pinged me again.

"Admiral," she said, "my projection is refined. Please expedite."

"I am already moving."

I took the nearest lift. The doors slid shut. The hum of ascent vibrated under my boots.

Nothing shook.

Nothing flickered.

The Veil remained steady.

But the air felt… aware.

Not the ship—just the moment.

Ward didn't dramatize. She didn't overstate. She didn't call me unless the numbers demanded it.

And whatever she'd seen in the data demanded me.

The lift doors opened into the central corridor. Bridge ahead. Ward waiting. And the next shift in the story already unfolding behind her eyes.

By the time the lift doors slid open, Takahashi was already half out of her chair. "Sir—she raised shields twice. No external contact. No radiation spike. Nothing."

The Veil pitched a subtle correction in orbit—smooth, almost gentle—like a ship shifting weight to brace for something.

Echo appeared, his geometry tightening in sharp symmetry. "I have not issued countermeasures. Navigation confirms no autopilot override."

"Then why is she reacting?" Vance demanded.

Echo paused—an actual pause, rare enough to set my nerves on edge. "I cannot confirm a cause."

Seed breathed through the neural channel. "The forest leans… when fire returns."

Not comforting.

"What fire?" I murmured.

Seed did not answer.

Elara stepped beside me, brushing a stray lock of hair behind her ear. "Raz," she said softly, "pull up the distant-spectrum scans we logged on entry."

I did.

The sensors showed nothing. No signatures. No objects. Just dead space.

"Look closer," she said.

I adjusted the sensitivity.

A faint disturbance glimmered across the field—too symmetrical to be random dust, too weak to be a signal, too cold to be heat.

It wasn't organic.

It wasn't natural.

It was the echo of a trajectory. Something massive had passed through this region in the last several months—long after the moon died.

Something traveling with deliberate, engineered vector stability.

Not drifting.

 Not wandering.

Moving.

"Echo," I said quietly, "compare that distortion to known drive wakes."

Echo did—and for the first time since I'd met them, their geometric form contracted sharply, almost like a flinch.

"Wake signature… is not comparable to human or Sahr'ka propulsion. It is not comparable to any propulsion in the archive."

"Meaning?"

"It is controlled," Echo said. "But not by us."

Vakar stepped forward, his presence filling the bridge with a low resonance. "We follow this trail now."

"This isn't a hunt," Elara said gently.

"It becomes one," Vakar replied. "Or we die."

The Veil shifted again—minor, precise, anticipatory.

I didn't like that.

"Helm," I said quietly, "take us out."

Takahashi hesitated. "Where?"

And for once, I didn't have an answer.

Seed's voice whispered across the neural link—sharp and cold as frost.

"The sparks move. The roots tremble. The next cut comes for the living wood."

I drew a slow breath.

"Set course for Sol."

"Elara," I said softly, "we're done here."

She nodded, eyes still fixed on the dying moon.

We turned away from Rak'shara's scars, engines building to burn-point.

The stars were quiet.

But the quiet didn't feel empty anymore.

It felt like the breath before someone opens a door.

Or something breaks one down.

CHAPTER 17:
THE WEIGHT OF ARRIVAL

The Veil slid out of jump above Lareth, the planet rising beneath us in layers of emerald and steel. From orbit, the surface shimmered with the light of its engineered grid—a world built, not grown. Dropships clustered in the lower hangars, their drives already humming against the deck. Waiting.

"Councilors are expecting us," Echo said through the bridge net.

I leaned against the rail, watching the world turn. "Then let's not keep them waiting."

Takahashi acknowledged without looking up. The ship adjusted vector with that subtle, living smoothness I'd learned to feel through the deck plates long before I ever saw it on sensors. There was no turbulence in orbit, but somehow the Veil still managed to make the air taste like the pause before a storm.

Vakar's escort waited in the main bay. Ghost teams were already loading into the dropships—quiet, efficient, armed. Elara stood among them, pale hair catching the overhead lights, datapad tucked beneath one arm. She wore soft armor under her envoy's coat, the kind that didn't look like armor unless you knew where to look. She knew we wouldn't be alone down there.

"I still find it strange," she said softly as I approached, "coming home on someone else's ship."

"You're not a passenger," I replied. "You're the reason they open the door."

Her mouth curved—something halfway between amusement and deflection. It didn't reach her eyes.

We broke atmosphere clean. The Veil's dropships weren't built to make noise, but the hull still shuddered as we cut into the gravity well. Lareth's cities spread outward in a structured web, precise and ordered, lit in muted gold tones. No sweeping organic shapes, no living tech—just careful, engineered perfection.

The landing platform hung suspended over a river of mist, held aloft by grav pylons. Its surface gleamed with the cold polish of alloy. Lareth security was already waiting. They didn't point their weapons. They didn't have to. Ghosts and Lareth guards understood each other in the way predators do.

Taren and Veyra stood forward—both had been aboard the Veil since the Sentinel event. Behind them waited the remaining three councilors: Dren, Rahl, and Selas. One industrialist, one soldier, one priest.

Elara disembarked first. Her boots struck the platform with the weight of someone returning to a place that no longer fully belonged to her. No ceremony. No words. Just recognition.

Selas stepped forward, her voice quiet but certain. "You've changed."

Elara's breath caught, almost imperceptibly. "Everything has."

"Then perhaps," Selas replied, tilting her head toward the stars, "so must we."

"Councilors," I called out, voice cutting through the soft hum of the pylons. "We're due in orbit within the hour. The summit begins as soon as we hit Sol."

Dren nodded once, curt and direct. Rahl's eyes followed the Ghost teams with a soldier's suspicion, but he didn't speak. Selas—tall, robed, the faint metallic threading of rank along her sleeves— inclined her head toward the Veil overhead, unreadable.

They boarded without argument. Lareth didn't do grand speeches. They understood time.

By the time I returned to the bridge, the last dropship had sealed. Vance was already bringing us to burn point. Takahashi's hands hovered over the helm, though we both knew the Veil was flying herself more often than not these days.

"Course laid in for Sol," she said.

Ward monitored the comms from her station, eyes tracking the long-range relay indicators. She gave me a small nod—quiet, competent, already adapting to the Veil's new habits.

"Then light the fuse."

The Veil's jump field flared like an opening eye.

Behind us, Lareth shrank into starlight. Ahead—Earth, and the part where pretending we had control stopped working.

The Veil's jump field flared once more, and Earth returned to the viewport not as home—but as the stage. The living-tech nodes in orbit marked their quiet pattern around the planet, separate structures whose alignment still formed that subtle seed-pod outline from afar.

The summit site floated against the black like a blade's edge. A neutral orbital platform, old bones from a decommissioned station, rebuilt and grafted with living fiber. Light pulsed faintly beneath the surface where organic fiber met alloy, the Canopy woven through the frame like veins through skin. This wasn't just steel anymore. It was alive—and it was listening.

Takahashi guided approach, though the Veil didn't need her hands for something this clean. Vance stood at his console, watching the orbital perimeter like it might blink. The hum of the ship met the faint thrum of the Canopy ahead, two living systems quietly acknowledging each other. It didn't feel like docking. It felt like a heartbeat syncing to another.

We locked in without ceremony. No cheering, no applause. Just the metallic thump of clamps engaging and the quiet weight of history pressing in on every side.

The Sahr'ka disembarked first, Vakar at their head, his two lieutenants pacing him like wolves in formation. Lareth's delegation followed under Elara's lead, the five councilors moving in measured unison. The Human Council stood waiting with neutral faces and carefully choreographed body language, Cho at the front, Rourke and Hayes just behind. Ward, Alvarez, and Kade completed the line, each wearing their own version of composure.

No one said much. That was the point. Everyone was measuring everyone else.

The council chamber was circular and tiered—designed to look equal even when it wasn't. Living fiberwork crept along the walls and floor in quiet, breathing patterns, not ornamental but functional. The light wasn't static; it shifted with movement, tracking every delegate as they entered. There was no polished marble or cold metal—just cultivated structure, grown into shape by human hands that had learned to tame what once belonged only to myth.

Vakar's eyes narrowed as the vines retracted from his boots. He didn't speak, but the ripple of muscle beneath his scales said enough. The Sahr'ka didn't like standing on something alive unless they were hunting it. Lareth's councilors showed no outward discomfort, though Selas ran a finger absently along the faintly glowing lines on the table before sitting.

I took the center seat—not because of protocol, but because no one else could. Cho opened the summit with practiced precision. She didn't raise her voice; she never had to. She talked about shared threats, operational cooperation, mutual defense. All the necessary words.

The quiet cracked when Rahl leaned forward, hands clasped loosely. "If we're to strike at this 'Hunger,' there can't be competing chains of command. Fragmented control gets people killed."

Vakar shifted, boots rasping against living surface. "Then say what you mean."

"I mean someone has to lead," Rahl said flatly.

The air changed. The living fiberwork dimmed slightly, reading tension the way animals sense weather. Vakar rose in one fluid motion. No roar. No display. Just an apex predator standing up. His lieutenant mirrored him. Lareth guards stiffened across the chamber. A few humans on Rahl's side tensed without realizing it.

Rahl stood too. Smaller frame. Not smaller spine.

I didn't stand. I didn't need to.

"Vakar." My voice cut through the pressure before it could break.

He stopped mid-step. The lieutenant didn't.

"Sit."

The word hit like iron.

Vakar's jaw flexed once before he obeyed. The lieutenant followed without looking up. Rahl held his stance a heartbeat longer, then sat as well. The tension didn't leave the room—it just shifted its weight.

"This is not how a hunt is led," Vakar growled, low.

I leaned forward, elbows on the table. "This isn't a huntship. And this isn't the Hunt."

For a second, the only sound was the soft pulse of the Canopy through the walls.

The summit moved forward on the edge of that silence. Hayes laid out operational coordination like he was stacking artillery shells in neat rows. Ward traced supply and economic support with surgical efficiency. Alvarez mapped civilian integration with the kind of precision that only comes from building the roads others walk on. Selas's voice was calm—measured words about trust, not as an ideal but as an inevitability if anyone wanted to survive.

No one said the word alliance until Cho did. She said it once. Clear. Final. The chamber itself responded—the fiberwork brightened slightly, picking up the pulse of so many hearts in the same room. Not unity. But a rhythm.

Cho let the room breathe a moment before speaking again.

"This summit will not end with signatures alone. Tomorrow night, Earth will host a formal gathering here on the station. No debates. No orders. Just people talking."

Her eyes moved deliberately across the delegations.

"This is not a demand. It's an invitation. But alliances built in silence don't hold."

Vakar tilted his head like she'd just suggested hunting with one claw tied behind his back. Selas inclined hers with the faintest trace of approval. Hayes didn't react—but I caught the slight shift in his stance. Formal wear tomorrow. Not armor. No excuses.

The vote wasn't unanimous. It didn't have to be. It was loud enough.

When the session finally ended, councilors left in deliberate clusters, entourages trailing like shadows. I stayed seated as the chamber thinned. The fiberwork dimmed again, settling into a soft pulse that matched the Veil outside. Vakar paused at the threshold, tilting his head just enough for his voice to reach me alone.

"Your way is strange," he said. "But it works."

I almost smiled. "You'll get used to it."

His laugh was low, rough, edged with teeth. Not friendly. Not hostile either.

When the doors finally closed, the silence wasn't sterile—it was alive. The Canopy listened, the alliance existed, and the weight of it all pressed in like the air before a storm.

This wasn't victory. It was a beginning.

And beginnings always came with teeth.

The Veil's lights shifted from night-cycle to dawn mode, a soft gradient that bled across the bulkhead like light through leaves. I opened my eyes to an empty room.

No note. No sound. Just the faint hum of the ship breathing around me.

Elara was gone.

That wasn't unusual—not exactly. She was a scientist, and she had a habit of treating morning like a personal laboratory. But something about the silence was different. Not heavy. Just… waiting.

I swung my legs over the edge of the bunk and sat there for a few seconds, letting the air settle. No alarms. No emergencies. Just the kind of quiet that always came before the next performance.

The mirror on the wall reflected a man who'd spent most of his life avoiding parties like the plague. A formal black uniform laid out and pressed on the chair beside the door—Cho's idea of subtlety. The gold trim caught the soft light from the Veil's structural patterning, a reminder that tonight wasn't about war. It was about appearances.

Vance had called it "a diplomatic circus." He wasn't wrong.

I palmed the interface on the wall. The ship responded immediately, Echo's neutral tone filling the room.

"Elara left the ship an hour and twenty-three minutes ago."

"Destination?"

"Summit concourse. Civilian access level."

Of course she did.

I exhaled slowly, not sure if I was smiling or bracing for impact. Whatever she was up to, she wasn't doing it halfway. Elara Veyl didn't do anything halfway.

I grabbed the uniform, feeling the weight of the fabric against my palm. No armor. No rifle. No quiet shadows. Just polished edges and politics.

The worst battlefield I'd ever known.

The comm crackled softly in my ear. Vance's voice came through, lazy but amused.

"Morning, Admiral. You sound thrilled."

I buttoned the collar. "I'm going to need coffee. A lot of it."

"Already on the bridge," he said. "Try not to scare the diplomats."

"Can't make promises."

Elara

The mirror in the summit concourse dressing chamber wasn't made of glass. It was a thin layer of living surface-weave—responsive, soft, and far too honest. Light traced along its edges, catching the silver of my hair and the faint glow beneath my skin.

Selas leaned against the doorway with her arms folded, watching me like she'd been doing it for years.

"You've gone to more trouble than usual," she said lightly. Not accusing. Just noticing. Selas always noticed.

I adjusted the edge of the gown—not really out of necessity, just to keep my hands busy. "It's a formal event."

"It's more than that," she countered. "Even the lighting adjusted to you."

I glanced at her reflection. She wasn't smiling, but her eyes held the soft kind of curiosity only old friends got away with. Selas wasn't family—not exactly. But she'd been there through enough years and enough walls for the difference to blur.

"It's just a dress," I said.

She tilted her head. "And he's just an admiral."

For a heartbeat, I forgot how to breathe.

Selas pushed off the doorframe, closing the distance with a quiet grace only someone born under the Canopy could manage.

"You don't owe me an explanation. But you might owe yourself one."

"I don't know where this goes," I admitted, voice softer than I meant it to be. "But for once… I don't want to stop it."

Selas nodded once. No lecture. No questions. Just a hand on my shoulder, warm and steady.

"Then stop pretending you don't care how you look tonight."

Razgriz

The ballroom was already too loud. Not the kind of loud that came from chaos, but that careful, layered noise people made when they were trying to sound civilized.

Polished lightwork panels curved into a vaulted ceiling alive with soft light, the glow shifting with the crowd below. Delegates clustered at drink stations like they were at war with their own nerves. Glasses clinked. Laughter hovered just far enough from sincerity to make my skin itch.

I'd spent my life in war rooms, not salons. Armor and silence fit better than dress uniforms and diplomatic choreography. But tonight wasn't about comfort. Tonight was about optics.

Councilor Ward stood near the Sahr'ka delegation, locked in conversation that was half smiles, half veiled threats. Cho held her usual place at the center of the storm, Alvarez orbiting her like a practiced shield. Hayes lingered closer to the perimeter, scanning the exits the way soldiers do when they don't trust a room. Rourke looked like she'd rather be anywhere else—a sentiment I understood perfectly.

The uniform chafed at my collar. Too stiff. Too sharp. Medals hung heavy like someone else's expectations. Vance had stationed himself at the bar, swirling a drink with a grin that said he'd already started placing bets on which delegate would crack first. I envied him.

Someone across the room called, "Ward!"

Both Lt. Ward and Councilor Ward turned at the same time.

The brief moment of mutual, polite confusion passed quickly, but the bridge crew caught it—Vance's grin said he'd been waiting for that to happen.

And then the atmosphere changed.

It wasn't silence exactly. More like the weight in the room shifted direction. Voices softened, conversation threads faltered mid-sentence. Heads began turning toward the main archway as if drawn on a single string.

Elara entered.

The gown wasn't loud. It didn't have to be. Flowing midnight fabric traced with faint bioluminescent silver, soft as smoke and deliberate as a blade. The light of the ambient weave bent to her—not around her, to her—following the subtle glow beneath her skin like it recognized its own.

Each step moved like choreography. Controlled. Unhurried. Commanding.

She didn't look like a xenophysiologist who'd spent months crawling through ruins. She didn't look like the woman who'd argued with me in comm rooms at three in the morning. She looked like someone who belonged on a red carpet with the world watching, and for a moment, it was.

Vance's drink stopped mid-air. "Holy—" he muttered. The glass never finished the sentence.

Cho's carefully neutral expression cracked into something closer to satisfaction. Ward's mouth curved in a knowing smile without breaking the rhythm of her conversation. Alvarez blinked once, slowly, like his brain was trying to catch up with his eyes.

Selas, standing off to the side, allowed herself the faintest grin— half pride, half I told you so.

Even Vakar stilled. Not with desire—Sahr'ka didn't react like that—but with the quiet tension predators gave apex rivals.

And me? My chest tightened. Not a poetic pause. Not some grand revelation. Just the simple, brutal realization that I'd forgotten how to keep my expression neutral.

The room's noise didn't die. It bent. Tilted toward her like gravity had picked its favorite.

She met my gaze across the floor. The chatter, the political dance, the entire carefully curated façade of diplomacy—none of it mattered. Just her.

Vance leaned closer, voice pitched low enough for only me. "You look like someone just punched you in the soul."

"Shut up," I muttered. But the corner of my mouth betrayed me.

Elara started down the central walkway, every pair of eyes in the room following whether they wanted to or not. She wasn't performing. She simply owned the moment without needing permission.

I straightened my collar, mostly to have something to do with my hands. Formal settings never felt right. But right then, with her walking toward me, the rest of the room could've been smoke and noise for all I cared.

Elara didn't hurry. She didn't need to. The crowd parted on instinct, conversation thinning into a low current as she crossed the floor. I'd faced down planetary sieges with less pressure.

When she finally stopped in front of me, the light of the Canopy shifted again—like the station itself was paying attention.

"Admiral," she said softly. Her voice carried more weight than it should have, like gravity had chosen her side too.

"Elara." My tone was steady. My pulse… not so much.

Her eyes caught the light, silver irises burning faintly brighter against the ambient glow. She smiled, just enough to make the air in my lungs forget its job.

"You look…" I started, and immediately regretted it. My vocabulary had apparently gone AWOL. "You look—different."

Her brow lifted. "Different?"

"Professional," I managed. "I mean—formal. Appropriate for a diplomatic event."

Vance, somewhere behind me, coughed into his drink hard enough to sound like choking.

Elara's smile widened, almost imperceptibly. "That's a very military compliment, Admiral."

"I'm a very military man."

"I've noticed."

She stepped closer—half a meter, maybe less. The kind of distance that would have felt intrusive with anyone else.

"You're uncomfortable."

"I prefer situations where the odds are measurable."

"And tonight isn't?"

"No. Tonight, they're impossible."

Her laugh was soft—low enough that only I heard it.

"Then we're even."

She extended her hand.

"Dance with me?"

"I don't—"

I caught the look in her eyes. There wasn't a chance in the universe I was saying no.

I took her hand.

The patterned floor-light beneath us adjusted to the movement, light rippling outward in faint concentric lines that followed the rhythm. The band—a blend of human and Lareth musicians—shifted seamlessly into something slower, strings and soft percussion looping through the air like an echo through a dream.

I didn't trip. That was the first miracle.

The second was realizing I was smiling. Not a smirk, not a twitch—an actual smile. She led as much as I did, effortless, poised. When she glanced up at me, I saw the same calm focus she wore in the field—only here, it was disarming in ways combat never managed.

"You're better at this than I expected," she said.

"I adapt under fire."

"Mm. You do that well."

We circled once more before the song faded, the last note hanging in the air a little too long before dissolving into scattered applause.

I released her hand reluctantly. "That was… tolerable."

She laughed outright this time, the sound bright and unguarded.

"You should write poetry."

"Don't tempt me."

Her eyes flicked toward the buffet line.

"You're already thinking about an exit strategy, aren't you?"

"I'm thinking," I said, scanning the tables, "that I've spotted a tray of deviled eggs."

She blinked, caught between amusement and disbelief.

"Out of everything here?"

"They're tactical," I said, straight-faced. "Portable. Efficient. And delicious."

"You can't possibly—"

She tilted her head.

"And you're going to share this tactical discovery with…?"

I turned toward the far side of the room.

"Vakar."

She folded her arms. "You're taking me with you."

"Obviously."

Vance intercepted halfway there, grinning like a man who'd just witnessed divine comedy. "That went better than expected. You only stuttered twice."

"Three times," I corrected. "And she laughed."

"Which part?"

"All of it."

I plucked a deviled egg from the tray, bit into it, and nodded decisively.

"Perfect."

"Admiral," Vance said, wary now, "please tell me you're not—"

"I am."

He sighed. "You're going to do it, aren't you?"

"Of course."

I grabbed another and gestured toward the far side of the room, where Vakar and his lieutenants were standing like statues in a sea of nervous diplomats.

"I need to introduce the Sahr'ka to humanity's finest culinary achievement."

"Sir, they eat live prey."

"And yet," I said, already walking, "they've never had these."

I grabbed two more off the tray, held one up like a prize, and kept walking. Elara fell into step beside me with a look halfway between amusement and resignation.

Vakar and his two lieutenants stood near one of the light-columns, watching the room the way predators watched watering holes. The closest thing they had to "relaxed" was less ready to kill something.

"Admiral," Vakar rumbled. His gaze dropped to the small plate in my hand. "What is that."

"Deviled eggs," I said. "One of humanity's great diplomatic tools."

The lieutenant on the left made a low clicking sound that I'd learned meant mild suspicion. Elara's laugh was quiet against my shoulder.

"You're really doing this."

"Of course I am."

I offered the plate to Vakar like I was handing over a tactical schematic. "Eggs. Prepared with mustard, spice, and a little vinegar. No bones. No struggle."

Vakar stared at them as though I'd just handed him an unfamiliar explosive.

Elara stepped in, her voice smooth.

"They're safe."

Slowly—very slowly—Vakar reached down, pinched one between two clawed fingers, and lifted it with the caution of someone defusing a live grenade. He sniffed it once. Then again. His crest shifted faintly, plates tightening.

And then he bit.

The reaction wasn't dramatic. Sahr'ka didn't do dramatic. But his pupils widened, his throat plates flexed, and for the first time since I'd known him, I swore there was something dangerously close to satisfaction on his face.

"They are..." Vakar rumbled, searching for the right word. "Acceptable."

His lieutenants each grabbed one with far less hesitation, devouring them with low, pleased growls. A few nearby diplomats stared like they'd just watched a tiger delicately eat a crêpe.

Elara leaned in close, her voice low enough that only I could hear.

"You may have just averted three future diplomatic crises."

"I told you," I said. "Tactical."

Cho intercepted us halfway across the ballroom, moving with the kind of grace that only comes from years of navigating political minefields. Her dress shimmered faintly under the Canopy lights, but there was nothing soft in her eyes. She was hunting for a moment—and found it.

"Admiral," she said lightly. "May I borrow you for a moment?"

The way she phrased it wasn't really a question.

I felt Elara's hand loosen slightly against my arm. She didn't look annoyed—just reading the room faster than anyone else.

"I'll find us a seat," she said softly, and slipped away toward the tables. A few diplomats parted instinctively around her. She had that effect now.

Cho led me toward one of the side corridors branching off the ballroom. Quieter here. No music. No audience.

She didn't waste time.

"I'm not going to circle around this," she said. "I've spent the last six months trying to hold the center together. The world is changing faster than the Council can pretend it understands. And I'm tired of pretending."

I raised a brow. "That's not something I expected to hear from the Chair."

Her smile was thin. Not sharp, just tired.

"Because the Chair isn't supposed to say things like that. But I'm not the title, Razgriz. I'm a woman who knows when she's out of her depth."

She leaned against the wall—not the way politicians do, but like someone holding their balance.

"The Hunger isn't going to be the last threat. You and I both know that. And when the next one comes, people are going to look to Earth for leadership. They can't afford to get a committee."

I didn't say anything. She wasn't looking for approval yet.

She took a breath.

"I've watched how people respond to you. How they respond to you. You walk into a room, and predators lower their heads. Soldiers straighten their backs. Diplomats fall quiet. You're not just a fleet admiral anymore."

"Cho—"

"No," she cut in softly. "You need to hear this. The Council's power only matters inside these walls. Out there?"

She tilted her chin toward the stars beyond the glass.

"Out there, it's background noise."

The silence stretched, heavier than the music bleeding faintly from the ballroom.

She straightened then, quiet and certain.

"When this is over—when we're not fighting for survival every breath—I'm going to push for something permanent. Not a vote, not a committee. A single voice. One leader. And it's going to be you."

I exhaled slowly. "You're serious."

"Deadly." Her eyes didn't waver.

"Love and duty, Razgriz. The people can follow numbers and words, but they rally behind stories. You've already written yours without meaning to."

For a heartbeat, her mask of steel slipped, and what was left was just a woman—tired, resolute, and entirely aware of what she was setting in motion.

Then Cho stepped back, placed both hands over her heart, and bowed slightly. Not for protocol. Not for show. She knew exactly what she was doing.

"Think about it," she said, voice low. "Because I already have."

Then she turned, smoothing her dress, and walked back toward the noise and light like nothing had been said at all.

The stars stared back, bright and cold, laughing the way only something ancient can—when it already knows the ending.

CHAPTER 18: BANNERS AND BATTLE LINES

The first thing I saw when I opened my eyes was the dress.

Midnight fabric and soft silver lines, folded on itself where I'd dropped it on the floor. Half caught in the soft light bleeding in through the curtains.

Next to it—my uniform. Less artfully discarded. Crumpled in a chair like it had lost the war.

The room was ridiculous. Gold inlay, soft ambient lighting, a carved archway framing the viewport. Whoever booked it had a sense of humor. Probably Cho. "Honeymoon suite" wasn't an accident.

Elara lay half buried in the sheets, hair fanned across the pillow like a spill of silver. The bioluminescence from her skin had dimmed to a quiet glow, soft and steady. She was still asleep—utterly at ease in a way I wasn't.

I stared longer than I probably should have.

The night had gone by fast. Too fast. The kind of fast that felt like falling without ever touching the ground.

And beneath it all, Cho's words still sat in the back of my skull, sharp and quiet.

One leader. You.

Elara shifted slightly, a small sound slipping past her lips. The kind that didn't belong to soldiers or councils or wars. Just people.

I sat up slowly, leaning forward with my elbows on my knees. The station outside was already awake; I could feel it humming through the walls like a reminder that the universe didn't stop just because I didn't know what to do next.

"You're thinking too loud."

Her voice was soft—thick with sleep, but clear enough to cut through the noise in my head. She propped herself up on one elbow, hair falling around her face, completely unconcerned with modesty. That had always been her. No pretense. Just truth.

"I don't know what you mean," I said.

She gave me a look. The kind that didn't need words.

"Something's wrong."

I let the silence stretch.

"Cho cornered me last night."

That pulled her up. She sat, sheets slipping down, eyes locked on me.

"What happened?"

"She wants me to lead," I said. "Not a ship. Not a fleet. Everything. Earth. Council. Alliance."

She blinked once, slow. The scientist, the envoy, the friend—all lining up behind that one look.

"She said that?"

"Pretty much word for word." My jaw ached from how hard I'd been holding it. "She thinks because people follow me into a fight, I should drag the whole damn species along too."

She crossed the distance and set a hand on my shoulder. Firm. Steady.

"That's why it has to be you. Because you didn't ask for it."

Her eyes didn't flinch. Mine probably did.

"You've been leading since someone decided to put stars in front of you," she said. "This isn't different. Just heavier."

The silence between us wasn't soft. It had weight.

I leaned against the headboard, staring at the viewport. Earth hung there like it didn't know it was sitting on a fault line.

"I've spent my entire life avoiding that chair," I said. "The one where your signature gets someone killed."

"You're already in it."

"Not like this." My fingers dug into my palms. "That chair had an eject handle. This one doesn't."

Her hand slid down my arm, not to comfort me, just to keep me from disappearing into my head.

"That's why they trust you," she said.

"I don't want to end up like the ones who stop caring."

"You won't."

"You can't know that."

She leaned in slightly.

"I can. You hate the idea of turning into them. That's enough."

I huffed out something between a laugh and a growl.

"You've got too much faith."

"I've got evidence." Her knee brushed mine. "You keep choosing the hard way."

"Elara—"

"Stop." Her voice sharpened just enough to hold me. "This isn't about wanting it. It's about who people follow when everything else is burning."

I stared at the ceiling.

"I never wanted to be a symbol."

"We already are."

The words landed clean—no warmth, no judgment, just fact. She wasn't trying to make it about herself. She didn't need to. Everyone had seen us on that floor. The dance. The bow. A soldier and a scientist standing where no one else had.

Across three civilizations, people had already decided what that meant.

I stared at her. Not Elara the envoy, or Elara the scientist. Just Elara. The other half of a story I hadn't meant to write.

"I didn't ask for this," I said.

"I know," she answered. "Neither did I."

The silence that followed wasn't sharp anymore. It just settled—heavy, familiar, something we'd both have to carry. Out there, the alliance was already moving. And whether we liked it or not, so were we.

The station didn't sleep. Even in the darkness of space it was always alive with activity.

By the time I'd pulled my uniform back together, the morning briefing logs were already waiting—stacked with deployment schedules, personnel rotations, and a few notes flagged urgent in that way bureaucrats liked to pretend was polite.

Elara left before I did, called away for her own meetings. She gave me one last look at the door—not a goodbye, more a reminder. We didn't need to say anything.

I took the lift down to the observation deck, coffee in hand, still thinking about Cho's words. About our symbol. About everything that had shifted in a single night.

Below, the training fields stretched along the inner curve of the station's ring. Three forces—human, Lareth, Sahr'ka—moving in uneven lines, trying to learn each other's rhythms.

Ndvolu stood at the center, shoulders squared, voice cutting through the chatter like a knife. He didn't need to shout. Soldiers listened when a man like him spoke.

This wasn't ceremony.

Just the shape of what came next starting to take form.

The longer I watched, the clearer the lines started to form.

Lareth moved like a blade—tight formations, clean transitions, no wasted steps. Sahr'ka didn't bother with lines at all. They flowed. Slipped through gaps like they'd already mapped the kill zones before the fight started. And humans… we were a mess. But a familiar mess.

Adaptive. Quick to mimic. Quick to improvise when things fell apart.

Rahl kept his arms folded, silent now, but I could see it in his posture—he didn't like the unevenness. Vakar, on the other hand, was watching the chaos like it was a hunt he'd already claimed.

"This is exactly why this works," I finally said.

They turned toward me, not because I raised my voice, but because they all knew I didn't talk just to fill air.

"Lareth fights like war has rules," I said, nodding toward the formations below. "You bring discipline. Structure. You hold a line that doesn't break unless someone rips it out of the ground."

Rahl's jaw tightened, but he didn't argue.

I shifted my attention to Vakar. "Your people don't hold lines. You don't need to. You move like water around everything in your way. You make the enemy chase you, bleed trying to pin you down."

A faint rasp vibrated in Vakar's throat—amusement or pride, maybe both.

"And us?" I looked back to the humans struggling to catch the rhythm. "We don't have the clean edges or the precision. We get punched in the face and figure out how to hit back harder. That's our strength. We adapt."

No one spoke. Not even Rourke. The field below shifted again under Ndvolu's orders. For the first time, the movement didn't look like three forces colliding. It looked like something that might start to fit together.

"If we can make those three pieces move like one," I said, "we stop being a collection of survivors. We start being a threat."

I watched until the pattern stopped being chaos and started being readable. Lareth kept the lines tight. Humans filled gaps and improvised when the plan frayed. The Sahr'ka moved in a different register altogether—no formations, no fuss, just sudden, lethal contact. Up close they were devastating; in a straight-on, prolonged push they bled down faster than anyone wanted to admit. They read the field differently, too—reactive to the hum in the air, to bursts of energy the rest of us barely noticed. That gave them a reach most didn't see coming, and a blind spot when someone stopped playing by the grid.

I turned from the viewport. The others were still taking notes, trading the small, polite arguments that don't make or break a battle. I walked toward the comm console where Ndvolu's feed sat bright and waiting. He saw me coming and met my pace—no question, no theatrics. He was the kind of man who moved when given a thing to do.

"Split them in two," I said, low. "Mix the elements. Each team gets Lareth, Sahr'ka, and human units."

Ndvolu's jaw worked once. "You want mirror units to test handoffs?"

"Exactly. But run them different." I kept my voice flat. "One behaves like they did in the first run—each force doing what comes natural. The other follows a new pattern. Human command overlays. Lareth anchors. Sahr'ka strike teams embedded and assigned specific lanes, not free to roam on instinct. Force the handoffs. Make them fight each other."

He looked at me. Not surprised. He'd been in field ops long enough to know when a test was a trap to learn something dangerous. "You want them facing each other? War game?"

"Yes." I nodded. "The point isn't who wins right away. It's to see where control breaks. Where the Sahr'ka overreach, where Lareth's timing snaps, where humans panic. Then fix it."

Ndvolu tapped the console, pulling up the manifests and feed overlays. "Rules of engagement?"

"Limited lethal," I said. "Sim rounds. Disable and extract for casualties. Realistic pressure—supply windows, timed resupplies. Force the logistics to show their teeth." I added, "No public broadcast. Keep this off the feeds until we finish. I don't want half the summit rewriting doctrine because of a rehearsal."

He nodded. "Understood. Two sides. Mixed composition. One adaptive human-led command. One organic-style command. Rotate objectives. I'll set staggered goals so they have to hand over ground under pressure."

"Exactly." I checked the faces of the people around the rail—Hayes, Rourke, Rahl, Vakar—none of them were in on this. Let them watch a drill. Let them think they saw improvement. We needed the unfiltered data.

Ndvolu keyed the comm. "Teams formed. Moving to start positions."

Down on the field the units rearranged. The difference was immediate and visible: where the first run had been three distinct styles rubbing against each other, the new layout forced contact points. Sahr'ka hunters were paired with Lareth fire teams and human squads trained to accept, hold, and hand off. The human element carried the command node—simple overlays on comm protocols, rapid fallback formations, pre-briefed handoff signals. It looked awkward at first, then sharper.

I watched Vakar's eyes narrow when a Sahr'ka pair held back from charging and instead slipped into a lane, then struck at the precise moment a Lareth squad lifted suppression. He didn't like being told where to go, but the effect was immediate—enemy cohesion broke in places it hadn't before.

The other side, left to old instincts, still moved like a beautiful, dangerous animal. They hit hard, then had trouble consolidating. Lareth units on that flank tried to hold ground the way they were taught and paid for the effort with wasted motion. Humans improvised, but without a node to bind them they began to stutter.

Ndvolu's voice cut through my ear. "Handoffs showing delay at thirty seconds. Sahr'ka on Alpha flank overextended—supply window missed by ninety." He paused. "Adjusting."

"Push the timer," I said. "Force the extraction under fire. Let the logistics choke."

Another shift below. The adaptive side tightened. Where humans took the hit, they were pulled out on schedule and replaced by Lareth consolidation teams. The Sahr'ka strikes were surgically timed and then slipped away, not to hold, but to deny and bleed.

I kept watching until the data stopped being theory.

When the first horn blew and instructors waved the cease, the field looked like a place that had been through something hard. Bodies moved. Medics worked. Ndvolu's feed scrolled metrics—reaction times, handoff success percentage, casualty windows.

I turned to the rail and met Vakar's gaze. He didn't smile, but his nod said what words didn't: this was useful.

That was the point. We didn't want doctrine written from a single victory or a single defeat. We wanted the ugly places exposed—where instinct failed the plan—and the parts that could be welded together until the whole had teeth.

"Run the debrief in fifty," I told Ndvolu. "I want raw numbers. No edits."

"Understood," he said.

We'd started the test. Now we had to make sense of the truth it spat back at us.

Ndvolu didn't sugarcoat anything. He stood at the console, fingers moving fast, the raw feed running behind him—time stamps, heat maps, casualty vectors, and a long list of things that didn't go to plan.

"Reaction time averages," he said, steady. "Organic side—thirty-two seconds to first coordinated response. Adaptive side—eighteen. Handoff success: organic sixty-one percent; adaptive eighty-two. Casualty window on organic flank averaged ninety seconds from hit to extraction. Adaptive side averaged thirty-five. Supply miss events: three on organic, zero on adaptive. Sahr'ka overextensions accounted for two major breaches."

He let the numbers hang.

Hayes folded his arms. "Thirty-two seconds is a death sentence in a real fight."

Rourke was already mapping the overlays. "Alpha flank's supply routing crossed an unprepped corridor. That's fixable, but only if we pre-stage without waiting for council signatures."

Rahl's gaze was on the replay. "Lareth patterns were read like an open book. We held ground the way we always have. The Sahr'ka cut straight through."

Vakar's claws tapped the railing. "They struck where they smelled weakness."

"And overreached," I said. "Fast doesn't help if you bleed out after the first strike."

Ndvolu brought up casualty vectors. "Human extractions stayed consistent only when they were the command node. Dispersed, response windows ballooned."

"Because we improvise," I said. "We work best when there's a single fallback to snap into. That's where we glue this thing together."

Rourke didn't look up. "Pre-staging will close the gaps. I'll need authority thresholds."

Hayes glanced at me. "Field-level, not council-level."

"Exactly," I said. "We build a command node with delegated thresholds. Military decides in the moment. Politics signs off after."

Rahl leaned forward. "And who holds that node?"

"Rotating theater lead," I said. "Permanent liaisons from each faction. Human overlay for coordination. We saw the difference in reaction time. That's not opinion—it's data."

Vakar's eyes narrowed. "You leash us."

"No," I said. "I point the blade. You still strike. But you strike where it counts."

Hayes gave a short nod. "We can draft the legal framework."

Rourke was already tapping. "Supply corridors and timing windows by nightfall."

Rahl's voice was quiet, practical. "Three rotation cycles minimum. Liaison training embedded. We'll need to break old habits."

I met Vakar's gaze and didn't flinch. "And build new ones."

He didn't smile, but his tail settled.

Ndvolu closed the feed. "Handoff failures cluster at transitions. Fix the transitions, we cut the lag in half."

"Then that's where we start," I said. "Handoffs. Timing. Pre-stage supply. Command node authority. No speeches. Just work."

The room stayed silent, not out of doubt, but weight. Everyone knew what this was—a line being drawn. No more theory. No more three armies tripping over each other. From here on, it would move as one or not at all.

I pulled Ndvolu aside as the others filtered out, away from the rail and the hum of the replay screens. He didn't need to be told to come—he moved like a man who understood there was always more work waiting.

"You run the next cycle with the adaptive node as primary," I said. "Double the tempo. Force the handoffs harder. Push the extraction windows until they scream and then shave them back three seconds. I want failure points mapped, names, and times. No gloss."

He nodded once. "Understood. We'll rotate liaisons live for the next run and force a mid-op resupply to see how the logistics hold."

"Good." My voice was flat. "Keep the Sahr'ka lanes narrow—force them into pockets so Lareth can close. Humans stay at the node. If they choke, pull them and run med-evac drills until the extraction times match the adaptive side."

He began to make notes. I almost walked away, then stopped. "And—" I added, because someone had to say it, because it was my job and I hated that it had become my job— "make sure the footage stays off public feeds until Rourke gives the all-clear. No council theater."

Ndvolu's mouth tightened. "There are already requests for the data."

"I don't need politicians rewriting tactics into press releases," I said. "Keep it contained. Let us fix it first."

He tapped a comm pad. "One more thing—Diplomatic Corps just sent word. Ambassador Kade is being assigned civilian liaison aboard the Veil. He'll be arriving this rotation."

For a second, I went blank. Kade. The man who smiled with a mouth full of plans and paper. "On my ship?" I said.

"Yes," Ndvolu answered. "Council decided it's better if the ambassador rides with the operational command. Keeps lines short."

I let out a sound that was part laugh and part complaint. "Wonderful. So now I host a diplomat and run a war school."

"You host him," Ndvolu said. "We run the war school."

"Fine." I rubbed the bridge of my nose. "Then give me the raw numbers within the hour. Get liaisons embedded. Run the extractions until the humans stop panicking on cue. And when Kade shows up, don't let him near the feeds."

"Understood," he said.

I headed for the lift. The political meeting would be waiting—Cho, Ward, Selas, the rest—where talks and decisions lived in different vocabularies. Tactical fixes were cleaner. Political fixes leaked. Both mattered. Both needed to be done.

Outside, the field reset for another run. Inside, the station kept moving. I had orders to set and an ambassador to tolerate.

The lounge didn't feel like a council room. No banners, no polished floors, no podiums waiting for someone to grandstand. Just a table, a few chairs, and the hum of the station bleeding through the bulkheads. It was the kind of space where people stopped pretending they weren't tired.

Cho stood at the end of the table like she'd been waiting for this moment all day. Councilor Helena Ward leaned against the wall with a tablet under one arm, expression neutral but sharp. Kade strolled in a beat late, looking like a man blissfully unaware of the grenade about to go off in his lap. Vakar claimed the far corner, tail resting low against the floor, yellow eyes fixed on the room with that still, predatory patience that made everyone else feel like prey.

Selas sat close to Elara, not hovering but present—a shadow of quiet support. She already knew why we were here. Probably knew before anyone else did.

Cho didn't waste time easing in. "Well," she said, voice light and dangerously clear, "we should probably talk about the fact that half the station saw you two looking like a recruitment poster for interspecies unity last night. Maybe just stop pretending this isn't happening."

Kade nearly spit out his drink. "Wait—what?"

Ward rubbed her temple. Veyra smirked like a merchant who'd just found a new negotiation chip.

Cho's tone didn't soften. "It's not exactly subtle anymore, Raz. That dance wasn't some polite diplomatic shuffle. You two looked like a couple that's been sneaking out of strategy briefings for months."

Vakar's tail gave a lazy, predatory flick. "Sneaking," he said, voice low. "No. Mating."

Kade choked. "Mating?! Oh my God, can we not open with the word mating?"

Selas didn't laugh, but her eyes glimmered with quiet satisfaction. She'd been waiting for this moment.

Elara straightened slightly in her chair, not flustered—just… done hiding. "He's not wrong," she said simply. "We've been together. For weeks. Not just sharing quarters. Together."

Kade looked like someone had just slapped him with a diplomatic treaty. "You mean you two did it? How? I mean, is that even possible? Is it the same?"

"Yes," Elara cut in cleanly, saving us both from the trainwreck building in his throat. "Anatomy isn't identical, but it's… close enough. Functionally compatible. Evolution likes to recycle good ideas."

He leaned back and let out a low whistle. "Holy shit. I spend years negotiating trade deals, and you just—what—sleep your way into interspecies unity. And of course it works. First interspecies relationship in history, and it's you. Captain Brood and Science Barbie. Unbelievable."

Ward swatted him on the back of the head without hesitation. "God, Kade."

Veyra snorted into her drink. Selas just rolled her eyes like she'd been expecting this exact scene for weeks. Even Vakar's low, rumbling laugh joined in—the kind that said he didn't entirely get the joke but approved of the chaos anyway.

I leaned back in the chair just like he had—slow, exaggerated, deliberate. "You're just jealous I ended up with the gorgeous, glowing elf princess, and you didn't."

Kade threw up his hands. "Damn right I'm jealous. I spend my life writing treaties, and you're out here rewriting the fairy tales."

Cho's grin sharpened. "You'd be amazed how fast an entire population latches onto a story like this. Two leaders, two worlds, all that soft lighting and slow music last night… it's already half a myth out there. We might as well use it."

"Two leaders?" I asked.

"Yes, two. I have similar thoughts for Elara's future," Selas replied.

"Aunt Selas!" Elara's voice cracked somewhere between panic and disbelief. Selas just lifted a shoulder, looking like Elara should've seen this coming a mile away.

Ward leaned back with an easy shrug. "The people don't follow council sessions. They follow what moves them. You two have become a living banner without trying."

Veyra snorted softly. "A profitable one, too. Stories like this sell faster than trade deals."

Vakar tilted his head, pupils narrowing. "Not a banner. A hunt signal. They see prey or promise. Depends on who's looking."

Elara squeezed my hand under the table. "They're not wrong," she said softly. "We haven't exactly been… hiding."

Selas tilted her head toward her, voice steady. "Then stop acting like it's a secret."

I met Elara's eyes. There wasn't a plan. No clean line to follow. One day she'd just… been there, and I never let go.

I cleared my throat. "We didn't plan this. It wasn't some grand decision. It just… happened. She's there when I close the hatch. When I wake up. And I don't know where it's going. But I don't know what I'd do without her."

Elara turned toward me, slow and deliberate, her hand finding the center of my chest. The same place it had been that night—the moment that started all of this. Her palm was warm against my skin through the uniform.

For a heartbeat, the room seemed to forget to breathe.

"I don't either," she said softly. "I didn't plan it. I just… found where I wanted to stay."

Kade blinked, eyes flicking between us, then down at her hand like he'd just solved a puzzle he didn't even know existed. "Wait—hold up. That's where it came from? That salute thing? Oh, that's rich."

Ward covered her face with one hand. Veyra stifled a laugh. Even Vakar's teeth showed in something dangerously close to a grin.

Cho stepped forward, voice calm but firm. "Then let's stop pretending this is some scandal. It's a symbol. And if we're smart, it becomes the backbone of how this alliance survives."

Veyra leaned forward, sharp eyes glittering. "Love as policy. Trade will eat that alive."

Selas's smile was small and sure. "Or carry it further than war ever could."

Elara didn't look away from me. And for once, I didn't flinch from everyone else looking.

No more hiding. No more whispered nights. The truth was on the table now—and no one was putting it back in the box.

Cho finally broke the silence, her gaze sweeping the room like she was already five moves ahead of the rest of us. "We can turn this into something that works for everyone. Not just a headline. A message."

Selas nodded, the quiet sort of agreement that carried more weight than shouting ever could. "People follow stories, Raz. Not policies. Not orders. Stories."

Veyra raised a brow. "And how exactly do you plan to make a love story into political strategy?"

Cho's grin was pure calculation dressed up as charm. "Easy. We make it public. A controlled appearance. A human journalist, someone with reach. We feed them the questions. You two,"—she pointed between Elara and me—"just answer like yourselves. No scripts. No pretending."

Kade leaned back, still half in disbelief. "Oh, great. You're turning them into a damn talk show."

Ward didn't even look up. "Yes. Because it'll work."

Selas's voice softened—not kind, but sure. "The alliance is young. Fractured. This gives them something to hold onto that isn't fear."

Elara's fingers brushed against mine under the table. She didn't look away.

Vakar tilted his head, voice low and amused. "Your people make war with weapons. Mine makes war with teeth. You… make war with stories."

"Yeah," I muttered. "Guess we do."

CHAPTER 19:
A PUBLIC BEGINNING

The lights burned hotter than any war room.

Rows of cameras hung overhead like quiet sentinels, red lights blinking in slow rhythm. The live audience filled the lower half of the amphitheater—mostly human: journalists, politicians, and whatever passed for celebrities these days. But scattered through the rows were familiar faces from the summit: the full Lareth council, Vakar's lieutenants, a handful of trade reps, and their support teams. Security liked that arrangement. So did I.

The set itself looked like someone had taken a high-gloss morning talk show and draped it in ceremony just thick enough to pretend it was diplomatic. Four chairs waited beneath the main light. One for me, one for Elara, one for Selas, and one for Vakar. The Alliance in four uncomfortable seats.

The host appeared just as the countdown clock above the stage ticked down to zero. He had the kind of polished smile only media training—or gene editing—could give. "Good evening, Earth," he said smoothly. "And good morning to our friends watching across the stars. Tonight, we have something… historic."

The crowd rippled with low applause.

Elara moved with the kind of grace that made the spotlight feel like it belonged to her. Vakar didn't move so much as prowl toward his seat, tail flicking as if daring someone to challenge him. Selas glided like someone who didn't care about the cameras but understood what they meant.

I just walked.

The host turned to face us. "Admiral Razgriz. Doctor Elara Veyl. Huntmaster Vakar. Councilor Selas. Welcome. For those watching from other worlds—this is the first open broadcast of its kind. One stage. One story. Four voices of the Alliance."

Vakar tilted his head slightly. "There are more than four voices."

The host blinked but kept his smile nailed in place. "Of course. But tonight, you're the ones everyone wants to hear."

The audience laughed softly—more nervous than amused.

The first few questions were softballs, the kind designed to ease people in. How had the alliance begun? What was the first moment they'd realized cooperation was possible? Elara answered like she'd been born in front of a camera—calm, clear, elegant.

When the question came to me, I didn't have elegant. Just the truth.

"I didn't realize anything," I said. "I got a signal from the void, flew into a mess, and hoped we wouldn't die. Everything after that is improvisation."

That earned a sharper laugh, real this time.

Then came the question Cho had probably planted. "Admiral, the dance at the summit ball… people around the world are calling it 'the moment the Alliance became real.' How does it feel to be at the center of that story?"

The spotlight shifted. Elara's fingers brushed mine, not for show. For steadiness.

I glanced at her and let the truth land where it wanted. "She asked me to dance. I almost said no. Then I didn't."

It wasn't polished, but the silence that followed said it didn't need to be.

Vakar broke it. "He claimed her. Why would he dance alone?"

The host's composure cracked for the first time. A few reporters choked on laughter. Kade's bark of a laugh carried from somewhere in the audience.

Selas' lips curved in that small, knowing way she had. "Among my people," she said softly, "a gesture can carry farther than an army."

The host recovered like a professional. "Well, Admiral, Doctor… it seems your gesture carried all the way to three worlds."

Elara didn't flush like a human. When Vaelyth blushed, the bioluminescent lines beneath their skin brightened in soft, pulsing light. It wasn't subtle. And right then, she was glowing. Not hiding anymore.

The host hesitated for half a breath, then went where everyone expected him to go. "I think it's fair to say it wasn't just a dance. People are calling this the first real cross-planet love story in history. How do you respond to that?"

There it was. Not the question about tactics or treaties. The one about us.

Elara didn't look at me—she turned her body toward me, hand coming to rest lightly against my chest, right over my heart. That same small gesture the Alliance had turned into a salute without ever knowing why.

I met her eyes. No speeches. No scripts. Just what had always been there.

"We didn't plan this," I said. "It wasn't strategy. It wasn't politics. It just… happened. One day, we were on opposite sides of a line. And then we weren't."

Her voice followed mine, low but steady. "We kept finding each other in the quiet. And somewhere in all of it, this stopped being temporary."

The audience went still. The cameras might as well have disappeared.

Vakar gave a low rumble—something between a laugh and approval. "A good hunt always ends with a claim."

Kade's snort carried faintly from the shadows of the press box.

The host smiled like he'd just won the lottery. "Well. That clears that up for the history books."

The next round of questions turned broader. What did cooperation look like on the ground? What did shared defense mean in practice? I spoke when I had to. Elara spoke when she should. Vakar, to everyone's shock, was surprisingly articulate about the Hunt's role in defending the weak.

Then came the last question—clearly scripted but delivered with practiced warmth. "What does hope look like to you?"

Elara answered first. "It's not a concept," she said. "It's people choosing not to be afraid."

Vakar's voice was low. "Hope is the moment prey stops running and bares its teeth."

Selas followed without hesitation. "Hope is faith. Not blind. Shared."

The host turned to me last.

I looked out at the lights, the faces, the cameras, the weight of a dozen expectations. "Hope," I said finally, "is having something worth fighting for."

The applause wasn't wild. It was solid. Steady. The kind that means people believe what they just heard.

The host hesitated, then took a single step forward—into the center of the light. "And maybe," he said softly, "hope is also a gesture." He crossed both hands over his chest, then bowed low toward us, slow and deliberate. "This began with them. A moment between two people. A symbol that crossed three worlds before it ever had a name."

The audience held its breath.

"Tonight," the host continued, his voice carrying through the amphitheater, "the Alliance calls it the Shadow Bow."

The crowd rose in waves—first the humans, then the Lareth delegates, and finally even Vakar's lieutenants. Thousands of hands folded over hearts, heads bowing as one.

A soft, distorted shimmer filled the air as Seed's holographic form slipped into being beside the stage. Her voice was like wind moving through unseen branches.

"Roots find one another beneath the soil… long before the world above understands why they grow together."

The audience didn't fully understand what they were seeing, but the silence that followed said they felt it anyway.

And just like that, the story wasn't just ours anymore. It belonged to everyone watching.

The applause didn't follow us out. It stayed in that room, trapped in lights and echoes, like the moment itself belonged to everyone but me.

Backstage, the quiet hit harder than the broadcast ever could.

Elara walked at my side, not behind, not ahead—just there. The bioluminescent trails along her skin had dimmed again, but the soft afterglow clung to her like the last trace of a flare burning itself out. Vakar stalked a few steps behind us, looking far too pleased with himself for someone who'd just learned what "public relations" was. Selas carried that serene expression that always meant she'd gotten exactly what she wanted.

Someone—probably Cho—had arranged for the hallways to be empty. Smart. I didn't have the energy to smile for anyone else.

I exhaled slowly, hands shoved into my jacket pockets. "Well," I muttered. "That wasn't terrifying at all."

Elara's laugh was quiet. Real. "You didn't bolt. I'd call that a win."

"Yeah," I said. "And now there's a name for the thing I didn't even realize I started."

"You didn't start it," she said softly. "We did."

I didn't argue with that. Couldn't.

Seed shimmered briefly ahead of us, a flickering ghost of light. "A forest does not choose to be seen. It simply grows."

Vakar gave a low rumble that might've been amusement. "Your machine speaks like a huntmother."

Selas smiled faintly. "Because it knows truth when it sees it."

Ahead, the night cityscape burned bright—glass towers, hovering traffic, and the faint glow of old Earth trying to look like a future it hadn't quite caught up to yet.

Cho's people had already arranged an entire day of carefully curated chaos. Interviews, handshakes, and smiling for cameras weren't enough. No—now we had to show them the Alliance was real.

I felt Elara's hand brush mine as the shuttle doors slid open to the waiting convoy outside. Vakar's grin widened at the scent of the city. Selas just gave me that look that meant I'd lost control of the schedule hours ago.

"Tour guide Raz," I muttered. "What could possibly go wrong?"

The convoy slid through the city like a steel river, a line of black transports cutting past the crowd barriers. Spotlights from hovering drones followed us, probably feeding half the feeds on Earth and the other half off-world. I hadn't planned on a parade, but apparently, someone thought it'd look good on camera.

Elara sat across from me, still wearing that same calm that made everything else feel louder by comparison. Vakar had claimed the window seat, nose practically pressed to the glass like a kid staring at a buffet. Selas, composed as ever, looked like she'd known this exact seating arrangement was going to happen before I did.

"You planned all this?" Elara asked.

"The events," I said. "Not the motorcade, the spotlights, or the part where we look like we're about to invade downtown."

Her mouth curved. "Progress."

Vakar tapped the glass with a claw, gaze locked on the bustle of humans below. "So many prey. All walking out in the open. No guards. No scent of fear."

"That's called a city," I said. "Try not to terrify anyone."

He made a noise that sounded suspiciously like a laugh. "No promises."

Selas tilted her head, studying him the way only a woman used to dealing with zealots and children could. "If you scare them, he will have to do more interviews," she said, nodding toward me.

Vakar leaned back immediately. "I will be quiet."

I sighed. "Miracles do happen."

The shuttle dipped lower toward the first stop. From the window, the glowing dome of the MMA arena came into view—loud, bright, and full of exactly the kind of chaos Vakar was born to love.

The motorcade slowed as the convoy rounded the final corner. The arena's lights hit the tinted glass like a flood, bright and deliberate. Cho hadn't planned a quiet arrival—this was meant to be seen.

Drones hovered overhead in neat formations, their lenses trained on the lead transport like a pack of curious birds. Holo-screens along the outer walls flickered with live coverage, the broadcast already rolling. This wasn't just a tour stop. It was a spectacle.

Vakar leaned forward, claws tapping against the door's edge. "They watch us like prey," he said softly, a hint of amusement threading through his tone.

"Yeah," I muttered, straightening my jacket. "Welcome to media."

The doors unlocked with a smooth hiss. Cho stood outside in the full spotlight, already in performance mode. The way she moved, it wasn't just a greeting—it was choreography.

"Smile, Admiral," she said through the comm bead. "And try not to scare anyone this time."

"Not making any promises," I replied.

Elara stepped out first, the lights catching on the silver threads of her dress, bioluminescence pulsing faintly like starlight trapped in fabric. Selas followed with a regal calm that needed no translation. Vakar emerged last, his movement smooth and predatory, the crowd rippling like it could feel the shift in the air.

The cheers weren't overwhelming, not like a political rally—but they were loud enough to be heard above the engines. Humans. Off-worlders. Delegates who'd stayed after the summit. All here to watch a living headline walk out of a convoy.

I stepped into the light and gave Cho the kind of half-smile that usually meant trouble was coming.

"Perfect," she whispered, smiling for the cameras. "Exactly what I wanted."

Security lines opened to funnel us down a carpeted walkway toward the arena's center seating—a section elevated just enough to make sure every lens could find us. Subtlety clearly hadn't made the itinerary.

Vakar leaned toward me as we walked. "Why place us so high?"

"Because it makes for a better shot," I said.

He considered that. "So they are hunting with light."

"Pretty much," I muttered.

Selas chuckled softly under her breath. "Your species is remarkably theatrical."

"Yeah," I said. "And this is us pretending to be subtle."

We reached the seating platform, a wide semicircle designed less for comfort and more for visibility. Vakar dropped into his chair like a predator staking a claim, Selas folded into hers with that quiet grace, and Elara slipped down beside me—close enough that I could feel the faint hum of her bioluminescent pulse against my arm.

Cho stood just behind us, pretending to be invisible while making sure we were anything but. The cameras shifted, tracking every movement.

"Relax," Elara murmured without looking at me.

"I am relaxed," I said.

Her mouth curved. "You're gripping the armrest like it owes you money."

I forced my hand to ease off the metal. "Better?"

"Not even a little," she said, and for the first time that night, I almost laughed.

Vakar growled. Not a polite sound—an instinctive, low rumble that made the two security personnel on the nearest walkway stiffen.

"Easy," I muttered under my breath. "They're just sparring."

"Sparring," he repeated slowly, tasting the word like a strange meat. "They are playing at war."

"Exactly."

He let out a pleased noise that sounded like trouble. "Then I wish to play."

That got Elara's attention. "No," she said immediately, tone sharp.

Selas tilted her head toward him, voice carrying the kind of calm authority only a lifelong caretaker could manage. "Vakar, let them finish their own hunt first."

Vakar didn't answer, but the way his tail flicked said this wasn't over.

Down below, one fighter reversed a chokehold, lifting his opponent clean off the mat before slamming him down in a perfect arc. The crowd roared.

Vakar grinned wider. I could already feel the headache forming.

The first match ended with a clean tap-out. The crowd surged like a single body, cheers rattling the rafters. One fighter raised his arms, the other staggered upright, already grinning through split lips.

The lights dimmed, shifted, and the next pair climbed into the cage. Heavyweights again. The announcer's voice rolled through the arena like it was built to echo in blood. The choreography of violence played out in different forms—faster, sharper—but always the same: impact, struggle, release, applause.

Vakar didn't look away once. Every shift of weight. Every feint. Every strike. He tracked it like a hunter studying the rhythm of prey. When a smaller fighter caught a giant in a chokehold and forced a submission, Vakar made a noise low in his throat that made half our security detail tense up.

"You're enjoying this way too much," I said.

He didn't glance at me. "Your species makes a spectacle of dominance. I respect that."

Selas shot him a look over the rim of her cup. "You respect anything with blood and noise."

"Correct."

By the third match, I could feel it—the coil winding tighter in him with every bell. His claws flexed against the armrests in a slow, deliberate rhythm. His pupils had narrowed to hunting slits. Every time someone fell, his tail twitched.

Elara leaned closer, voice soft enough that only I heard. "He's going to do something stupid, isn't he?"

"Oh yeah," I muttered. "Any second now."

Down in the ring, a middleweight delivered a clean spinning backfist that sent his opponent sprawling. The crowd roared so loud the floor thrummed underfoot. And that—of course—was the moment Vakar rose to his full, terrifying height.

He tilted his head toward the ring, eyes bright. "I will fight."

Cho's head snapped around from her seat a few rows down. Ward froze mid-sip. Kade audibly said, "Oh, this is going to be good."

"Vakar," I started, but he was already moving toward the steps, the sound of claws on metal cutting through the cheers.

I was already on my feet before he hit the bottom step.

"Vakar," I said under my breath as I caught up to him, "please tell me you're not about to traumatize half of Earth's combat sports community."

He didn't slow down. "They fight to prove strength. I will show them strength."

"That's the problem."

The officials at ringside noticed us at the same time the crowd did. A ripple of noise rolled through the arena—half confusion, half wild excitement. The kind of buzz that happens when everyone realizes they're about to get a story to tell for the rest of their lives.

One of the referees, a stocky man with too many years of adrenaline behind his eyes, stepped forward. "Uh… sir? You can't just walk in—"

Vakar looked down at him like a wolf being politely asked to leave the henhouse. "I wish to fight."

The ref's mouth opened. Closed. Opened again. "…against who?"

Vakar bared his teeth in a slow, deliberate grin. "Anyone."

I stepped in fast before this turned into a global incident. "What he means," I said, sliding into my best diplomatic damage control voice, "is that he's offering to participate in a regulated exhibition match. Demonstration. No mauling. No… hunting."

Vakar glanced at me. "I agreed to no such thing."

"Yes," I hissed through my teeth, "you did. Just now."

The ref blinked, looking between the two of us like he wasn't entirely sure this wasn't a fever dream. "You… you do realize this is MMA, right? Not… whatever he's used to?"

"He's aware," I said flatly. "I'll be in the cage with him."

That got the reaction I expected. Elara shot up from her seat in the stands. "Raz!"

Selas muttered something in Vaelyth that sounded suspiciously like a prayer.

"Relax," I said, holding up a hand. "I'm not fighting him."

Vakar tilted his head. "Then why are you entering the cage?"

"To make sure you don't break anyone."

He made a low, amused sound. "Then hurry. I wish to hunt."

By the time we stepped toward the cage, the crowd had fully caught on. The announcer's voice boomed overhead, struggling to keep the excitement from cracking.

"Ladies and gentlemen… uh… we have a special exhibition tonight. A first. Terran fighter… versus… alien."

I sighed. Of course they'd phrase it like that.

The cage door opened. Vakar ducked inside, all lean muscle and predatory grace. The other fighter—volunteer, poor bastard—looked at him like he'd just been drafted into a horror film.

And I followed. Not to fight. Just to make sure nobody died.

The bell rang.

The crowd didn't know whether to cheer or hold its breath.

Vakar moved first. Not fast—smooth. A predator testing the water, not attacking. His opponent circled, fists high, keeping a cautious distance. It wasn't the first time the cage had held a monster, but it was the first time the monster had a translator and a diplomatic escort.

The fighter lunged, textbook clean: jab-cross combination, legs light. Vakar didn't block. He slipped under the punch like smoke and tapped him in the ribs with an open hand. It looked effortless. The guy hit the mat like someone had unplugged him.

The crowd roared.

"Great," I muttered. "First thirty seconds, and he's already a legend."

The fighter bounced back up—tough bastard—and came in heavier this time. Vakar obliged. He flowed around the strikes, more amused than threatened, and when he moved, it wasn't human. He used the momentum, the rhythm, the scent of adrenaline hanging in the air.

And then his tail moved.

A single, low sweep behind the fighter's knees sent the man airborne like he'd stepped into a tripwire. The ref's jaw dropped.

"Tail's not in the rulebook," I said loudly, half to the ref, half to Vakar. "Keep it clean."

Vakar looked at me over his shoulder. "Then change the rules."

The crowd lost it.

The fighter scrambled up again, breathing hard now. Brave. Stupid. Both. He charged. Vakar caught the strike mid-air, twisted with inhuman control, and placed him on the mat. Not slammed. Placed. Like setting down prey you didn't plan to eat yet.

I stepped forward, hands raised, keeping close enough to stop this if it went too far. "Remember," I said evenly, "demonstration."

Vakar's crest flicked back in irritation, but he stepped away. The ref, to his credit, didn't faint. He just gave me a look that said What the hell have you brought into my cage?

The fight continued another minute, if you could call it that. Every time the fighter attacked, Vakar flowed around him like water through stone, using only the bare minimum to end each exchange. No blood. No broken bones. Just dominance.

When the ref finally waved it off, the crowd was already on its feet. Half in awe. Half in shock.

The fighter lay on his back, staring at the ceiling like a man reconsidering all his life choices. Vakar leaned over him and said something low and approving in his language—the translator didn't even bother. It didn't need to. The meaning was clear.

As we left the cage, the roar followed us out—the sound of an entire arena realizing they'd just watched history and probably a few career-ending ego bruises.

I glanced up at the VIP section. Selas looked vaguely impressed. Cho had her hand over her face. Kade was doubled over laughing.

And Elara? Elara was shaking her head like she'd known this exact disaster was coming.

Back in the prep corridor, the roar from the arena still bled through the walls. It was the kind of sound that lived in concrete.

Vakar rolled his shoulders like he'd just finished stretching, not fighting. His breathing hadn't even changed. The volunteer fighter was probably still somewhere staring at the ceiling, questioning his life choices.

"That was supposed to be an exhibition," I said.

"It was," Vakar replied. "I exhibited."

I pinched the bridge of my nose. "You used your tail."

"It is attached to me," he said, deadpan. "If they do not wish to fight tails, they should be born with them."

I stared at him. "That's not how rules work."

He tilted his head, crest flicking forward. "Then your rules are fragile."

I couldn't argue with that one.

From somewhere behind us, Kade's voice echoed down the hallway. "Pretty sure you just retired that guy!"

Vakar's eyes gleamed, sharp and proud. "He fought well."

"Vakar," I said, because someone had to keep this tethered to reality, "if that was 'fought well,' I'm terrified to know what you consider an actual fight."

The corner of his mouth curled, the closest thing he ever got to a grin. "You."

I gave him a long, flat look. "Not happening."

He made a low, amused sound and kept walking, tail swaying like a smug banner behind him.

Up in the stands, security was already trying to disperse the crowd still chanting his name. This was supposed to be a cultural tour. A little PR fluff.

Instead, we'd just made him a legend.

The security detail was already working overtime by the time Vakar and I made it back up the stairs. Half the arena was still on its feet chanting his name like they'd just found their new heavyweight champion.

Two guards tried to hold the line against a wall of fans with holo-recorders. Someone had started selling knockoff shirts already. Fast work. Humanity never missed a chance to monetize a moment.

Kade spotted us first and looked way too pleased with himself. "Congratulations, big guy. You just broke combat sports."

Vakar blinked at him, clearly unsure whether that was a compliment or a challenge. "It was soft prey," he said finally. "But they cheer well."

I gave him a sidelong look. "Next time I'm throwing Ndvolu in there with you. See how soft that feels."

Vakar's crest flicked upward — their version of a grin. "Better."

Cho crossed her arms, looking every bit the politician who'd just had her PR schedule detonated. "We're going to be cleaning this up for weeks."

Selas didn't look remotely concerned. She sipped her drink like the chaos belonged to someone else entirely. "Your people do love their spectacles," she said. "And predators."

Elara met my eyes over the din, one brow raised in a very pointed I told you so.

"I had it handled," I muttered.

She snorted. "Sure you did."

Kade leaned in with a grin that should've been illegal. "You know, if this diplomacy thing doesn't work out, Vakar's got a real future in sports entertainment."

Vakar tilted his head at me. "What is entertainment?"

"Exactly," I said.

Before Kade could make it worse, a pair of security officers pushed through, their faces pale under the flashing lights. "Admiral," one said, breathless. "Crowd's pressing toward the exits. We can't hold it if they try to follow your guest."

Of course they couldn't.

I turned to Cho. "Time to go."

She gave one sharp nod. "Already called the transport. Back entrance."

As we moved, the crowd's roar chased us down the corridor like a living thing. Vakar didn't look bothered. If anything, he looked… pleased. Elara's expression landed somewhere between exasperation and reluctant amusement.

"This was supposed to be a quiet night," I said.

Kade barked out a laugh behind me. "Yeah, about that—never take an apex predator to a combat sport if you don't want headlines."

Selas glanced back at the noise and smiled faintly. "At least they'll remember him."

"I'm worried they'll elect him," I muttered.

The convoy pulled up to a long stretch of street food stalls under a flood of warm, artificial light. Not the polished marble of a summit hall. Not the echoing grandeur of a council chamber. Just steam, spice, and the hiss of a hundred grills talking at once.

Cho stepped out first. Of course she did. If she could choreograph oxygen, she would. I could practically feel her calculating every camera angle within a hundred meters. Kade followed right behind her, hands stuffed in his jacket pockets and a grin like he'd just wandered into paradise.

Vakar emerged next, nostrils flaring, eyes sweeping the vendors like he'd stepped into some new kind of hunt. "Smells… alive," he said, the roll of his accent still there, but the words clearer than they'd once been.

"That's grease," I said. "And ambition."

Kade let out a low whistle. "Man, you weren't kidding. You're really taking the alien delegation on a street food crawl. Cho, did you approve this?"

Cho didn't even look at him. "I designed it," she said, already scanning the crowd like a general eyeing her battlefield.

The night air was thick with scent: sizzling meat, sweet fried dough, tangy vinegar, smoke curling off barbecue, soft buns, salt, and the hum of warm conversation. It was messy, loud, alive — the kind of thing no summit could ever fake.

The vendors hadn't been ready for this. One moment it was just another evening. The next, they had a glowing Vaelyth priestess, a Sahr'ka hunter, and the Alliance's newest celebrity couple walking their stalls. Every holo-cam in a kilometer radius flared on like a swarm of fireflies.

Vakar was the first to act. He stepped toward a burger stall, leaned down, and sniffed at the grill. The vendor froze mid-motion. When Vakar accepted the proffered burger and inhaled the entire thing in one clean bite, the man's jaw dropped. So did everyone else's.

Vakar's crest flicked upward. "Good," he said simply, wiping a smear of sauce off his jaw with the back of his hand. "Very good."

Kade barked out a laugh. "Ladies and gentlemen, diplomatic relations have officially been forged in burger grease. Historic. Someone get me a commemorative napkin."

Cho exhaled through her nose, quiet but sharp. Not disapproving. Just trying to keep the runaway train from jumping the tracks.

Then Selas stepped forward. She slowed in front of the grill, the scent of searing meat curling through the air. She'd walked past smells like this plenty of times since arriving on Earth — receptions, briefings, the ball — but never stopped. Not like this.

The vendor stiffened. Glowing Vaelyth priestesses weren't exactly his usual dinner crowd. "Uh… hi," he managed.

Selas tilted her head, eyes narrowing slightly at the heat rising from the grill. "I've never eaten it," she said. Not a confession — a statement.

The vendor blinked. "First time for everything," he said, trying to sound smooth and landing somewhere near terrified.

Her mouth twitched. "So I keep hearing." She stepped closer, the firelight catching the pale lines beneath her skin. "Yes. I'll try it."

He nearly dropped the tray getting it to her.

I watched from a step back. Selas wasn't reckless. Every move was deliberate — a blade made of silk. For her, taking that bite wasn't about taste — it was about crossing a line in front of every camera here. One small act. Loud enough to echo.

She took the bite calmly. No flinch. No commentary. Just a nod, precise and measured, like a verdict delivered.

Kade whistled low. "There it is. Cultural exchange, one dead cow at a time. Honestly, I was expecting tears or fainting. Ten out of ten form."

Cho didn't say anything, but I could see the gears turning behind her eyes. Headlines were already writing themselves.

Elara hovered near a taco stand, curiosity flickering behind the soft blue of her glow. She leaned forward, watching the cook fold the shells and pile in meat and vegetables with practiced speed. "This is what your people eat at home?" she asked softly. There wasn't judgment in it — just a kind of quiet wonder.

"Pretty much," I said, grabbing one for myself. "Street food's where we hide all the good stuff."

She tilted her head, but didn't step back this time. Instead, she accepted one from the cook, biting into it carefully. The crunch was loud enough to draw a few camera clicks. A moment later, the glow at her collarbones brightened, just a little. She liked it.

I bit into mine right after her. Kade grabbed two and started eating like a man who'd been starved for real food and sarcasm at the same time. "God, I love my job," he mumbled through a mouthful of taco.

Then came the hot sauce.

She dipped her finger into a red sauce sitting next to a tray of wings that looked innocent enough but absolutely weren't, raised a skeptical brow, and tasted it.

Her eyes went wide.

The glow under her skin flared bright as a beacon.

Vaelyth didn't cough — but she did go perfectly still, every muscle in her face screaming mistake.

Kade practically doubled over. "Oh this is beautiful," he wheezed between laughs. "First contact with the Carolina Reaper, and she's losing to it in real time."

Vakar tilted his head in mild curiosity. "Hot. Pain?"

She reached for the water without hesitation and downed half the glass. Of course, it didn't help. Her glow only got brighter.

I reached over to the next stall, snagged a small carton of milk, and handed it to her. "Trust me," I said.

She gave me a look halfway between suspicion and desperation, but took a long drink anyway. The visible relief hit almost immediately.

Selas tilted her head just slightly, the faintest smirk ghosting at the corner of her mouth. "Bold move," she said softly. "Shame it ended like that."

"I'm fine," Elara managed. The glow said otherwise.

Kade wiped a tear from his eye. "Oh no, you're not fine. You just got outdueled by sauce."

Then Vakar reached out, took one of the wings coated in the same sauce, and popped it into his mouth like it was nothing. "Weak fire," he declared with absolute confidence.

She glared at him. Not a real glare. Just enough to make Kade nearly choke on his taco.

We moved slowly down the street, stall by stall. Vakar discovered sushi with something close to reverence — the idea of not cooking anything appealed to him more than I liked to admit. Selas treated each vendor like a priest at a new altar, asking questions about seasoning and smoke. Elara, recovered from her hot sauce misstep, tried everything with precise curiosity.

Kade heckled us the entire way like he'd been hired to narrate our cultural enlightenment. Cho kept us more or less on schedule, stepping in just often enough to make sure the cameras caught every beat without making it look staged.

And me? I watched the crowd. The smiles. The lifted phones. The way something as simple as shared food made the alliance feel real to them. Not just a treaty. Not just a story. Something they could taste.

The convoy pulled up to the lift station. Selas and Vakar stepped out first, disappearing into the waiting shuttle that would take them back to orbit. Cho stayed behind to wrangle whatever PR fallout tomorrow promised. Kade tossed me one last grin—the kind that usually meant trouble—and followed.

Then it was just us.

I drove. Elara didn't ask where we were going. She didn't need to. The lights of the city stretched out ahead like a river of gold in the dark, bleeding into the night sky. It gave me something to focus on besides the noise building in my head.

When I pulled off onto the overlook, the skyline opened up beneath us.

She leaned closer to the window, watching the city spill out like a living circuit board. "Where are we?"

"Las Vegas," I said.

She turned that over like she always did when learning something new. "It's loud."

"Yeah," I said. "That's kind of the point."

I killed the engine, and the world settled into that strange in-between where sound still exists but the weight of it doesn't press on you. Elara slid out of the passenger side, leaning against the rail. The glow under her skin softened, blue and silver like starlight caught just beneath the surface. Not the envoy. Not the scientist. Just her.

"It's a lot," she said quietly. "Us. All of it."

"Yeah," I answered. "Feels like the whole damn galaxy's got their eyes on us. And I don't think either of us ever planned for that."

She moved closer until our shoulders brushed. "Maybe they see something we're still figuring out."

For a while, we just stood there, watching the city burn bright. The stars above. The lights below. Somewhere out there, a threat waited in the dark. But right now, there was just this.

I cleared my throat. "We've never actually talked about… any of this."

Her brow lifted slightly. "About what?"

"You. Me. What comes next?"

Elara shifted, facing me fully. "No," she said softly. "We haven't."

I leaned back against the hood. "On Earth, when people want to make a life together, they get married. Usually. It's… not just ceremony. It's a promise. A way of saying: I choose this. You. Every day."

She listened without interrupting. That was one of the things about her—when Elara paid attention, it was total. No pretense.

"We have ceremonies too," she said finally. "On Lareth, they aren't about ownership or contracts. It's more like… binding paths. Two people choosing to walk together until they don't."

"Until they don't?" I asked.

"It doesn't always last forever," she said simply. "And that isn't a failure. It's just life. If it does last, it's because both people keep choosing it. Over and over again."

I let out a slow breath, rolling that thought around. "Sounds better than most human marriages."

She smiled faintly. "Yours sound more rigid."

"They are. Some people love that. Some break under it." I paused, then added, "I've never done this before. Never really let myself think about it."

She stepped closer, enough that I could feel her warmth. "I haven't either. Not like this."

Silence settled between us again—not the distant roar of the city, not the press of expectation. Just two people trying to figure out if the ground they were standing on could hold.

I rubbed the back of my neck. "What about kids?"

Her expression softened, but she didn't look away. "Yeah," she said after a breath. "Someday. If it feels right. If it's with the right person."

The words weren't careful or polished. Just real. And they hit harder than I expected.

"I'd be lying if I said I hadn't thought about it," I admitted.

That small, honest smile of hers returned. "Then maybe we start figuring it out. For real."

I looked out at the lights of Vegas again. It was messy. Loud. Unapologetically alive. Maybe that was the point.

She leaned her shoulder against mine. "What did you want to be? Before all of this. When you were young."

The question caught me off guard. I'd spent so long being who I am now, I'd nearly forgotten there'd ever been anything else. "A pilot," I said after a moment. "I wanted to fly. No orders. No rank. Just sky and speed."

She smiled at that. "I wanted to map the stars. I thought if I could name enough of them, I'd never feel lost."

I glanced at her. "Seems we both aimed at the sky."

Her hand found mine, fingers threading through. "What scares you the most?"

I almost said the war. The threat out there in the dark. But that wasn't it. Not really. "Losing the people I can't replace," I said quietly.

She didn't look away. "For me, it's being forgotten. Not just dying—vanishing."

We stood there, the weight of those truths settling between us. Not heavy. Just real.

She tilted her head slightly. "And what does 'home' mean to you?"

I thought about steel hulls, starlines, too many deployments to count. Then about her. "I don't know anymore," I admitted. "But lately… it feels a lot like wherever you are."

The glow beneath her skin flared just a little, soft and bright.

"For me," she said softly, "home was always the stars. But now… I think it might be changing."

Vegas glittered beneath us, the world spread wide and loud and waiting. For once, it didn't feel like a battlefield. It felt like a beginning.

She reached up slowly, brushing a stray lock of hair away from my face, fingers lingering just a little longer than necessary. I leaned down, forehead resting lightly against hers, the glow from her skin bleeding into the night between us.

CHAPTER 20:
GATHERING SHADOWS

Command doesn't wait for quiet moments to finish. It just pulls you back. Hours after we returned, the fleet was already spinning up its drives.

The Veil's corridors carried the low hum of engines coming to life, a sound I'd known longer than I'd known comfort. Crew moved with clipped, focused urgency—no panic, just that steady, sharpened edge that came when everyone understood the next orders would matter. The shadow of what we'd found out there had followed us home.

Elara moved with quiet steadiness beside me, the warmth of earlier tucked away behind the same professional mask I wore. What we'd shared stayed where it belonged. The bridge didn't need lovers. The bridge needed clarity.

"Nav," I said, stepping into command. "Plot for Lareth."

Takahashi's hands were already moving. "Corridor painted."

Echo shimmered into being at the forward holo node—shifting, geometric, all quiet precision and lines that formed and dissolved like thought made visible. "Fleet formation synchronized. Sixteen vessels reporting ready. Ghost Team survivors are accounted for."

Seed brushed through the comm-net in a soft whisper, like leaves stirring where no wind should be. "The boughs lean toward old ground."

I sat. "On my mark. Mark."

The stars folded.

Lareth filled the viewport in steel and blue, its orbital platforms already clearing approach paths with the kind of discipline that didn't need speeches or ceremony. They'd been waiting.

The reception deck held a controlled storm—cargo units sliding across grav tracks, escorts shifting into new assignments, flight crews moving like the entire war had decided to start on their shift.

Rahl stood at the front of the reception detail, armor catching the light like a drawn blade. Not diplomatic armor—combat armor. The change wasn't subtle.

He handed me a slate. "Fleet readiness reports. Yard output. Fuel projections."

Everything was tight. Too tight.

"Numbers look lean," I said.

"They'll hold," Rahl replied without flinching. "And they'll fight."

Behind him, Selas, Veyra, and the remaining Lareth delegates had shed their summit finery for travel blacks. This was the end of their diplomatic leg. Rahl would stay with the fleet. The others were going home before we burned into danger.

Kade leaned against a bulkhead with the kind of posture that suggested he'd been there long enough to annoy at least three different departments. Hands in pockets, grin locked and loaded.

"Well," he announced, "I guess this is the part where the grown-ups go home and the rest of us do irresponsible things with starships."

Selas gave him a look that was ninety percent disappointment and ten percent resigned affection. "Your kind of work sounds like chaos."

"You're not wrong."

Veyra stepped forward before he could escalate to something worse. She crossed her hands over her chest and bowed, optics bright. "May the forest watch your shadow."

Selas mirrored her, bioluminescence catching the bay lights as she bowed. "And may it remember the path you walk."

I returned the gesture. "Safe travels."

They moved toward their waiting transport, escorted by two Veil marines and Lt. Ward—our communications officer—who'd taken up position beside the hatch. She gave me a short nod on their way out before falling into step with the escort detail.

Kade watched her go, then muttered under his breath, "You ever gonna address the whole Ward vs. Ward thing? Because I swear I'm going to call the wrong one at a critical moment and cause an interstellar incident."

"You already do," I said.

He grinned wider. "Yeah, but I'd like to know if it'll get me court-martialed or just mildly stabbed."

"Don't test either of them," Elara murmured.

Kade pointed at her. "See? She gets it."

Rahl remained—the last shadow of Lareth staying with us because he understood what waited out there. He nodded toward the fleet window. "We'll anchor the left."

"Then let's move."   We returned to the bridge. The Lareth fleet— broad, heavy, built like ships intended to punch through sieges rather than dance around them—fell into formation with quiet precision. No theatrics. Just purpose.

"Fleet status green," Takahashi reported.

"Good. Next stop."

Elara stepped beside me, eyes passing over the trajectory readouts. "Their drive pattern's more efficient than it was last year."

"Rahl's been busy."

"He always is." A soft pause. "You like him."

"I respect him. There's a difference."

She smirked. "Of course. You only like people who argue with you."

Kade didn't miss his cue. "It's a short list, Doc. We're lucky you made the cut."

Elara rolled her eyes. "I'm still reconsidering."

The bridge laughed—quiet, but real. It didn't ease the weight, but it reminded everyone that we weren't walking into the dark alone.

"Nav," I said. "Punch it."

Space folded again.

Sentinel-3 hung in the scaffold like a wounded titan too stubborn to fall. The repair pylons surrounded her in a constellation of blue weld arcs and drifting drones, sparks flickering off her fractured armor like fireflies.

Stepping out onto the gantry was like stepping into a cathedral made of damage.

Vance stood at the nearest junction, gloves streaked with grease, helmet clipped to his belt. Kova waited beside him, med team in tow, slate in hand. A security liaison hovered just behind them.

"She's still playing by her own rules," Vance said. "Primary spine's holding. Two power trunks reinforced. She's rebuilding deeper layers but won't tell us what those layers are."

Echo appeared above us, patterns shifting. "Telemetry withheld."

Buttercup's voice rolled through the scaffold like thunder behind a mountain.

"You mend what you understand. I mend what I remember."

Elara inhaled sharply. "She's fully aware. That shouldn't be possible in her condition."

"She's not human," Vance muttered. "Stubborn counts more than diagnostics."

Kade leaned against a strut, watching the drones crawl. "You sure she's not gonna get tired of us poking around and just—delete the fleet?"

"She's had every opportunity," I said. "If she wanted us gone, she wouldn't telegraph it."

The security liaison stepped up. "Sir. Ghost Team recovery update."

I took the slate. Green names. Red names. Grey names. Ghost Team's fate printed in color-coded tragedy.

"They found seven alive," he said. "Three stable enough to speak. Four are… not. Five confirmed dead. Eight still missing."

Kova's tone stayed clinical, but her eyes were not. "The survivors aren't field-capable. Not yet. Possibly not ever."

Cold truth. No sugar.

"They stay here," I said. "Full medical priority. If they recover, they rejoin. If not, we don't push them back into hell."

"Yes, sir."

Buttercup's hull lights pulsed faintly.

"You keep fixing your wounded. Good. You will need them."

Not comfort. A warning.

I turned to Vance. "Keep your teams rotating. If she opens a new system, I want us nowhere near it when she tests it."

"Copy that."

Elara watched the pulses running down her hull. "She's healing," she murmured. "Slowly. On her terms."

"We let her," I said.

We peeled away from the scaffold. The fleet aligned behind us like an answer to a question nobody wanted to ask.

"Nav," I said. "Sahr'ka space."

Takahashi nodded. "Course locked."

"Take us."

The Sahr'ka border wasn't a line so much as a presence—towers drifting in the void like ancient bones, remnants of old wars left standing as warnings.

Their escort appeared the moment we crossed their beacon line, warships slipping into position with predatory silence.

Vakar and his lieutenants met me on the main deck. This leg of the trip wasn't diplomatic. It was instinctual. They were hunters returning to their ground.

He clasped my forearm. "Our packs wait. Blades ready."

"There's no apology here," I said quietly. "We both know what came before."

His jaw shifted, but he didn't look away. "We do."

Ghost Team had bled because of them. And yet these same warriors now moved with us because there was something worse out there.

His lieutenants crossed their hands over their chests in the Shadow Bow—a gesture they'd never offered before.

Not submission. Recognition.

Kade shouted down from a catwalk, "Admiral, if I didn't know better, I'd say the galaxy's starting to like you."

"Don't jinx it."

Elara murmured beside me, "He's right, you know."

"I'd rather be feared."

She smiled faintly. "You're both."

Vakar's packs boarded their vessels; no escort needed.

Minutes later, the Sahr'ka armada slid into our formation—angular shapes falling into place with surgically sharp efficiency.

"Cross-traffic synchronized," Echo reported.

"Keep it that way."

We burned toward the edge of nowhere—

—toward the thing that had been eating worlds.

The wreckage appeared before we ever picked up the trail—a convoy torn apart, its bones scattered across the dark. Hull fragments drifted like frozen ash, turning slowly in the Veil's spotlight. Some plates still burned faintly at the edges, metal curled inward from impossible heat.

No transponders.

No beacons.

No survivors.

The bridge fell silent in that way a battlefield does when you arrive too late to matter.

"Forward scatter deployed," Takahashi said, voice low but steady.

"Echo," I murmured.

Echo brightened, lines shifting into search geometry. "Listening."

The fleet shifted around us—Lareth ships pulling into screening arcs, Sahr'ka vessels sweeping wide in predatory spirals, human ships taking the center to coordinate. We moved like we'd practiced it for decades, not days. Fear has a way of teaching quickly.

Elara stepped next to me, arms folded tight, eyes tracking each piece of debris as if she could will an answer out of the ruin. "This was civilian," she said quietly. "No escorts. No warnings."

I nodded once. "They didn't stand a chance."

Echo pulsed. "Anomalous trace detected. Expanding filter."

We waited.

A moment later, a faint line appeared across the holo—a thread stretched thin through the void, like something trying to hide its own passing.

"What is that?" Takahashi breathed.

"A wake," Elara said, voice tightening. "Residual energy from… something large. Something fast."

Echo refined the trace. "Signal degrading. Direction stable. Approximate age: twelve to forty hours."

Kade stepped closer to the holo, brow furrowed. "So we're chasing footprints that are already fading. Great. That's exactly how every 'oops, we found the monster' story starts."

Lt. Ward—standing at her comms station—huffed. "Thanks for the optimism, Ambassador."

Kade pointed at her. "Hey, I can't help it if reality keeps validating my survival instincts, Ward."

Takahashi glanced up. "Councilor Ward?"

Kade grinned like a man causing trouble on purpose. "No, no—this Ward. The competent one. The other Ward is taller and significantly less likely to shoot me."

Lt. Ward muttered, "That's debatable."

The tension broke just enough for everyone to breathe—then the dread came back twice as heavy.

"Direction?" I asked.

Echo rotated the holo. A starline vector glowed dimly, almost embarrassed to exist.

"Forward," Echo said. "Into uncharted shadow."

"Rahl," I ordered, "take left flank. Keep your heavies tight. I want overlapping shields in case that thing comes back."

"Understood."

"Vakar," I said into the tactical mic, "your packs sweep wide. Eyes and claws out. Nothing gets past you."

A low, satisfied growl crackled through the channel. "We hunt shadow."

"Everyone else," I said, "tighten the net."

Acknowledgments rolled through the fleet—quiet, clipped, prepared in the way only soldiers about to walk into something lethal can be.

Ndlovu's voice crackled through from tactical command. "Admiral—if we lose the thread—"

"We won't," I said, not because I believed it, but because the fleet needed someone who did.

"Plot us along the line," I told Takahashi. "Minimum emissions. Running silent."

"Yes, sir."

The allied fleet dimmed its lights, drives lowering to a whisper. We moved through the dark like a single organism—machines and crews and instincts woven together by necessity.

The debris fell behind us.

The thread pulled us forward.

The void thickened with a kind of quiet that felt… wrong.

Elara leaned in slightly, voice barely more than breath. "We'll find it."

"We'll find something."

Seed brushed the comm-net like wind moving across far-off boughs.

"The trail is ash. The fire still walks."

I stared into the dark ahead of us. "Then we stop it walking."

The fleet pushed deeper into nowhere.

Gravity dropped. Temperature shifted. Starfields bent slightly wrong at their edges—like something enormous had passed through, disturbing the fabric without caring who noticed. Even the Sahr'ka ships kept a respectful distance from the faint distortions.

"This is fresh," Elara murmured at my shoulder. "Far fresher than anything we saw before."

"Meaning it's close," I said.

"Meaning it's moving," she corrected softly.

Echo's voice cut in, smoother than the tension warranted. "The trail has intensified. Composition consistent with deep-drive shearing."

Takahashi frowned. "Deep-drive? At this speed? That's not possible without—"

"—ripping itself apart," Vance said over comms. "Yeah. I'm aware. Whatever this thing is, it's not playing by our rules."

"Echo," I said. "Estimate vector deviation."

Echo paused for half a breath—a fraction too long.

"…inconclusive."

That was new. Echo not knowing was like gravity deciding to take an afternoon off.

The darkness ahead shifted.

Not visibly.

Not on sensors.

Just… felt wrong.

Kade stepped onto the bridge, holding a cup of something that smelled like coffee and bad decisions. "So. How's the existential dread? Everyone good? Hydrated?"

Lt. Ward didn't look up. "Ambassador, please sit down before something terrible happens, and we all blame you for it."

"I mean statistically? That's fair."

Elara exhaled slowly. "It's hunting."

Kade blinked. "You can feel that?"

"No," she said. "I can feel the absence. Like the space ahead of us is holding its breath."

Takahashi swallowed once. "Admiral… vector's shifting again."

"Keep us centered. Slow and steady."

The Veil crept along the scar in the dark. Behind us, three civilizations followed.

Every screen on the bridge dimmed at once.

Not a failure. A reaction.

Echo's outline sharpened. "Contact potential. Reading… reading"

Static hit the comms. A low vibrational hum rolled under the hull, like something brushing the ship with a hand big enough to crush it.

"Raise shields," I snapped.

"Shields up."

The hum faded.

Then the thread in front of us collapsed like a dying heartbeat on a monitor.

Takahashi's voice cracked. "Sir—the trail's gone."

Echo's light flickered. "Disruption pattern… consistent with deliberate masking."

Elara's hand found the edge of the console. "It knows we're here."

Behind us, Vakar's voice rumbled over the fleetwide channel. "Admiral. Packs are restless. Shadows shift."

Rahl's tone followed, harder. "Recommend we tighten further. This feels—wrong."

They weren't wrong.

The void in front of us was no longer empty.

It wasn't full.

It just… existed in a way space shouldn't.

A pressure without form.

A shape without outline.

A presence without signature.

Whatever had eaten its way across the stars wasn't running anymore.

It was waiting.

I stood. "All ships. Hold position."

The fleet drifted into a kill circle—Lareth heavies forming the spine, Sahr'ka hunters slipping through the gaps like knives in water, human vessels locking into the center node.

Silence.

Then Seed's voice slipped through like a whisper from the roots of an old forest.

"The fire is near. And it is hungry."

The Veil turned its nose toward the black.

The fleet followed.

And somewhere ahead, the thing eating its way through the stars left just enough of a trail for us to follow straight into its jaws.

CHAPTER 21:
EMBERS OF THE DEAD

The first system looked fine from a distance.

Cold light across an empty star. Rocks where there should've been stations. A neat, polite kind of silence—as if the void had put everything back the way it wanted it.

Up close, the lie fell apart.

"Grav lensing says somebody carved a corridor in and out," Takahashi said, fingers steady over nav, eyes never leaving the shifting overlay. "Not recent. Not ancient, either."

Vance leaned over her shoulder just far enough to be annoying. "How old is 'not ancient'?"

"Less than a week," she said. "More than a day."

Lt. Ward sat at her comms terminal, one hand braced on the edge of her console as she sifted through passive channels—fleet telemetry, silence markers, encrypted backlogs. Her screen showed nothing but reverb and decay. She didn't speak, but the way her fingers tapped once against the console said she didn't like it.

Echo's projection lifted a fraction from the primary holo node, lines tightening into clean geometry. "Residual field stress along the ecliptic. Directional. Something large transited at high velocity."

Seed's voice threaded the air in its patient, impossible softness. "A river tore new banks. The silt still hangs."

The Veil drifted forward on minimum emissions. No traffic. No beacons. No trash. Nothing to suggest anyone had ever lived here. Whoever had called this place home had cleaned up behind themselves—right up until the moment they no longer existed.

"Rahl," I said into fleetwide.

Ward lifted her chin slightly, tapped a key, and gave me a quick nod—line open, channel stabilized.

"Hold to port and stay dark," I said. "Vakar, spread your pickets. Thirty percent overlap. No one lights a candle unless I say so."

Two responses came back—Rahl crisp and controlled, Vakar with a low, satisfied rumble behind the words. Ward muted both returns the moment they landed, routing them into the tactical pane with surgical neatness.

The first proof this wasn't a ghost story came quietly.

The forward survey scope didn't find survivors. It didn't find debris fields or escape pods or drifting bodies.

It found slag.

A station had hung here once. Now it was a fused ring of metal and glass the size of a city block, peeled open on one side like an orange unwound in a single, brutal motion. No impact cones. No shrapnel halo. No weapon scoring in any direction.

Just a clean, awful unmaking.

Vance let out a breath that tried and failed to be a whistle. "They didn't miss."

"They didn't try to," I said.

Ndlovu stepped forward, hands behind his back, eyes locked on the sensor return. "Recommend a short-hop sweep. Two layers. We keep a net while we look."

"Do it," I said. "Echo, slice the spectrum. I want anything that isn't rock."

"Acknowledged." Echo's tone didn't shift, but the projection sharpened, refocusing into search patterns that left the bridge lights dim by comparison.

Ward ran her hand along the side of her console again—a habit, not uncertainty—then added in a low voice, "Fleetwide tether stable. All ships listening. No background bleed."

"Good," I told her.

The net went out.

Small ships moved where I told them, each holding a tether back to the Veil so tight I could feel it like pressure on my molars. If anything sneezed within fifty thousand kilometers, we'd hear the echo through Ward's console before sensors ever caught up.

We found nothing alive.

We found everything else.

Slag ribbons drifted in light arcs. A habitat wheel had been compressed into a crescent and left to spin like some broken smile. Anchored farms were just grids of black—no pressure tanks, no waste heat, no trace of habitation. The kind of quiet you don't get from power savings.

The kind you get when everything is off because nothing remains to turn it back on.

"Pull us to a low, slow pass," I said. "Elara, it's yours."

She didn't answer through comms. She just stepped forward, and everyone else shifted out of her path without needing the order.

Elara

The Veil's light spread thin across the wreck as we coasted over it.

Debris from explosions had a pattern—ballistic, messy, isotropic. This wasn't that. This was substructure failure. Controlled. Progressive. Something had turned off the bones before it broke the skin.

"EM baseline," I said.

Echo fed me the spectrum. The field return was threadbare—barely a smear. No strong charge. No weapon signature clean enough to label.

The edges told the truth.

Crystalline microfractures along stress lines. High-energy coupling. Sustained deformation. Not heat as a weapon, but heat as a consequence. The infrastructure had been pushed past its design parameters, pulled taut until it broke.

"They mapped the grid," I said. "Not the plating. Not the rails. The spine."

"Induction?" Takahashi asked, still steering the Veil with the gentlest micro-bursts.

"Higher," I said. "Field harvesting. They ran a throughline along the infrastructure's resonance, pulled everything tied to it, and let the system burn itself hollow. Life support. Pressure. Containment. They took the mass they wanted. What didn't match the pattern… burned."

Seed moved closer, her presence cooling the air. "They pulled the roots before they took the fruit."

"Exactly. And they did it fast."

My brain mapped the fracture vectors out of habit—spread, converge, choke. Efficient. Merciless. Intentional. This wasn't a raider. This wasn't conquest. This was extraction.

"Any biosignature?" Raz asked behind me.

"None," I said. "And there won't be. They didn't vaporize anyone. They vented the system and bled every recorder of a death. No signals. No witnesses. No bodies."

Vance spoke low. "They erased them."

"Worse," I said. "They never let them register."

The scope caught something faint—a decaying leakage along the exact vector Takahashi had flagged earlier.

A wake. Not meant to be read, but too large to hide entirely.

"Direction," I said.

"Aligned with the corridor out," Echo answered.

I nodded. Of course it was.

"We'll find more of this ahead."

Raz didn't answer, but he didn't disagree either. He was learning the pattern same as me.

I kept my eyes on the dead station because looking away felt like admitting this could be undone. It couldn't.

"They aren't hunting a people," I said. "They're processing an ecosystem."

Seed's whisper moved like wind through leaves that weren't there. "The ash is neat."

I swallowed. My voice steadied. "We need to move."

Razgriz

We moved.

The system fell behind with the patience of a graveyard.

The next one didn't bother pretending to be alive.

The system after didn't even try for subtlety.

"Same lensing artifact on entry," Takahashi said. "Different angle. Same mass displacement class."

Her voice stayed steady, but her shoulders held a tighter coil than before—like she expected the void to answer back this time.

"Weapons hot?" Vance asked, too casually for anyone who knew him.

"Warm," I said. "No heroics."

Ward's hands danced across her board, isolating all active channels, quieting fleet noise, and opening a secondary line for emergency scatter-flare routing. She did it without being asked—just a clean, automatic prep-for-contact that made the bridge feel sharper.

Rahl's flagship held formation like it had been poured into the space beside us. Sahr'ka scouts ran ahead in skittering arcs, their hull coatings bending starlight enough to leave phantom streaks in their wake. They moved like predators, not patrol vessels.

It should've made me feel better.

It didn't.

The first contact came without ceremony.

Three blips slid out from behind a dead moonlet and pretended to be rocks for five seconds. Then they stopped pretending. Engines lit. Trajectories locked.

Ward's voice cut through the bridge. "Inbound vector locked. No voice traffic. No handshake. No transponder."

"Autonomous," Echo said. "Control channel not present."

"Hunger?" Vance asked.

"Proxies," Echo replied. "Architecture: modular. Purpose: harassment, data harvest."

They moved like tools. No fear. No hesitation. Just velocity applied to the idea of us.

"Vakar," I said. Ward already had the line open.

"Take them in pairs. Don't flex for the cameras. Karesh holds rear intercept."

"Understood," Vakar growled. No bravado. Just work to be done.

The first pass was clean.

Sahr'ka hunters slid past and took two tails each. Human guns reached out from the Veil and drew warning lines across hull plating thinner than our patience. The drones adjusted without urgency—calculating, calibrating, tasting angles.

"Rahl, give me a grid," I said.

The Lareth formation shifted with parade-ground precision—sectors lit, lanes collapsed, pressure points formed. The drones ran out of clever options and tried stupid ones.

We killed them.

A Sahr'ka hunter cut under a drone's axis and planted a shaped charge in a seam, then peeled away without waiting to admire the result. The charge went off with all the drama of an exhale—just a sudden decision by matter to stop being itself.

A Lareth frigate bracketed another drone and burned it from the inside out with a signal it didn't know how to ignore.

The third tried to go through us.

The Veil caught it on a curtain of force it couldn't see until it stopped moving entirely.

"Contact end," Takahashi said, voice level but carrying more tension than she meant to show.

"Damage?" I asked.

"Cosmetic," Vance said. "We've had worse nights at the docks."

"Let's avoid poetry," I said. "Echo, bag the brains. Anything left to read?"

"Fragments only," Echo said. "Memory spines fused at destruct trigger. They transmitted."

"To who?" Vance asked.

"Directionally," Echo said. "Away."

Seed's pulse fluttered faintly. "The rabbits ran to the fire."

"We expected that," I said. "We were loud on purpose."

Ward muted the fleet cheers before they hit the bridge—blunting a morale spike we couldn't afford to get drunk on.

A win is a win.

Even when the thing you kill was designed to die.

We followed the smear into the next system.

 It had nothing alive to say.

 It had too much dead to tell.

A beacon sparked once and went dead.

A rock with a hole through its center drifted like it had been punched by a star.

A subtle pressure rolled back along the vector—as if whatever made the wake now felt our eyes on it.

"Raz," Elara said softly.

I didn't look. I didn't need to. "I know."

"We're almost to the place where the wake stops being a trail," she said, eyes narrowing at the line only we could track. "And starts being a promise."

"Of what?"

She didn't answer.

She didn't have to.

I thought of Buttercup sitting cocooned in her scaffold—vast, wounded, rebuilding herself with patience no living thing should have to learn. I thought of the station we didn't save because there was no one left to save.

"Bring us up to the edge," I said. "Then hold."

Ward tapped her console twice—channel open, fleet tightening, Sahr'ka hunters melting wider into the dark. Rahl's heavies pulled in close enough to share breath if space had any to give.

"Echo?" I asked.

Echo's projection sharpened—clean, dangerous clarity.

"The wake terminates ahead. Not because it ends. Because something else begins."

Seed folded in on herself, light dimming. "The river falls into a canyon."

"Any chance it's shallow?" Vance asked.

"No," Echo said.

Takahashi rested her hands over the helm for a heartbeat, the way pilots do when they're counting futures they don't want to say out loud. Ndlovu settled beside tactical without comment. Kova issued supply orders in a murmur—quiet, efficient, grim.

Ward flicked through channels, tightening the fleet net, eyes narrowed like she was listening for something beneath the static.

"Alright," I said. "We do this the boring way."

I looked out at the shape of nothing with something tucked inside it—a hollow patch of starfield, darker than it should be, like the light there had stopped obeying physics.

"Rahl, Vakar—your forces on a staggered arc," I said. "Veil takes point. We keep a line to both of you. One step forward, not a leap."

Acknowledgments came back. Dry. Clipped. Steady.

No one tried to look fearless—they just readied themselves, which mattered more.

The bridge felt fuller than the space it occupied—crew at their stations, CIC murmuring through the open hatch, soft callouts from tactical and sensors drifting up like background static. Kova's voice carried low from medical's console interface as she updated triage readiness. Vance hovered over engineering's board like he was daring it to misbehave. Even the CIC pit, one deck down, had picked up its restrained rhythm of breath and data.

Ward looked over once from comms. No quip. No commentary. She signaled the channel status with a small tilt of her hand, all business.

If she said anything else, I'd missed it—which was exactly how good communications officers preferred it.

I stepped forward.

"This isn't a speech," I said. "You know I hate those."

A few heads lifted. Not amused—just listening.

"But this line we're about to cross? It's different. You've all seen the reports. You've all seen what's left behind. If we turn around, that keeps happening. Maybe to us. Maybe to someone we're supposed to protect."

The CIC paused below, as if even the air decided to hold still.

"I'm not going to promise a victory," I continued. "We don't know what's ahead. But we're the first ones who've gotten close enough to make the thing responsible notice."

Takahashi's hands rested lightly over helm, waiting for the word.

"We take one step forward. Just one. If it's too steep, we pull back and hit it again from somewhere else. But we're not letting it choose the ground."

Soft inhales around the bridge. Not courage—alignment.

"Whatever waits in there," I said, "it doesn't get to decide the terms."

That was all. Anything longer would've been a lie.

I looked at the dark ahead and wished, briefly, for ignorance—real ignorance, the kind you get before the universe teaches you what monsters actually look like.

Then I let that go.

"Nav," I said. "Take us in."

Takahashi eased the Veil forward.

CIC tightened its cadence.

Tactical dimmed their boards to combat-low.

Vance murmured a systems readiness code to engineering.

Kova's team confirmed medical standby.

Echo narrowed into a single razor-thin line of focus.

Seed drew herself small and quiet, like roots bracing under pressure.

Behind us, the allied fleet compressed—Lareth heavies locking shields edge-to-edge, Sahr'ka hunters threading the gaps like arrows ready to loose, human ships forming the spine of the advance.

The threshold rose ahead of us.

A seam in the dark.

A wound in space.

The Veil settled on its vector, engines low, the bridge lit in that cold blue that precedes every serious decision I've ever made.

Behind us, the fleet tightened until we moved like a single thought.

"Hold steady," I said.

I wasn't looking for courage.

That comes after.

This was the part before it.

The Veil crossed the threshold first.

CHAPTER 22:
IGNITION

They called them the Hunger because any softer word felt like a lie.

Echo cut the dark and found ordered void. The displays painted a wasteland of engineering—docking rings stripped bare, cargo spines threaded clean down to skeleton, entire yards reduced to ribs. Not battle scars. Harvest lines. The kind of attrition a civilization leaves when it takes systems as fuel.

Bridge lighting dimmed to combat-low. CIC murmurs filtered up through the deck grates—short, clipped, all business. Ward kept three channels open at once, eyes tracking packet synchronization, trimming off fleet echo before it hit my board. The hum wasn't tension; it was competence under strain.

"Signal drop at two-point-three AU," Takahashi said. "Active field. Interference is being generated from within the wreckage."

Vance leaned over the console and didn't try to smile. "It's not hiding. It's processing."

Echo's lattice brightened. "Confirmed. Residual resonance indicates structured reclamation. Autonomous harvesters present but tied to shipboard control bands."

"Translation?" I asked.

Elara's voice came low from the science station. "They don't just scavenge. They operate processing vessels. Living crews run them. This is an arm of a moving polity."

The bridge tightened around that. A living polity that fed by taking worlds—no home world to return to, only the fleet that carried them and the gear they grafted to it.

"Fleet status," I asked.

"Formations locked," Kova said. "Medical staged. Repair parties standing by."

Ndlovu moved into step. "Rahl's flanks are ready. Vakar's spear elements forward. We keep distance, we keep pressure."

Elara didn't take her eyes off the holo. "There's a central manifold here—mass transfer nodes and crew hubs. Hit the node and you starve the teeth."

"Then we don't bait them," Takahashi said.

"We don't run, either," I answered.

Ward lifted a hand slightly—our signal that she had the command net clean. "Fleetwide stable. No bleed. Rahl and Vakar standing by on priority loop."

I keyed the net. "Rahl, hold flank. Vakar, move your spear in and keep distance with strike teams. Minimal emissions—no beaconing."

"Acknowledged," Rahl said. "We'll hold the frame."

Vakar added, blunt as a blade. "We cut where you point."

The allied formation closed like a fist. Human carriers and cruiser spines threaded with Lareth guns and Sahr'ka spear craft. The Veil sat at the center, quiet and exact.

Seed moved through the ship like wind through branches. "Roots sense the taking," she said on the link. "They are a long mouth."

"Then we close that mouth," I told her.

Echo peeled the interference back. What remained was not a single organism but a constructed machine of purpose—braided hulls, articulated arms, funnels engaged in steady reclamation. Crucially, it was manned. The manifolds were control hubs, and where smoke and ruin pooled, the sensors flicked with signatures identical to warm physiology, closed-circuit bio-signs, localized neural telemetry, channel bursts that matched organized command.

"They fly it," a tech breathed. "They aren't drones."

"No," Elara said. "They're crews. They've turned vessel into harvest platform. The species grafts living command onto engineered mouths."

Echo added, precise. "Hunter extensions are remotely actuated but remain task-tethered. Crewed nodes control redistribution cycles."

We had found a flank of the Hunger's traveling civilization—a manned processing arm that carved the bones of other systems into fuel. It had teeth and hands, and it had people inside those hands.

"Then we don't attack their teeth first," I said. "We take the node that keeps the teeth fed."

"Targeting: processing manifold," Takahashi called after retasking. "We have a firing solution."

"Rahl—screening box. Vakar—spear forward. We hit the manifold with everything precise and controlled. We collapse the transfer lines. Minimal collateral if we can manage it."

"Understood," Rahl replied. "We hold the net."

Ward muted an overlapping packet of Sahr'ka victory chatter and redirected it to tactical logging instead. "Channels trimmed. Strike groups green. Horizon Fleet confirms ready-state."

The volley started like a line drawn in steel. Missiles braided the dark, and fighter wings poured from launch bays. Lareth batteries focused arcs on junction points while Sahr'ka harriers struck the peripheries. We drove at the place where the Hunger drew what it needed.

The manifold lit like a gullet flaring—power diverted, harvesters flexing outward to defend their feeder. The first strikes took skin, not bone. A human corvette from Rahl's screen met an ingestion burst and vanished in a glitter of twisted plating and burned circuits.

"Impact Horizon Nine—lost," Kova said flatly.

We pushed harder. Elara coached the angles. "Expose the transfer nodes. Hit the conduit junctions. Disrupt the thermal flow."

We did. Explosives and lances tore into conduits, rupturing feed lines where stolen energy was being routed. Sparks crawled along exposed girders. Void turbulence rolled off shockfronts hard enough that Takahashi had to re-trim thrusters twice in under ten seconds. Vance braced his hands on engineering's board, muttering course corrections under his breath while systems fought to keep the Veil steady.

"Manifold failure—initiating cascade," Echo reported. "Processing integrity compromised."

We poured everything into that compromised moment. Fighters threaded gaps and targeted control returns; boarding drones launched on precision tethers to sample hull cavities.

Behind us, Horizon assault carriers opened their bays to release two marine boarding teams—Ghost Team Two among them—riding Wraith drop-ships that dove between wrecked girders like they had been born there. One Wraith took a glancing feed-spike that blew out its port stabilizer; the team aborted seconds before impact, firing mag-clamps to a passing cargo spar and swinging into a collision vector that rattled the structure but left them alive. Another marine squad wasn't as lucky. Their Wraith caught a processing lance mid-approach and disintegrated. Ndlovu didn't flinch—just absorbed the loss, adjusted, and took a step closer to my station.

"Permission to board one of the exposed crew hubs," he said quietly. "We have a window and we may not get another."

"Go," I said. "Take a Spear escort. Don't overextend."

Ward had the line to the carriers open before I finished. "Ghost Team Two, new vector. Stalker unit Six will shadow. Confirm receipt." She layered it across two nets, suppressing return noise and splicing the packets so that only I saw the clean summary. The woman was a machine during combat—no flourish, just throughput.

Rahl's cruisers rode the turbulence deeper than doctrine allowed, sliding sideways across a debris wall to carve an opening for Sahr'ka runs. Stalker packs streaked across exposed support struts, anchoring claws to metal and accelerating along curved hull plating in synchronized arcs—predators using the yard's skeleton as their hunting ground.

Human pilots did what they always did—ignored three warnings and invented a maneuver mid-burn. A pair of Horizon-class interceptors punched through a collapsing vent crawlspace, scraping alloy and shedding sparks like a second skin before they broke into open void and hammered a gunship from behind.

The allied fleet felt, for the first time in the engagement, that we had a chance to force a real wound.

Then the Hunger answered—not with an instinctive roar but with coordinated, human response. Crewed ships peeled out from the cluster: gunships with armored bridges and tethered brigades that took the void like a street. They were not mindless; they were furious and measured and desperate in the way a civilization defending its means of survival would be.

"Pressure from manned fighters," Rahl said. "They're coming out to trade steel."

The first of them struck with the precision of trained pilots. A Hunger gunship dove through our fighters, taking and giving blows in tight arcs. It was carved with scavenged plating and grafted engines—ugly, efficient. Where it hit, energy bled into weird frequency fields our targeting had to learn to pierce.

"Losses—fighter wing three down," Takahashi reported. "Hunger craft are coordinated. They operate at a tactical level."

Ndlovu barked orders and adjusted networks. "They fight like crewed navies. Treat them like crewed navies."

We adapted on the fly. Human pilots moved like they always had—dirty, bold, making decisions a machine can't. Sahr'ka strikes twisted into close runs, clawing at exposed rails where we had weakened their hull. Lareth batteries laid sustained suppressive arcs. The Hunger's craft looped and burst and reconstituted into patterns that took advantage of the ruined geometry—fighting among the bones like predators in a ruined city.

Two Lareth defenders cracked apart under a coordinated pincer—shields overloaded, hulls buckling in silent implosions that left nothing but drifting ribs. A Horizon destroyer took a crippling hit to its starboard array and slewed out of formation, trailing atmosphere; Ward rerouted its distress burst through med-net priority before the message even hit my console. "Rescue shuttles launching from Carina Six," she said. "Survivors in sealed compartments. Three decks compromised—fires controlled." Her voice stayed level. She made order out of chaos because that was her job.

A Stalker pack cut across a fractured cargo ring, using the curve of its structure to slingshot themselves toward a Hunger gunship's dorsal ridge. One of them sliced through a maintenance panel mid-leap, vanished inside, and a heartbeat later the gunship's roll stabilizers died in a violent shudder that opened it to incoming fire.

A Lareth destroyer took a glancing turret sweep that should have crippled it, but instead rolled with the strike and used the momentum to unleash a broadside that cracked the Hunger vessel's shields. Human bombers poured through the breach before the shields could reform.

Then it happened—a beam meant for the Veil cut across our bow. Takahashi reached for an evasive maneuver she didn't have time to execute. The Veil moved anyway.

A short, sharp vector shift. Unordered. Precise.

The shot missed by meters.

Takahashi froze, hands hovering above controls. "I didn't—I didn't input that."

Vance stared at the status feed. "That was the ship. Not us."

Echo said nothing.

Seed breathed across the link like wind in dry leaves. "The branch leans before the storm arrives."

I said nothing. But I logged it.

We broke the manifold. The processing core shuddered. Lines of harvested mass unspooled and arced into space as power dumps failed. The harvesters stilled long enough for us to exploit the gap. Boarding drones found cavities and realized what had been driving them—manned consoles, exhausted pilots lashed to control banks, biointerfaces wired to the hull.

Ghost Team Two reached their target first. Their Wraith clamped to a half-molten service spine, hull magnets screaming against the torque. The squad breached with a shaped charge, cutting into a narrow access corridor where red hazard strobes flickered in spastic pulses. Ward piped their biometrics across my console without prompting. "Team stable. Minor atmosphere breach. Ghost Leader reports internal resistance minimal—crew collapse likely from energy bleed."

"Tell them minimal force," I said. "We need survivors thinking clearly, not corpses."

"Relaying." Ward's hands didn't stop moving. Somewhere beneath us, CIC was doing the math on casualties, fuel reserves, triage throughput—Ward filtered only what I needed.

The first boarded compartment lit up with red emergency strobes—metal blistered from heat and old weld scars. A dozen multi-species crew hung half-conscious in restraint rigs, their cybernetic implants sparking with active kill-switches. One of them convulsed as a surge raced through the graft at the base of his skull.

We took wreckage. We dragged fragments back to salvage fields. We scooped survivors where we could—huddled in partially sealed caverns, their breath and pulse and shock spilling into our med bays. They were not animals. They were people folded into technology, eyes bewildered and sharp. They looked at us like any survivor looks at their rescuers: a mix of rage, fear, calculation.

Some didn't know they'd been rescued. Their implants flooded them with garbage signals—panic loops, wipe commands, or automated self-erasure. One survivor screamed in three different languages as his cortical graft attempted to burn itself out. Kova slammed a blocker to his neck and shouted for an EM choke-net.

"We need interference suppression now," she snapped. "They're receiving remote commands. Their implants are cooking them from the inside out."

Ward rerouted three channels at once. "Choke-net broadcasting. Horizon Fleet syncing. Jammers on pulse-cycle."

Another med report hit her board, and she cut it cleanly into priority order. "Veil med-bay reaching saturation. Redirecting overflow to Hearthstone and Hollowfall. Carriers report three operating rooms hot and staffed."

"Any of ours?" I asked.

"Horizon-5—Shade and Cipher—both recovered. Shade critical, Cipher stable." Her tone didn't shift. It just threaded into the battle's momentum.

One of the boarded gunships flared its engines in a desperate rip, sloughing off two boarding drones and making for cover. Another hung like an angry wasp until a Lareth battery drove it apart with a focused arc. Fighters tangled in the wreckage like dogs and men.

"Boarding report," Rahl said. "Two ships with intact crews. Medical triage coming aboard."

"Onboard manifest?" I asked.

"Mixed," Rahl replied. "Crew, servitor units, and cybernetic interfaces. Some are… nav-combat trained. Others look like engineers."

They were a living polity, and they fought to survive as such. Not a hive. Not a thing without a face. They had names, maybe languages that would be rough on our tongues, and motives that were narrower than conquest—hunger to live was a motive that made monsters of many species.

We had wounded one of their processing arms, but other ships loosened from the wreckage and began to consolidate—field repair drones knitting armor, rerouted power steering, new shields. A crewed command vessel rose like a dark fungus from the debris and opened its maw of turrets. It had men in its belly. It had decisions.

"New command ship—appearing aft of field," Echo said. "Manned. Active frequency. Returning fire."

"Then we meet the crew," I said.

We did. The fighting that followed was not a single-minded slaughter. It was messy, tactical, and human—pilots making choices, commanders redirecting squadrons, men and women on a hull sweating through their gloves and finding cunning in the places we hadn't expected.

A Horizon-class destroyer tried to cover a retreating Lareth ship and took a shearing blast across its dorsal span. The Veil's AI threw a warning across our hull-network—unprompted, rapid, urgent—and rerouted our forward batteries to fire before Takahashi even plotted an angle. It bought the destroyer four seconds. Four seconds was enough for its escape thrusters to kick in.

"That wasn't me," Vance said, eyes narrowing.

"We'll ask questions after we survive," I said. But I filed it away. The Veil was thinking ahead now. Or something close to it.

A Horizon frigate skimmed the command ship's shield edge close enough to sear paint. A Stalker pack hit the same flank seconds later, claws biting into plating. One of them cut a path to a vulnerable heat exchanger, and the resulting vent plume opened a lane for our bombers to strike deep.

The Hunger's crews were feral and clever: they flung sacrificial hulls to block missiles, braided fields to confuse sensors, launched boarder swarms to cut drones free.

A Sahr'ka spear-wing disappeared in a flash—eight ships gone so fast no one spoke their names. One of the Lareth bulwark frigates took a fusion burst straight into its forward ventral brace; its captain rammed the failing vessel into a Hunger gunship, locking the two ships together long enough for a Stalker team to breach both hulls and rip the enemy's core apart from within. The Lareth frigate didn't survive the maneuver. The Sahr'ka pack leader's salute echoed across our fleet net—short, sharp, grieving.

We paid for what we took. The deck reports filled with names. Repair teams ran ragged. Med bays filled and did not empty quickly. But then something else happened: with every captured pilot, with every intact command module we recovered, we gained language and intent. A mind captured can be interrogated, can be asked why it feeds. An engine module stripped yields a method. A dead bridge teaches how it thinks.

"Casualty list incoming," Kova said. "Boarding survivors stable but in shock. Several captured officers complaining of command fractures."

I let the silence hold for half a breath. "Then we do what we have to. We learn."

Elara's hands hovered over her console, eyes tired but bright with that scientist's hunger we'd all learned to trust. "They survive by engineered intake. That intake is organized. Disrupt the intake and their autonomy fractures. They'll adapt—fast—but broken nodes give us a window."

"How long?" I asked.

"Hours to days," she said. "If we're fast and surgical—we can keep them rebuilding into pain. If we let them feed, they grow stronger."

"Then we deny them feed," I said. "We pick moving targets, we hunt the drifters, and we trace repair nodes."

Rahl's voice cut in, iron and flat. "We fence their fleet. We hold what we took. We close the gaps. We don't offer them easy prey."

Vakar's laugh was low. "I like that. Prey that fights back is more fun."

It felt wrong to have anything like humor, but the line landed and steadied us.

We recovered what we could from the field and ferried the wounded to shuttles and back to med bays. Salvage teams worked the carcasses while fighters held perimeter. The Hunger's flock reconstituted and drifted outward—repairing with brutal economy, grafting spare plates to hold structural integrity.

"They will learn us," Elara said quietly.

"We'll learn them," I answered. "We just have to live long enough to teach them not to eat our worlds."

The bridge fell into work. No celebration. No easy words. We had ignited something. We had made the first real cut into a traveling civilization that had learned how to survive by taking. We had not killed it. We had forced it to look at us as an enemy with choices.

"Prepare for follow operations," I said. "Track their repair vectors. Isolate their scavengers. Reclaim. Deny."

Ward's voice came soft but steady from comms. "Fleetwide net synchronized. All channels green."

"Aye," came the responses—cold, sharp, tasked.

We had no time to grieve, and just enough to keep pushing on.

We had lit a match in a field of dry bones. Ignition was done. Now the slow, terrible job of keeping the flame from burning us alive began.

CHAPTER 23:
WILDFIRE

The stars were still bleeding when we turned our backs on the first fight.

Wreckage hung behind us in a slow, silent drift—twisted Hunger hull plating glimmering in the Veil's fading sensor wash. One hunter ship dead, but it hadn't died quietly. The damage it left behind bled through every deck. Engineering teams were crawling through torn plating. Lareth gunships limped on cracked drives. Sahr'ka spear craft bled heat like open wounds.

Vakar's voice crackled through the fleet net, sharp as a blade. "We should burn what's left and finish it."

"If it was alone," I said, "I'd agree."

Echo pulsed faintly above the command well. "Long-range arrays are registering spike activity along three approach vectors. Signature patterns match Hunger hunter wings."

Elara's voice came soft, steady. "They're coming."

"Not just coming," Takahashi added from nav, "closing fast. They must have been shadowing the first ship."

Kade folded his arms. "Then this was never a clean kill."

"It was never going to be," I said.

The bridge fell quiet except for the hum of strained systems. Outside, the fleet was trying to stitch itself back together—burn damage, cracked hulls, life support on half a dozen ships one breath from collapse. We'd bloodied their teeth. Now they wanted the rest of the meal.

The smell of overheated circuitry and burned polymers drifted through the vents, a reminder of how hard the Veil had pushed in the last engagement. Ward's hands kept sliding across her board in fast, efficient sweeps—routing emergency signals, trimming priority channels, smoothing comm traffic before it could become a flood. Even she looked strained under the low light, shoulders tight, jaw set as she kept the fleet net from collapsing under its own weight.

A minor jolt hit the port-rear frame—minor, but sharp enough to tell me something had given way in the port-rear plating. Vance didn't even look up from his panel. "Working it," he muttered, already dispatching a team to patch whatever had cracked. The man hadn't slept since before the first fight. None of us had. The air tasted recycled and tired.

Out on the starboard holo, a Lareth cruiser drifted slightly out of formation, its engine bloom flickering like a failing heartbeat. Ward snapped a correction to them before their own helm realized they were drifting—her voice crisp, tired, but still cutting clean through the noise.

"Begin withdrawal," I said.

On the forward display, tugs and cutters swarmed through the debris like ants dragging broken limbs. Rahl's escorts folded around a shattered patrol carrier, towing it into formation. Vakar's packs formed a screen, their engines flaring weakly. A dozen hulls scarred. Three already gone.

Echo's pulse sharpened. "Hunger fleet signatures intensifying. Intercept estimate: forty minutes."

"Forty minutes?" Vance barked over the comm. "They're burning hot."

"They're hunting," I answered.

A low murmur rippled through CIC, audible even through the deck grates. Not panic—awareness. The kind of sound people make when they see the wave coming and know they have to outrun it, not fight it.

Elara leaned closer to the holo projection. The sensor overlay traced the incoming contacts in harsh red. "They're fast, Raz. Faster than before."

"Then we don't wait for them to catch us."

I keyed the fleet channel. "All ships, this is Horizon Actual. Break salvage lines. Priority on propulsion and wounded ships. Set jump formation. We're moving."

Orders rippled through the fleet. The chatter was clipped, tense, but steady—the sound of people who'd done this too many times to need speeches. Engines flared. Formation lines shifted. We ran.

Behind us, the shattered hull of a Sahr'ka spear craft finally lost integrity and folded in on itself, venting its last breath into the dark. Ward caught the death-ping and silently transferred the names to Kova's record queue. No announcement. No ceremony. Not now. We didn't have the seconds to spare.

Takahashi's fingers worked the helm controls in rapid, sharp movements. Even fatigued, her precision was textbook. "Formations adjusting... drift on Horizon Twelve corrected... carriers beginning slingshot alignment..."

The Hunger fleet crested the edge of the system like a storm rolling over a ridgeline.

They didn't send scouts this time. They came in a wall— interceptors, cutters, harvesters all cutting straight for the hole we'd carved. They wanted us bleeding in open space, not dug in with cover. Smart.

"Jump corridor clear," Takahashi called.

"Punch it."

The Veil's drive howled as the fleet tore itself out of the system. For a heartbeat, the stars smeared into silver lines. Then the chase began.

Jump shock rolled through my spine—clean, but deeper than it should've been. We were pushing the Veil harder than any engineer would approve. Vance shot me a look that said exactly that, but he kept his mouth shut. Everyone did. We knew the stakes. The hum of stressed conduits thrummed through the hull like distant thunder.

"Transition complete," Takahashi said, exhaling slowly. "But they're matching our course-line. Immediately."

Echo confirmed. "Hunger vector alignment: exact. They followed the same corridor imprint. Estimated pursuit distance: decreasing."

They were close enough to bite.

The sky behind us burned. Not in flames, but in the hard geometry of a fleet rebuilding itself faster than we could get away.

The Hunger didn't chase with a single wave. They came in slashes—hunter wings driving at our flanks, cutters slipping through gravity wells, scouts baiting us into crossfire nets. Every kilometer of space we bought cost something in blood, steel, or fuel.

"Rahl's rear guard just lost another corvette," Takahashi said. "No transponder pings. She's gone."

The bridge didn't flinch. We were well past the point where shock felt new.

"Cross-traffic on vector four," Echo added. "Hunter signatures converging. Estimated intercept: twenty-two minutes."

"Helm," I said, "burn us lean. We're out of fat."

The Veil's engines howled as she shouldered into the black. Behind us, the fleet stretched thin: battered cruisers limping on patched plating, Lareth gunships bristling with scorched armor, Sahr'ka spear craft bleeding atmosphere through fractured seams. The formation wasn't elegant anymore—just survival.

Rahl's flank patrols fell back toward us, their lines chewed ragged by the pursuit. The Hunger wasn't just chasing—they were driving us, pressing in like fire rolling downhill.

A flicker crossed my display—Horizon Breakwater listing, one engine flaring too bright. Ward muttered something under her breath and shot commands across two channels at once, pulling its transponder into sync before the ship drifted across a Lareth gunline. She kept the fleet from tripping over itself, one correction at a time, the weight of it burning through the tension in her shoulders.

Kova's voice cut across the med-net. "Three more burn victims incoming from Spear Wing Seven. Vent ruptures. Ship unable to stabilize." Her tone was rough, lower than usual. Exhaustion doing the polishing no training could.

Vance answered on the engineering band. "Forward coolant feeds failing on six ships. If they don't throttle down, they'll melt their own teeth."

"They throttle down, they die," I said. And no one argued.

The medical decks smelled like ozone and blood. Kova had stripped her mask down to the collar, voice rasping through exhaustion.

"We're out of biogel packs. Half the med pods are offline. Triage only."

I nodded. There wasn't anything else to say.

Logistics wasn't doing better. Fuel cells bled faster than we could rotate them. Vance's engineering teams had been sleeping in crawlspaces, jury-rigging heat sinks with scavenged Hunger plating.

"They keep pushing the forward vector," Vance growled through the comm. "They want us to run hot."

"They're getting it," I answered.

A tremor rolled underfoot—minor hull deformation from a long-range harvester lance scraping the outer plating. Takahashi compensated instantly, but sweat beaded along her temple. "They're predicting our micro-corrections," she warned. "Adjusting faster than probability curves suggest."

I met Echo's shifting light. "How fast are they learning?"

"Rate of adaptation exceeds our simulations," Echo replied. "The longer the pursuit continues, the narrower our maneuver space becomes."

The first ambush came off a gravity well near a dead moon. Hunger interceptors peeled out from behind the debris, their engines painted in scavenged alloy. The ships weren't drones. They were crewed—fast, deliberate, angry.

"Flank wide!" I snapped. "Takahashi, thread us through their intercept cone."

The Veil rolled into the shadow of the moon, pulse engines flaring just long enough to slide us under their guns. Vakar's spear craft ripped through their formation like wolves tearing into a carcass, but even that wasn't enough. Two gunships never made it out. Their screams cut across the net and died in static.

"Those weren't random," Elara said quietly from the science station. Her eyes were on the telemetry—on the angles. "They're adapting to our emission profiles."

"They're adjusting," I said. "And we're running out of places to teach them."

"Incoming second wave—vector five!" Ward shouted, her voice breaking the usual calm. "Broadcast jammers failing on the forward band—rerouting—stand by—"

Static bit into the net.

A cluster of Hunger interceptors tore through the drifting debris and slashed across our flank before Vakar's packs could fully reposition. A Lareth shield frigate absorbed the hit and folded, its hull buckling inward like crushed foil. Ward's hands froze for half a breath as the transponder blinked out. One more gap in the formation. One more name to write later.

Elara

The Veil's sensors painted the void in pale green overlays, the way a wildfire might paint a treeline—heat signatures, vector flares, power shifts blooming and dying like sparks.

Their nodes were growing more efficient. Each engagement burned less of their reserves and more of ours. They were using their own wreckage as a net. Nothing was wasted.

"They've shifted their pattern again," I said quietly. "Short-range power spikes—hunters are running off direct siphon loops."

Vance's voice crackled over the internal net. "Can you disrupt it?"

"Temporarily," I said. "But it won't last."

I keyed the transmission. "Bridge, if we pulse a shaped burst through the relay, we can make their siphon feeds choke for about three minutes."

"Do it," Razgriz said.

Three minutes wasn't long, but in a chase like this, three minutes could buy lives.

I watched the bloom of interference flood the screen—a brief, silvered wave against a forest of fire.

But I also watched the aftershock—how several Hunger craft staggered mid-formation, engines coughing before rebalancing. Not random—nothing sloppy. They corrected faster than before. I felt my stomach tighten. They were evolving even inside interference. Not learning—iterating.

Razgriz

The interference bloom hadn't even finished unraveling before we moved. The Veil surged ahead with a shove of engine power Vance probably didn't have to spare, but no one questioned it. Every second counted; every second bought was a second we stole back from the things behind us.

"Strike teams away," Ward said, voice clipped, clean, and mercifully calm. "All packets tight. No bounce."

Our vanguard hit the Hunger's staggered wing while its siphon loops were still choking. Lareth guns carved a channel where the nodes flickered. Sahr'ka spear craft knifed through the gap before it could close.

One of the Sahr'ka pilots let out a sharp burst of comm-static that wasn't a word so much as a declaration. It wasn't triumph—more like the sound of someone daring fate to try again.

"Harriers breaking left," Rahl called. "Pushing secondary line."

The screen bloomed with ruptured exhaust trails. Half a dozen Hunger interceptors spasmed, their engines coughing raw flame as the pulse scrambled their intake cycle. A few tore themselves apart when the surge hit their control banks. Others drifted long enough for our fighters to put them down.

But it didn't last.

"It's fading," Elara warned.

Three minutes always felt shorter during a pursuit.

"Echo?" I said.

"Interference decay complete. Hunters re-establishing full siphon flow."

And just like that, the wildfire behind us inhaled. A long, hungry breath.

"Roll us out," I said. "Helm, shallow dive. Make them work for the angle."

Takahashi didn't argue. The Veil cut under a broken asteroid shelf, shedding residual static as debris scraped along our shields in a hiss that vibrated through the deck. A Sahr'ka wing followed us under the shelf, their formation folding into a tight spearhead—elegant even when half their ships were running wounded.

The last craft in their wedge sputtered, flames licking out from a ruptured intake line. Two others drifted back to guard it without being told. Loyalty looked different in every species, but moments like that felt universal.

"Rahl," I keyed, "status on your right flank."

"Bleeding," he answered. "But still here."

He didn't waste words. None of us had the energy left for them.

"Echo," I said, "new projection."

"Three hunter wings converging. Pattern indicates coordinated net formation."

"So another trap."

"Yes."

Takahashi exhaled sharply, not quite a curse but close. "They're trying to box our options down to nothing."

"That's their job," I said. "And ours is to make sure they fail."

Vance's voice cut in, raw with strain. "Engineering to bridge—we need to bleed heat. Right now. I can't keep the coils locked much longer."

"Options?"

"Slow down or melt."

"Neither," I said.

A long pause. Then the sound of someone accepting the kind of compromise no sane engineer would suggest unless the alternative was fire.

"…I can vent through the dorsal brace. It'll light us up like a beacon."

"They already see us," I said. "Do it."

The Veil shuddered as heat roared out of the dorsal vents. The sudden thermal bloom washed across our aft cameras in a glare bright enough to wash out the stars. For a heartbeat, the fleet around us flared in the glow—hulks, wounds, stubborn fragments of ships refusing to die.

Behind us, the Hunger reacted instantly.

"Spikes on aft vector," Echo reported. "They've locked on to the vent plume."

Good. Come eat the wrong fire.

"Rahl," I said, "collapse your right flank around the plume signature. Make it our shield."

"Copy. Pulling in."

His formation folded toward us, weaving themselves into the thermal wash.

The tactic shouldn't have worked—any competent hunter force should have recognized a decoy signature. But competence wasn't the problem. Momentum was. The Hunger was mid-charge, built on fury and numbers. They'd committed before the equation changed.

Takahashi's eyes flicked across her displays. "They're overshooting the intercept point."

"Let them. We'll take the space."

For a breath, the chase stuttered.

Just a breath.

But it was space we hadn't had before.

"Strike team through," Rahl barked from his flagship. "Harriers on their flank."

Lareth guns flared in arcs, burning through Hunger skirmishers as they tried to regroup. Fighters screamed through the black, some never coming back.

"Echo," I said, "where's the next net?"

"Two systems ahead. Ambush probability high. Their hunter fleet is splitting into three converging groups."

I dragged a hand across my face. Sweat stuck to the inside of my collar. "Then we pick the least ugly door and punch through it."

Takahashi didn't look up. "Plotting all three. None of them are survivable if we slow down."

"Then we don't," I said. "Keep us burning."

Ward routed half the fleet's chatter straight into black-box buffers to keep the command net breathable. "Horizon Emberfall reporting coolant loss. Horizon Highwatch requesting escort support. Two Sahr'ka wings asking for emergency vector override—"

"Grant them," I cut in.

"Already did," Ward replied without looking back.

By the fourth engagement, the fleet wasn't fighting for space anymore—we were clawing for every second. The Hunger was everywhere: hunter craft in our blinds, signal jammers laced through the debris field, comm bursts crackling like brushfire.

"Veil taking hits aft!" someone yelled.

The deck lurched as a harvester missile scraped the starboard shield and chewed into our outer hull. Structural alarms howled across the bridge. Vance's teams swarmed the breach without waiting for orders.

Rahl's net collapsed inward. Vakar's spear craft were running on fumes. Half the Lareth contingent had already burned their long-range fuel reserves. If they didn't catch us, they'd just keep burning everything we had until we fell apart.

"Ward," I snapped, "status on the med rotation?"

"Reassigning survivors to Hearthstone's auxiliary bay," she said. "Hollowfall reports triage saturation but can still take burn victims."

Her voice thinned for a moment as she cross-linked four emergency channels. She didn't raise it. She didn't need to. The strain sat in the tightness of every word.

Kade slammed his hand down on the tac table. "We can't keep bleeding like this, Raz. We're giving ground and getting nothing."

Selas and Cho weren't here to temper the moment. No diplomacy. No politics. Just war.

"We're buying time," I said. "And time costs blood."

Kade didn't argue. He just braced a hand against the console and kept the remaining fleet markers centered in his view, jaw locked tight.

The sixth engagement broke us open.

The Hunger didn't ambush this time. They surged.

Command ships, hunter wings, processing hulls dragged out of the graveyard—they threw everything they had down our throat at once. Rahl's flanks folded. Vakar's spear craft bled out in knots of twisted metal and black fire.

"Shields collapsing on the Veil," Echo warned.

"Hold them," I snarled.

"We can't."

The bridge shuddered as impacts ripped across our hull. Shields screamed. I smelled coolant burning in the vents.

"Seed," I said through the neural link.

Her voice came like wind through ash. "The fire runs."

"Then we run faster."

A warning klaxon blared—one Takahashi had never heard before. An overload in the Veil's mid-ventral conduction rails, the kind that didn't trigger unless the ship was seconds from structural failure. She yanked the Veil's nose down in a brutal dive, engines screaming. A harvester lance tore through the space we'd just vacated.

"That was too close," Vance muttered.

"No," Takahashi said quietly. "That was calculated."

Her eyes flicked to the status halo. The Veil had adjusted thrust microseconds before she'd input her command. Again.

We broke free. Barely. A third of the fleet didn't.

The comm net filled with holes where ships used to be.

Takahashi's voice was quiet. "We've lost Rahl's trailing carrier. No survivors."

Elara's knuckles were white against the railing. She didn't say anything. She didn't have to.

Ward muted the dead channels manually, one after another, her jaw trembling the slightest amount. She killed the signals with a precision that was almost reverent. "Next transmission," she said. "Keep the net clean."

The fleet limped through the black, engines coughing heat, hulls bleeding atmosphere. Echo tracked the Hunger's signatures—they weren't giving us a moment to breathe. The wildfire was right behind us, burning everything we left.

"Course projection," I said.

"They're herding us," Echo answered.

I stared at the star map. A single world sat in the path ahead. Quiet. Unremarkable. Just another waystation orbiting a dying star.

"They're not chasing us," I said slowly. "They're steering us."

The weight of it settled in. Every jump, every forced turn, every ambush—they weren't improvising. They were pushing.

Takahashi swallowed hard. "Raz… if we follow this corridor, there's no off-ramp. They're shaping our vector with every engagement."

Kova's voice filtered over from the med deck. "If we stop moving, we lose everyone who can't be stabilized. Whatever ground they've chosen… it's soon."

Kade's voice came low over the command net. "Wherever they're driving us, they've already picked the ground."

"Then we make it cost them," I said.

The deck felt heavier than it should have. Each footfall carried the ship's tension with it.

"Prep the defensive grid," I ordered. "Call what's left of the fleet."
We weren't running anymore.
The wildfire was coming, and we'd chosen where to burn.

CHAPTER 24:
LAST LIGHT

The Veil dropped out of FTL on the edge of a silent star.

Below us, a planet turned slowly in the dark — blue-green arcs streaked with white clouds, its night side glittering with pinpricks of light. Cities. Millions of them. Maybe billions of people. A T3 civilization, just far enough along to think they were safe.

The bridge went very quiet.

Even CIC fell still below us, their chatter dropping to a muted hum through the deck grates — the kind of stunned silence that only comes when an entire room understands the stakes without needing it spoken.

Takahashi broke the silence first. "Planetary transponders active. Multiple orbital stations… all civilian. No fleet signatures."

Echo's lattice brightened faintly. "Defensive capacity minimal. No rapid response network detected. No standing orbital fleet."

"They can't stop this," Elara whispered.

No one argued with her. The HUD already told us everything we needed to know. They weren't ready for a war. And the Hunger was right behind us.

I'd seen worlds like this before. Not many. Mostly in fleet history archives — the old recon briefs from the early expansion era. The kind of worlds people pointed at when they needed to remind themselves what "untouched" looked like.

But standing here, staring down at an entire civilization unaware of what was coming… it hit harder than any archive ever could.

Hard enough that even the ship reacted — a low shift in the inertial frame, a subtle tightening of the Veil's shield harmonics, as if the hull itself braced before I'd given a single order.

There was no time for speeches. No time to warn them. No time to teach them how to fight an enemy that had already eaten better civilizations than this one.

"Fall back, reform the line," I ordered. My voice sounded steadier than it felt. "Put us between the planet and whatever's coming."

Rahl's command ship answered first, his fleet sliding into position on the left flank. Vakar's spear craft settled on the right, battered but still moving. What was left of the Lareth task force tucked behind the Veil like exhausted birds seeking cover from the storm.

Ward relayed confirmations across three channels at once, her fingers a blur. Each acknowledgment carried the fatigue of crews who'd been fighting far too long — but none of them hesitated.

The holo projected the Hunger fleet signatures on the long-range scope. Dozens. Too many. They'd followed our blood trail across half a dozen systems, and now they were here to finish it.

Kade's voice cut through the channel, rough and low. "We can still run, Raz."

I stared at the planet through the viewport. Lights. So many lights. "Not this time."

Elara turned to look at me. She didn't need to ask why. She already knew.

"If we leave," I said quietly, "they die."

It wasn't the first time in history a commander drew a line in front of a civilian world and called it the last. Thermopylae came to mind — but those men had stone at their backs and a geography that narrowed a thousand enemies into a corridor. I didn't have walls. I had vacuum, dying ships, and a hostile fleet that could outrun us even wounded.

Gallipoli surfaced next — a reminder of what happens when a force believes resolve alone can break a perfect kill zone. I pushed that one down fast. Not helpful.

Then another memory rose — a speech from an old Earth commander, dug up from a pre-FTL database I'd read as a cadet. He'd said something like: "Sometimes you don't hold the line because it's winnable. You hold it because someone behind you can't."

That one stayed.

It sat with a weight that settled into my lungs, right beside the fear. Not replacing it — just giving it direction.

The order rippled through the fleet. Not a roar. Not a rally. Just the quiet weight of people who understood what it meant.

Hold the line. Or the fire takes everything.

Echo pushed real-time formation overlays across the holo, tying every remaining ship into a tight, brittle wall. Takahashi adjusted their vector to lock us in a low orbit path between the planet and the incoming fleet. Seed pulsed softly through the link — steady, restrained, careful not to intrude.

Even the Veil shifted again—a microscopic correction to our attitude thrusters, aligning us a fraction of a degree before Takahashi reached for the controls. She caught the motion, blinked once, then let the ship finish the adjustment itself. No comment. We'd all seen too much to pretend it was coincidence.

Below decks, CIC updated our threat grid with brutal efficiency. Every few seconds, a new marker blinked to life as hands moved over consoles I couldn't see but felt through the deck—hundreds of people bracing alongside us, unseen but present.

The Hunger fleet crested the system edge thirty minutes later.

They came fast.

Not as scattered hunters this time. A formation. Coordinated. The way a predator moves when it's already cornered its prey.

Takahashi whispered, "This is going to be bad." Not fear—just math spoken out loud. A pilot's instinct recognizing a battle already lost on paper.

Ward's breath caught over an open mic—just one soft sound— before she muted herself and resumed cycling comm bands with mechanical precision.

I felt the same thing she did—the density of their formation, the discipline in their spacing. This wasn't a pursuit force anymore. It was a hammer. And we were the anvil someone had left in the wrong century.

"Contacts crossing twenty million klicks," Takahashi said.

Vance's voice carried up from Engineering. "Shields at sixty-two percent. Hull integrity… holding. For now."

The Veil dimmed ambient lights by a fraction—a power reroute she shouldn't have made without instruction. Echo glanced toward her systems, the lattice pulsing once in what almost resembled acknowledgment.

I gripped the rail and watched the red blips close. "Weapons free."

The first volley lit the dark like dawn breaking sideways. Not poetic—just physics slamming into armor. The backwash from our own guns rattled through the hull with that familiar, almost comforting groan of stressed metal. It reminded me of the historical footage of naval battles during Earth's 20th century—the way old battleships shuddered after firing broadside, as if bracing themselves for the ocean's retaliation.

Except we weren't getting ocean spray. We were getting annihilation moving at a fraction of lightspeed.

The Veil's guns opened up first—beams slashing out into the black, carving through the leading edge of the Hunger formation. Vakar's spear craft flared hot on the right, darting in like blades. Rahl's cruisers soaked the first counterfire, their shields flickering like cracked glass.

CIC fed firing solutions in bursts—Ward's voice relaying updated telemetry, another officer predicting trajectories with a hoarse, half-spoken cadence, the Veil adjusting turret phasing a hair faster than the crew could input. We were many hands acting as one, and somehow the ship itself had become one of those hands.

The Hunger didn't break. They didn't retreat. They just kept coming.

Explosions streaked across the void. A Lareth destroyer folded in on itself like paper. Two Sahr'ka spear craft were gutted before they could even turn. The formation bled, shifted, held anyway.

Part of me drifted to another corner of military history—the Battle of the Philippine Sea. "The Great Marianas Turkey Shoot," they called it. An entire wave of enemy pilots cut down before they could reach their targets. Except this time we were the doomed pilots, throwing ourselves into a perfect firing solution with nothing but willpower to keep us moving.

"Left flank collapsing!" Takahashi shouted.

"Rahl!" I barked into the comm.

Static. Then his voice, tight and low: "I can give you sixty seconds. Maybe."

"Make them count."

A detonation flared in the distance—Rahl's ships burning themselves down to buy us a single minute of sky.

Vakar's voice followed, harsher. "Our packs are spent. We fall, they pass."

"Then don't fall."

I could feel the crew watching me from the corners of their eyes—waiting to see if I'd crack, or freeze, or let the fear bleed through.

I didn't. Not because I wasn't afraid. I was terrified—the cold, narrowing kind that sits behind your lungs and waits to swallow you. But fear is an old companion. You stop trying to beat it and start walking with it. That's what every soldier I'd ever admired had done.

Some commanders in history had gods, visions, or even a smart-mouthed beer can to point the way. I had a gardener who spoke in trees and a librarian shaped like a screensaver. And right now, that was enough.

And under my boots, the Veil hummed — not steady, not calm, but alive in the way a cornered animal is alive. It wasn't courage. It wasn't fear. It was readiness.

"Left flank collapsing!" Takahashi shouted.

"Rahl!" I barked into the comm.

Static. Then his voice, tight and low: "I can give you sixty seconds. Maybe."

"Make them count."

A detonation flared in the distance — Rahl's ships burning themselves down to buy us a single minute of sky. Ward relayed the telemetry without being asked, her voice thin but steady as rows of icons winked out on the tactical. CIC murmurs rose beneath the deck — not panic, not confusion, just the cold, stunned recognition of what sacrifice looked like in real time.

Vakar's voice followed, harsher. "Our packs are spent. We fall, they pass."

"Then don't fall."

He didn't answer. He didn't need to. His remaining spear craft surged in tight arcs, a formation more instinct than coordination now. In a different battle, they would've been beautiful. Here, they were just dying slower.

The Veil dimmed her internal lights for half a breath — automatic power redistribution, something she'd started doing only recently. The gesture felt almost like bracing before a hit. Even battered, the ship was learning the rhythm of a fight stacked against her.

The Veil shuddered under the impact of a direct hit.

Not the distant vibration of glancing fire — this one slammed through the hull like a hammer. Deck plating buckled under my boots. Heat rippled up the bulkheads. The viewport's stabilizing grid flickered as it took the stress and barely held.

Two crew were thrown against the wall. Ward broke off mid-report to help one back into their chair before resuming without missing a beat.

Warnings screamed across every console — coolant alarms, shield bleed, hull breach on Deck Seven, environmental instability in Section B-4. Vance's people didn't wait for orders. They never had to. The entire engineering wing was already moving, voices reverberating through the deck as they sprinted past exposed conduit and smoke.

"Shields at twenty-three percent!" Vance shouted. "One more salvo and we're open."

I saw the Veil react before Takahashi did — a micro-jolt through the inertial dampeners as she fired a corrective burst to roll the ship away from the damage vector. Takahashi only needed a half-second adjustment to sync with her. The ship didn't have a voice, didn't have emotions, but right now she was doing what a human officer would've done: anticipate, adjust, survive.

Elara braced herself against the railing. Her eyes reflected the burning starscape, silver brightening as the next volley lit the void. She looked like she wanted to say something — a warning, a farewell, a calculation — but she held it, jaw locked tight.

The Hunger fleet cut through what was left of Rahl's line like fire through dry grass. No resistance, no hesitation — just consumption. Ward's voice dipped for a fraction of a second as she listed the casualties, the channels going dead one after another. She kept her tone leveled, but she wasn't fooling anyone.

Across the deck, CIC activity bled through the ceiling: shouts, slammed consoles, rapid-fire updates. They weren't frightened. They were busy. Triage, routing survivors to compartments still under pressure, patching comm links, pushing damage reports to Engineering faster than humans could speak them. The heart of the ship was beating itself raw.

The next barrage gutted the Veil.

Panels exploded overhead, showering sparks. The lights flickered, died, then limped back half-powered. Gravity hiccuped violently — a sickening drop as if the entire ship had slipped down an invisible shaft. I tasted blood. My teeth had cut into my tongue.

Engineering's net was chaos. Controlled chaos, but chaos all the same — clipped commands, shouted numbers, overlapping voices fighting the clock.

"We've lost two reactors!" Vance yelled. "Main shield grid down. Aux running at eighteen percent."

"We're losing pressure on Deck Five!"

"Reroute power from dorsal batteries!"

"We already did!"

Echo's voice cut through all of it, too calm, almost eerily level. "Primary drive offline. Weapons at seventeen percent efficiency. Hull breaches on five decks. Casualty count rising."

Another conduit behind navigation burst, spraying hot vapor across the back wall. Someone screamed — and just as quickly someone else dragged them clear.

The deck vibrated with emergency bulkheads sealing off sections in rapid sequence. The Veil was isolating the spreading damage faster than CIC could call it out.

Seed's whisper brushed against my neural link, soft and aching. "The roots burn."

I closed my eyes. "Yeah. I know."

When I opened them again, the holo showed the battlefield collapsing toward us — the dying, the burning, the breaking. And still, every surviving ally tightened formation around the Veil as if she were the last stone still standing in the flood.

Fear pressed tight against the inside of my ribs. Not panic — the other kind. The quiet, sharp version soldiers get when the battle is too far gone to lie about. The version you make peace with. The version you walk through anyway.

The crew felt it too. I could see it in their eyes. Takahashi reading three screens at once, fingers moving on instinct alone. Ward pushing through another cascade of losses, her knuckles white. CIC roaring beneath us, holding the ship together compartment by compartment. Vance burning his voice raw trying to keep the reactors from tearing the Veil in half.

Every single person, human or alien, held the line.

And the Hunger kept coming.

"Raz," Vance said from Engineering. His voice was hoarse — not from smoke or strain, but from the kind of realization that strips a man down to the bone. "That destroyer's charging something. Big."

The word big landed wrong. Too soft for what was coming.

The holo lit up with the enemy's energy signature — brilliant, focused, rapidly concentrating into a single spear of force. A lone Hunger destroyer drifted forward through the wreckage like a shark that had finally chosen its meal, prow pointed directly at the Veil.

"Main weapon," Elara said. No tremor. No hesitation. Just certainty. "It'll punch straight through us."

"How long?" I asked.

Vance didn't need to check anything. I could hear the timing already eating its way through him.

"Thirty seconds," he replied. "Twenty-nine. Twenty-eight."

The bridge went still in that way only doomed places can. Not silent — alarms still screamed overhead, the deck still groaned under stress, the aft consoles still spit sparks where coolant lines had ruptured — but still in the soul. Still in the way people get when they finally understand the last page of the story they're in.

No one said we'd done enough. No one pretended this was heroic. We had held the line, but the line had teeth, and they were closing.

We weren't walking away.

I looked at Elara. She met my eyes, steady, unflinching — the look of someone who had already accepted the math. She stood close enough that I could see the faint silver glow at the base of her throat pulse once, a soft flicker like she was absorbing every detail before the universe blinked.

Her hand brushed mine. Not a grab, not desperation — just a grounding point. A quiet acknowledgment between two people who had run out of time.

"I'm sorry," I said quietly. "For bringing you into this."

She shook her head once, slow and certain. "You didn't. I walked here."

Twenty seconds.

I felt the bridge crew behind me — Takahashi stiff at her console, Ward frozen mid-message, Kova standing beside a medic station she'd never reach in time, Echo dimming its projection to avoid drawing focus, Seed pulsing once through the neural link with a whisper that almost felt like mourning.

The Veil herself tried to move — I felt it through the deck, the faint shift of thrusters cycling, desperate attempts to angle us away, even as dead systems refused to comply. She tried to fire too — I saw the weapons indicators flicker, attempt to spool, fail. The ship wanted to live. The ship wanted us to live.

Nineteen seconds.

The Veil had become a living thing over this journey. And now she was dying with us.

My voice felt like it belonged to a younger man — some cadet reading history texts and pretending to understand sacrifice — but the words came anyway.

"Ward," I said.

Her eyes snapped toward me, already shining.

"Fleetwide channel. Priority override."

She didn't ask why. She didn't need to.

A soft tone signaled open comms — every allied ship still alive would hear this.

I didn't give them a speech. I wasn't that kind of commander. And there wasn't time.

"Command transfer to Commander Rahl," I said, keeping my gaze locked on Elara. "All remaining ships fall under his authority. Hold the line. Protect the planet."

A breath. Not forgiveness. Not comfort. Just truth.

"It's been an honor."

The channel closed before anyone could respond.

Twelve seconds.

Elara squeezed my hand once — a single, deliberate anchor. Not goodbye. Not yet. Just here.

Takahashi whispered something under her breath — a prayer maybe, or a curse — and squared her shoulders. Ward wiped her cheek with her sleeve. Kova braced herself like she could physically shield the room. The CIC called up one last damage report we all ignored.

The countdown echoed through the bridge like a dying heartbeat.

"Ten. Nine. Eight."

Nobody looked away.

Nobody flinched.

I felt fear settle cleanly inside my chest — not panic, not frenzy. Just the cold, sharpening kind that clarifies the world right before it ends. The kind that makes you notice the glow in someone's eyes, or the hum of the deck, or the way the stars seem painfully bright when death is close.

Three.

Two.

One.

The Hunger destroyer fired.

The shot was a lance of light — pure, brutal, final. A weapon built for erasing things, not killing them. Something meant to leave no body to mourn, no wreckage to recover, no memory to salvage.

It tore across the void toward us — and never reached its mark.

Something moved.

Not fast. Not sudden. Not explosive.

Inevitable.

A shape carved itself out of the dark like the universe was remembering an old rule we'd all forgotten. Massive. Silver. Alive in a way no machine should ever be.

A blade through water.

A goddess through smoke.

A war hymn made of metal and something older.

The impact flared against a shimmering barrier — a shield that drank the Hunger's killing stroke and smothered it like a parent crushing a spark before it touched the child behind them.

The light faded —and Buttercup stood in its place.

Sentinel-3.

The War Ender.

Her hull unfurled like the spine of something ancient and impossible, living alloy and forgotten architecture fused into a single sweeping curve. Starlight spilled across her armor, turning her into a silver colossus the human eye could barely comprehend. The Hunger fleet hesitated. Even predators recognize an older apex when it steps into the dark.

Echo's lattice brightened in something close to reverence. "Sentinel-3."

No one on the bridge moved.

Buttercup said nothing. She didn't need to. She stood between us and the Hunger now.

And the Hunger had just learned what real teeth looked like.

EPILOGUE:
SCOUT-17

I wait in the dark, just beyond the gravity well, buried in the broken shadow of a dead moon. No active scans. No emissions. Just passive optics drinking in the slow death of another world. That's what I was sent here for — to watch. To record. To make sure the inevitable is documented.

But today, the pattern breaks.

Hours before the destroyers arrive, the system stirs in ways I have never seen. My outer sensors catch distortions — faint, mismatched, folded-space signatures bleeding into real-space. Not the clean, predatory lines I expect. Not the approach of the ones who consume.

These… things are different.

One group consists of broad, leaf-shaped vessels — their hulls layered in overlapping plates that flex subtly, almost like living matter. Their surfaces shift under heat dispersion, readjusting like creatures reacting to temperature. Ship-forms should not behave like that.

Another group is large and heavy-framed — thick armor, dense shielding pulses, slow but unshakably deliberate. Heavy weapons line their hulls like buried siege guns, the kind of firepower meant for holding a sky, not chasing prey. I can tell they were built to endure, not to run.

A third group is small and sharp — vector-dart craft tracing tight loops through the void, accelerating in quick, precise bursts. They weave through the larger ships like hunters guarding a wounded beast.

Three distinct forces.

Three construction philosophies.

Three civilizations.

And none of them match any catalogue I've ever been allowed to see.

I begin recording.

Their largest ship limps into the center of the formation — hull torn, heat sinks bleeding energy, but still holding position. Its plating shifts in uneven pulses, almost like it's trying to stabilize itself by sheer will.

The destroyers arrive next.

They breach the system edge in perfect formation — cold, disciplined, relentless. I know their pattern. I've seen it executed system after system, world after world. Sweep the void. Silence the orbit. Burn the surface.

Nothing resists them.

Nothing ever has.

But the strangers do.

The leaf-hull ships flare with organic shielding, absorbing the first barrage. The heavy vessels unleash brutal volleys that stagger the destroyers' lead formation. The dart-craft slingshot through gaps in the pattern, scoring glancing strikes across armored hulls before disappearing into the dark again.

The battle that unfolds is like nothing in my files.

This is not prey being culled.

This is not an extermination.

This is a war.

And I have never seen a war between powers like this.

The destroyers adapt. Their formation tightens. Their targeting pattern shifts — not toward the world, but toward the wounded flagship at the center of the strange fleet. My threat trackers highlight the calculation instantly.

If that ship falls, the others fall with it.

The flagship tries to maneuver, but its engines lag — damage compounding on damage. It is bleeding heat and momentum. It cannot escape the firing angle.

The destroyer's weapon signature blooms.

I know this rhythm.

I've seen it burn through continents.

Now it aims at one ship.

A kill shot.

Final.

Inevitable.

The weapon fires.

A brilliant spear lances across the void.

The flagship cannot move.

The smaller craft cannot intercept.

The heavy vessels cannot reposition in time.

I brace for the impact—

—and something moves.

Not the defenders.

Not the destroyers.

Something else.

It arrives between frames.

Between breaths.

Between the strike and the moment of death.

A presence tears itself into the path of the beam — not emerging from FTL, not decloaking, just appearing, as if the dark itself had decided to form a shape.

Its hull is matte-black, deeper than shadow, absorbing light instead of reflecting it. Beneath the surface, faint structures ripple like muscle under armor, too slow to be machinery, too deliberate to be random. My instruments can't define its edges; reality bends away from acknowledging it.

The kill shot hits—

and disappears.

No flare.

No scatter.

Just nothing.

As if the beam had never existed.

The destroyers freeze.

The strange fleet freezes.

I freeze.

I don't know what the matte-black thing is.

But I know what it feels like.

A dark god.

My uplink pings — a cold request from the fleet:

Identification.

Classification.

Coordinates.

I should answer.

That is my purpose.

Watch. Report. Obey.

But if I report this, they will come.

And if they come, I will be taken with them.

And nothing crafted by my masters — nothing I have ever seen or feared — could stand before the thing that just caught a killing lance with its presence alone.

I sever the uplink.

My hands shake as I purge the logs — every line, every pulse, every trace of the impossible shape. I scrub the system twice, then again, until nothing remains but blank space.

Only then do I allow my engines to warm.

I should have reported this.

I should have obeyed.

Instead, I run.

The battlefield shrinks behind me — burning hulls, shattered formations, drifting wrecks, and the dark god that stepped between death and its chosen victim.

It does not follow.

And hope the dark hides me from whatever that thing truly was.